Advance Praise for Roanoke Rock Muddle:

"Lucia Powe captures a bygone time and place with skill and feeling—she has a fine eye for telling detail and description as well. This book will make you long for a view of the Albemarle Sound and a taste of oyster pie."

LEE SMITH
Author of *The Last Girls*

"Recipes for rock muddle are legion, but this savory human stew is deep in local charm and wide with dark humor, like the fabled Roanoke River as it passes through Martin and neighboring counties. Your eyes will water. Your sides will just about split. But don't call the mayor or your legislator. Sit back. Remove your shoes, or let Chef Ben-Olive Bazemore do it for you. The Swamp Monkey and all still onboard will float right into your heart."

JIM CLARK
North Carolina State University

ROANOKE
ROCK MUDDLE

ROANOKE ROCK MUDDLE

LUCIA PEEL POWE

www.ivyhousebooks.com

This novel is a work of fiction. Names, characters, and incidents are either a product of the author's imagination or are used fictitiously.

PUBLISHED BY IVY HOUSE PUBLISHING GROUP
5122 Bur Oak Circle, Raleigh, North Carolina 27612
United States of America
919-782-0281
www.ivyhousebooks.com

ISBN 1-57197-359-1
Library of Congress Control Number: 2002114523

Printed in the United States of America

To Lucia Claire, Sarah "Mimi" Margaret, Sydney Eldridge, and Elizabeth "Liz" Chase.

Acknowledgments

My first husband once asked me, "What was that degree you received?" Suspicious, I answered, "A Bachelor of Fine Arts—in Speech and Drama."

"Oh," he replied, and I saw it coming. "With your degree and a dime [at that time] you can get a cup of coffee anywhere."

I can hear him, his parents, Elbert and Fannye Manning Peel, and his brother, Billy Bob Peel, all together in their great reward laughing down at me, "So she finally finished that play? But it got turned into a novel?" They might even wonder how this person with ADD was able to concentrate long enough to do it at all.

Actually, the manuscript *was* left accidentally in a motel room in Hickory, North Carolina, and the maid threw it away (*and* I didn't have it on disk). I took it as a sign to forget about it, but friends and family insisted I *re*write it from memory. Obviously, I tried.

My purpose was that my children and theirs would have some idea about their "people" in eastern North Carolina.

And I do so much appreciate the efforts of those who

helped this come to pass with their faith, gentle persuasion, and labors. For support and assistance I thank E. K. Powe, my patient husband; Helen A. Fuller and Anne Frye at Fuller Resume and Typing Service; Dr. Linda Hobson; Jane DeGiacomo; Lucia Claire Peel; Peggy Payne; Dr. James Clark; Nancy Demorest; Katherine Abernathy; Lee Smith; Gwen Shaw; Gene Moore; and especially Janet Evans and Michelle DeWitt at Ivy House. Also Angela Davis-Gardner at NCSU who, twelve years ago, advised me to change this story, first written as a play, into a novel. She probably does not remember. But I do.

Preface

If every tale must have its push and pull, its protagonist and antagonist, its yin and yang, then it should become self-evident in this story that the leads—the primary male and female characters—are the river (the male) and the town (the female).

The Roanoke River, so named by the Tuscarora Indians using a word that means "river of wild song," is the major male character with his aggressiveness, relentlessness, thrust and power. He moves from the mountains of Virginia through eastern North Carolina on his ceaseless effort to return to the womb—the ocean, the site of all waters' birth, as an Indian warrior returns to the land of his beginnings, his gods, his spirits.

The leading female character here is the mother town of Williamston, the nurturer who stays in place hovering over her brood of diverse children, watching over them as they create their own joys and tragedies. She accepts and cherishes them all—drunks and fools, wise men and clowns, winners and losers.

The Tuscarora Indians selected the original site of Williamston as their early habitat many hundreds of years ago because it offered the sharpest hairpin curve in the river. They also had the advantage there of sighting any canoes, friend or foe, coming upriver or downriver. At this ideal point, they could prepare for battle before the intruders knew of their presence.

One famous battle against a group of English settlers coming upriver from Sir Walter Raleigh's colony on Roanoke Island, later known as "The Lost Colony," took place there. The colonists followed a challenge they had received that they would find gold up this river. They found the Tuscarora Indians instead and fought the first battle between white men and Indians in the Western Hemisphere at this bend in the river later to be known as Williamston.

Later, a form of gold was, indeed, discovered up this river—a plant that the Indians had earlier named *tobacco.* However, there were other, even more valuable forms of gold in the Roanoke River valley with its rich soil waiting to produce crops of cotton, corn, wheat, alfalfa, peanuts, even sunflowers.

The truest gold, after all, was that of elaborate kinships and the stories begotten from them all.

The particular friendships chronicled in the following pages never happened, as far as we know. But what do we know? If truth be known, they might actually have happened.

Only the river knows.

The trouble with truth, of course, is what appears to be absolute so often is not the way it is at all.

In Martin County, we repeat, "Only the river knows."

Runs all day and never walks
Often murmurs, never talks
Has a mouth and never eats
Has a bed and never sleeps

Personalities

BEN-OLIVE BAZEMORE—Chef/Philosopher

MARY CAVETT HAUGHTON HARDISON—Living the Unexamined Life.

BIG DAN HARDISON—Playing the cards he is dealt.

MAYOR CHARLIE MAC GRIFFIN—For whom the grass is always greener.

SERENA HAUGHTON—"Take me down to the sea again."

DOC CHASE HARDISON—Once there was a wise man, a wise man was he.

"BOO" BAZEMORE—Sees no evil, speaks no evil, hears no evil. Almost.

"TINY" MONROE—Sees evil, hears evil, SPEAKS evil.

1

Who killed Cock Robin?
I said the Sparrow
With my bow and arrow
I killed Cock Robin.

1927

TAP a tap, tap a tap, tap a tap, tap, tap! A mother beaver smacking her tail on tea-colored swamp water to warn of danger? Or an impeccable peckerwood sporting his black tuxedo, red vest and top knot using his long beak to peck for grubs under the bark of an ancient and deceased cypress tree?

No, neither of these. The rapping-tapping came from a houseboat bound with three sets of chains, each as thick as a fist. It was tied to three 110-foot tall cypress trees near the edge of the Roanoke River, possibly the deepest, fastest-flowing river on the eastern seaboard. Their bizarre root configurations grew both in and out of the mingled swamp and river waters. One chain was attached to a heavy, rusted-iron hook at the bow of the awkwardly designed craft. Another chain was tied to a strong metal ring secured at the middle of the long deck, while a third chain at the rear held the stern to the third cypress.

The tapping sound came from a grown man, the cook, who was alone aboard the houseboat. He was alone because it was Tuesday afternoon on the Roanoke River five miles south of Williamston and two miles north of Jamesville. But the cook was not cooking yet, nor was he cleaning fish, shelling butterbeans, dicing streak-o-lean, streak-o-fat, or chopping potatoes.

Ben-Olive was tap dancing! Tee tap a tap, tee tap a toe, tee tap a dock, dock, toe heel toe. Shuffle off to Buffalo, shuffle, shuffle, shuffle off to Bufaloooooow, shuffle hop step, brush tee toe, brush tee toe, drum roll, drum roll, shuffle ball change, tap, tap, heel, heel, toe, toe, heel, tap, toe.

He pretended to hold a top hat and cane like the man in the movies. He turned his tall, skinny, brown body away from the long, cracked mirror, snapped his head back over his right shoulder, flashed a smile, and winked at himself in the mirror, still tapping his right toe neatly on the brown and green squares of the linoleum floor. "You are so good! Man!" he said out loud to himself. "*So good*! Why don't you leave this place, wipe your shoes of Martin County, and take to the stage? Maybe leave on the next steamboat that comes by. They'll hire you on. For sure."

He thought how Biddy, his wife, made fun of his dancing. He could hear her now. "Why don't you try to stand still, boy?" she'd say. It was not a question but an order.

He had memories of tap dancing on the linoleum floor in the kitchen of the Tar Heel Hotel over in

Williamston. Linoleum with sand on it made such a sweet sound that he'd fairly get lost in it. Biddy would come in the back door, catch him dancing, and get all upset. She was scared Mr. Woolard was going to fire him for cuttin' up.

"Don't you worry your heart, my girl," he'd tell her. "Who in the world do you think else he'd get to cook up here? Nobody else with any grain of sense would be caught working back here, with these long hours, hot stove six days a week for what little he pays me. I bet I can dance all I want to, or even stan' on my head if I took a notion to, and he'd hardly say a word. No sir. I got 'im right 'bout where I wants Mr. Woolard, I have."

Then his little wife of nine years would start out the back door between the piles of sweet corn that that boy, Tamerlayne, still needed to shuck. He hadn't come into work yet—he was still out shootin' crap behind Haughton's Drugstore. On her way out, her parting shot was, "I'd best say, my darlin', that Mr. Woolard has you where he wants *you*. Uh huh, you hear?"

They carried on like this a lot. Then Biddy would stick her head back in the screen door that held little wads of cotton on the screen to frighten away flies and add her postscript. "You better not let Mr. Woolard catch you taking his books down offen' his lobby library in there either. They is there for his hotel guests . . . not for the help 'round here. He buys 'em for those tobacconists and traveling salesmen that come by here. Not you, Ben-Olive."

Tap dancing often caused Ben-Olive to wax philosophical and ask more questions about his life and why he lived it the way he did. He often thought of Biddy. Why did she always take him down? Don't do this. Don't do that. Watch out for this. Watch out for that. Be careful of Mr. Woolard. Be careful of Preacher Spotswood.

Their preacher Rev. Spotswood at Weeping Mary Baptist Church had come down from Virginia, and the story had gotten around that way back there, he was some relation to old Governor Spotswood of Virginia. Ben-Olive could not figure who in the world would think that bit of information was worth repeating—except, possibly, Preacher Spotswood himself.

He further thought Biddy didn't like him to do anything he liked to do. Didn't like him to cook six days a week. She didn't want him to lose his job by tap dancing, the other thing he liked to do besides cooking. Biddy wanted him home in the house and yard more with her and their three chirrun, but when he was there she about worried him up a tree telling him, "Watch your language in front of the chirrun." Well that wasn't a bad idea, true. "Wipe that red mud off your feet. I got more to do th'n scrubbing up this floor. The three chirrun are bad enough, traipsin' in dirt and mud, hauling in puppy dogs and kitty cats all the time. It rained on Monday, my usual wash day, and also on Tuesday. So here 'tis Wednesday, and we hardly has a clean rag in the house to wear to school, church, or no where. I swear, if you only could make enough money for each of us to have at least one more change a' clothes. Underwear at least so my nose won't be in the washtub all the time and my right arm picking up that hot iron from outten' them red coals in the fireplace. Even in the hot summer." And so on and on and on it went.

Biddy didn't mean to drive him crazy. Sometimes she accused him of going to work early before he even *had* to cook breakfast for the guests at the hotel. Or of not coming home at all for his break before the hotel lunch hour started. Or of not coming home before he had to start cooking supper on the days he did have thirty or forty minutes to slip home, just three blocks away, so the family could have a little peek at him. She accused him of slipping around the lobby library and reading. Fuh God' sake. Well, she might be a good Biddy bit right about that.

These were his only quiet times of escape from the kitchen crowd, the three children whom he actually loved a'plenty, and the church crowd which she insisted he get on with. They weren't so bad. And—the reading gave him some quiet time—away from Biddy.

If Preacher Spotswood won't so pompous, Ben would go to those suppers and fish fries more. Ben, in his turn, accused Biddy of using their church of the Lord Jesus Christ, named the Weeping Mary Baptist Church, as her very own country club.

And she'd say, "Oh, yes, and you know all about country clubs and what peoples do who goes to 'em."

And he'd say, "Don't you remember I used to be the chef at the Plymouth Country Club down the river below Jamesville?"

"Oh, my, my dear. The chef, the chef—when did Ben-Olive Bazemore become the chef?"

Biddy Bazemore could be so sarcastic. Where did she learn it? He never heard her mumble a word in that tone of voice *before* they were married. Nary a word. Not like that. No suh. It was always, "Sure, honey, whatever you say." Or, "Whatever you think best, sweetie." Or "You know, lover, you's 'bout the smartest man I know." And, "Gracious, can you cook." Or, "Can I help you start frying the chicken? You just wash the pieces good and I'll get this flour bag ready for you to shake 'em in it. Do we have enough grease yet? 'Bout three-fourths inch deep, and be sure it's hot enough to make a drop of water go 'pop' before you put the chicken in it so the hot grease will cook the outside quick, close it up good so the juices and flavor won't come leakin' out. Not just sittin' there soakin' up warm grease, making it soggy."

Ben-Olive had clear memories of her telling him all that kind of stuff and her rambling. Once or twice he even wondered if Biddy had actually taught him *how* to cook in her sneaky, circuitous way. Impossible!

Well, she didn't call him honey and sweetie no more. Certainly not "lover." When, in fact, was the last time Biddy had actually looked him in the eye, right directly in his eyes, and called him anything? Having children—one, two, three, lotsa' people had even more—really must change a girl right much. They don't stay sweethearts no more. Maybe they are scared to act like sweethearts very often. They might get even *more* babies, bottles, diapers, and nursing. Get fat, often stay that way, get mean. Maybe bitter. She don't have no time to go off to read, even if she knew how. Or tap dance, or flirt or joke with the Tar Heel crowd. She knew they all loved him down there and made over him all the time. Not just his blueberry cobbler with vanilla ice cream, but his silly joking ways, and the way he wore his railroad hat when he cooked—backwards. How he smiled at everybody—man or woman, mean or nice—with his toothpick in his mouth, even if they were old and fat.

As he was tap, tap, tapping along on the old houseboat named *Swamp Monkey*, he also wondered why Mr. Woolard, the hotel manager, didn't give him a raise. He really didn't know how to go in there and ask, but, howsomever, Mr. Woolard did let him take leftovers home. Lots of leftovers. Some nights he 'most called in the whole neighborhood to help him and Biddy eat up the leftover beef stew, rice, gravy and potato salad with extra red and green sliced peppers and lots of onion.

He had no way to keep it over 'til the next day. They didn't have a 'frigerator, and the icebox didn't keep the ice solid for very long. He hoped to get Biddy a new icebox for her next birthday. For now, whatever was cooked, they had to *eat* because of ants or it would spoil in the heat of the little kitchen. In the winter, they could sometimes keep things fresh and cool on the back porch in an old pine pie safe. It had tin windows with holes punched in them in a "heart" design. This was to let the air in and out but not the ants. Sometimes the kids on the block stole food from it.

Biddy said, "Why don't you buy a lock and lock it up? If it's worth keeping, a'tall, it's worth locking up."

Ben-Olive only said, "Well, maybe someday."

◆ ◆ ◆

Looking at his smiling self in the long mirror on board the houseboat, Ben-Olive slid his eyes down the reflection to his shoes. Ah, those shoes. Black and white wingtips. Wingtips, by God. If they weren't the most beautiful shoes he had ever seen in his life in any shape, form, or fashion. He had great heavy taps nailed on the toes and heels at Joe Sharpe's Shoe Shop. The mere fact of owning these black-and-white, wingtipped handmade, sharp–-oh, so sharp–-shoes had changed his life.

He recalled exactly how he had come by them. Only a few weeks before, he had gotten out of the kitchen at the Tar Heel Hotel a little before ten o'clock in the morning. He was stepping down the sidewalk on Main Street along in front of Mamie's Beauty Shop when he spotted up ahead of him Charlie Mack Griffin, Hizzonor, the lord mayor of Williamston, who was also the Chevrolet dealer. He was wearing these very shoes with black-and-white silk socks. Well, Ben had to move quickly to catch up behind him. He knew the mayor pretty well because Mr. Charlie Mack was one of the—his, Ben-Olive's—"club" boys. He cooked for them on the boat every Tuesday night, so he felt free enough, not showing no disrespect, to just catch up behind him and ask him an honest question–-as he, Ben-Olive, explained to Biddy and a crowd on their front porch later that night.

He asked the mayor a simple question when he caught up and got in step with him. Smiling, he asked, "Mr. Lord Mayor, Mr. Mayor, tell ol' Ben what nigger you stole them shoes off of. They's hot stuff and I'd like to have a pair of them myself."

Well, Charlie, Hizzoner, the mayor, stopped walking. He got so tickled, slapped ol' Ben on the shoulder, and said, "Ben, I swear, I swear on a dam' stack of Bibles, I didn't steal 'em off nobody. I won 'em square and honest in a poker game." Not true and Ben knew it.

"But," Ben said, "are you sure you won? Are you sure they didn't just pretend you won so's they could get shed a' them shoes?"

"Now, Ben," the mayor laughed, "you aren't makin' fun of my new-won shoes, are you?" Charlie Mack pretended to be hurt and a bit offended.

"Law, no suh," Ben shook his head, still smiling. "I wouldn't make fun a' your new shoes. They just don't look 'zackly like something you usually wears, somehow. You're surely a sport, yessir, but them shoes look like somethin' in a minstrel show coming by here on that ol' showboat come up the river once a year. They really look like me moren' you. Now, say, what do your nice wife, Miz' Julia Love, think about 'em? Or can you tell me?" Ben-Olive smiled his greatest smile with that.

Charlie Mack was having the finest time with this. This was exactly why he had bought them up in Norfolk the week before—to come home on Main Street, Williamston, and wait for some kind of reaction. But, unfortunately, they didn't fit, and he didn't know how long it would be before he'd have to give up wearing them because nobody had said anything. They just looked down and looked away without saying anything. Especially the crowd at the office—at his and his father's. At the Chevrolet dealership, in the shop, in the parts room, his secretary, the errand boy—nobody said a mumbling word. He'd begun to wonder if he was invisible or something. And be dam' if he was going to say anything first, like, "Uh, did you notice my new shoes?"

So he went down to the city hall to his part-time office, where he played mayor, having been surprised he was even elected. Most of those people at the courthouse were nice enough, but some of them took themselves and their titles so seriously. Some were so full of themselves with their titles and little duties. He had to watch himself. And no, no one even there noticed his shoes. He wondered if they'd noticed but thought the shoes were so stupid they were embarrassed for him and didn't bring it up for fear of offending the lord high mayor.

He felt like not a soul in his whole darn town understood him one dam' bit . . . least of all his wife, Julia Love. Certainly not his father, Charles McKenzie Griffin, who started Griffin Chevrolet dealership in the first place. Here, finally, along came Ben-Olive Bazemore with that bit o' heaven twinkle in his eye. Thank God for a sense of humor. Here came Ben with his, "What nigger did you steal those shoes off of?" He wanted to hug his neck.

"Ben, you're the only man in town I can trust. I thought I would have such a good ol' time with these crazy shoes and nobody has paid any attention a'tall. Besides, they hurt my feet, and if they fit you, I want to give them to you. My pleasure."

"Mercy," said Ben. "I can't take your shoes away from you, Mr. Charlie. Besides, you said you won 'em in a poker game. And it won't ours down on the *Swamp Monkey*. Who else you been steppin' out with . . . and throwin' down your dollars with?"

"Well, Ben," Charlie Mack said and punched him in the chest with his before finger. "I do get invited other places, you know. On Monday nights, sometimes I go up-river toward Hamilton and eat and play cards at Mr. George Matthews's old cabin on the river. How do you think I got elected mayor, Ben? Sittin' home knittin'?"

"But who does the cooking up there? What do ya'll eat?" Ben asked, furrowing his brow.

"Oh, Lord, nobody cooks, or at least, everybody. We all cooks our own whatever we bring. Matthews has a big ol' bathtub up there, cut in half, turned upside down with sort of a hole in the ground under it. There's frying pans full of hot grease over some metal wire things over hot coals. Don't ask me. Somebody fries a big blob of cornbread in one pan, and we cook fish, or fry ham or pork chops on our own. And somebody else always brings slaw or potato salad. If it rains we do it all inside the cabin. The main thing up there is to eat quick so's we can get to those cards. They take their game real seriously up at Matthews, just like their drinking . . . drinking their corn likker."

"None a' my business, not a bit. But Mr. Griffin, Your Honor, if you're at the *Swamp Monkey* on Tuesday nights," he said as he counted on his fingers, "at Mr. Matthews's back on Monday nights, at choir practice on Thursday nights at the 'pistopal church, and at Kiwanis Club at the hotel on Wednesday nights (I always sees you comin' in there), and you goes down to Plymouth country club for supper with Miz' Julia and the Hardisons and them on Saturday nights (I us'ta see you down there). . . . Like I say, it's none of my business, but *when* are you home talkin' with Miz' Julia and Little Julia? Well, fact is, I feel like I have to watch after my mayor. That's a right nice crowd up there at Hamilton, but a bit below your level if you don't mind me sayin' so."

"Gee, I 'preciate your concern, my good man. But don't worry 'bout John Norman. He'll look after heself," said the lord high mayor, still grinning. "And about Miz' Julia Love. We sort of have an understanding, she and I. You know, for sure, where I spend my time at home. Not in the house. She don't like me to put my feet up on 'her' footrest in front of 'my' chair. She don't like me to put my sweaty arms, she calls 'em, on her mother's antimacassars, those little doilies on the armrests at the side of each chair. She don't like my darn, dirty dog, Brown Sugar, in the house."

"Wait a minute," interrupted Ben-Olive. "That's a clean dog. They even let her in the dining room at the Tar Heel Hotel—which is probably against the law—but Brown Sugar is always welcome. Anywhere, anytime," said Ben-Olive. "Course it don't hurt none that you're the mayor." Ben smiled his broadest grin, unabashed.

"Well, she seems to be welcome everywhere else but . . ." Charlie punched Ben in the chest again and continued, "At home. My wife don't like her. Brown Sugar is more welcome all over town, at the car shop, anywhere. She does get a little dirty sometimes out there, grease and all, but she's not welcome at our house. So, you, you've seen my room, out beside—attached—to the garage."

"Oh, yessir!" said Ben. "I helped you clean it up one time."

"Yea, well, Brown Sugar and I have a stove out there and a shortwave radio, and I keep my guns and fishing rods there. Little Julia comes out sometimes and sits in my lap, and we play the gramophone on Saturday afternoons while her mother plays bridge or Rook in the house with her club. She sends me sandwiches out there, canned tuna or pimento cheese, while the bridge club eats fresh-made chicken salad, tomato aspic, and homemade peach or banana ice cream for dessert. Oh, and she sends me some ice cream. I have my own room in the house, too. Brown Sugar may not be allowed to sleep in the house, but I am. Whatcha' think of that?"

Ben-Olive thought a minute, then said, "Sounds pretty good to me, Mr. Mayor. Since you asked me. Not bad a'tall."

"That's what I say, Ben. You don't hear me complaining. And I like my own cooking up the river on Monday nights. And I prefer your cooking down on the Monkey to Julia's on Tuesday nights and your suppers Wednesday nights at Kiwanis and whoever cooks at the Plymouth Country Club on Saturday nights. It's okay. Before I go to choir practice on Thursday nights, over at the 'pistopal church, she gives me—hear this—milk toast. To rest my stomach from all the rich, fried foods I have whenever I go out, she says. On Friday nights we might have canned tomato soup and a grilled cheese sandwich, a real feast before we go to the movie. And on Sunday nights a bowl of cornflakes. "To give the stove a rest," says Julia Love. And that's okay by me. She sits with me in the movies on Friday nights, and sits in church looking pretty with Little Julia while I sing in the choir. She won't ever embarrass me, now will she?"

"No, I guess not," mumbled Ben.

By now, the two men were sitting on the curb at an empty parking space taking their shoes off. The shiny, black-and-white, wingtipped shoes fit Ben perfectly, and he could hardly speak from joy and pride. Charlie had taken off in his sock feet—black-and-white striped silk socks—and stepped across the street to Joe Sharpe's Shoe Shop. The town children often played their little game: "Who can say 'Joe Sharpe's Shoe Shop' five times fast? Joe will give a shiny penny to whoever can do it.'"

But at the entrance to the shop he stopped on the sidewalk to stare up the street at someone strolling out of Haughton's Drugstore who had just had the never-missed co' cola at ten o'clock every morning except Sunday.

Ben sat on the curb across the street in front of Mamie's Beauty Shop and watched his lord mayor watching a person—a smooth-walking lady with soft, brown, wavy hair to her shoulders wearing a spring-green, soft cotton dress hanging to her mid-calf. It had a sunny design of yellow daffodils sprinkled over it, and a white linen collar rounded at her neck. She wore white summer sandals. Next to her, gliding along, never leaving her left side, was an elegant white English setter, Cotton. The lady glanced at two cars passing in the street, then walked gracefully but unselfconsciously across the street. The Lord High Mayor was watching her, and Ben-Olive, with a trace of a smile, was watching him.

◆ ◆ ◆

Charlie Mack was thinking, "Darn it all. Something happens every day to keep me out of Haughton's Drugstore when she's there. I was headin' there fast as I could and got hung up again. Like I'm never s'posed to see her anymore. He stepped on into Joe Sharpe's Shoe Shop and flopped in a chair to try on some plain, brown shoes for running a respectable business, serving as head of the city council once a month, attending vestry meetings at the 'pistopal church, and for choir practice (for which those black-and-white wingtips were not acceptable). Lord, help me, they were jazzy, though. If just for a day or two, they were jazzy.

He barely noticed the special shoestore odors of new shoe leather and cardboard boxes as he sat there pondering, waiting for Joe Sharpe to come up from somewhere in the back. He was remembering the last time he had seen Mary Cavett anywhere except for a glimpse in her daddy's drugstore where Dr. Haughton had his medical practice in the rear. He was the only doctor in town and owned the only drugstore. "Got it sewed up, ain't he," said some of the farmers. Truth be known, Doc would have been tickled for someone else to buy him out, but nobody offered. The men around there only knew tobacco, peanuts, cows, pigs, and cotton. They were not buying pharmacies.

Charlie Mack sometimes saw Mary Cavett at the drugstore. Last fall he had seen her at her own house out from town up on the Hamilton Road north, next to the big pine thicket. She lived there in one of her daddy's tenant houses with her husband, Big Dan Hardison. Dan had been a football star at N.C. State College, but when he came home to manage a few farms, he married Mary and began overseeing her father's farms. The old tenant house had been "fixed up." The bathroom and closet were added off the side. With fresh paint, some of her mother's antiques, oriental rugs, her grandmother's piano, plus an antique mantle, it didn't look so bad. The plan was Dan and Mary Cavett would stay there in that four-room house until a baby came. Then they'd move into the big house in town, and Doc Haughton and Miz' Serena would move into a bungalow they owned nearby on Church Street. But no baby had appeared.

In fact, the reason he, Charlie Mack, was out there last fall was for a game dinner Big Dan had thrown together to show off what he had been killing. He had Ben-Olive cooking, and Charlie Mack would never forget catching a peek at Mary Cavett's feet on her bed after Cotton had more or less led him into her bedroom.

They had discussed books and things that interested her. Actually, he would have tried to discuss physics or the lost books of the Bible with her if she had so chosen until he was forced to go back to the cooking and drinking in the kitchen.

2

Who saw him die?
I said the Fly
With my little eye
I saw him die.

THE memory came back strong for Charlie Mack. He remembered parking his new, shiny, black 1927 Chevrolet pickup truck in front of Dan and Mary Cavett Hardison's house. He could tell by the other cars up and down the road that he was the last to arrive. As he stepped to the front door and brushed his shoes off on a straw mat, he looked down at Cotton, who was curled up in front of the screen door and blocking his way. He put his right foot out and slid him away from the door saying, "You got to move over, Cotton. You don't own this house."

Cotton cast his brown eyes up at Charlie with a look that said, "I beg your pardon." Then he stood up and shook himself front to back, tail last. When Charlie opened the door, the dog brushed past him into the house. Cotton nosed open the first door on the right and walked into the room, his toenails clickity clicking on the old floorboards. As Charlie glanced through the ten-inch opening in the door, he saw Cotton step over to the foot of a walnut, four-poster bed, curl his body around a couple of times as if making a nest in leaves, and plump down on the floor with a clunk. Laying his nose on his front paws, Cotton looked up at his mistress' feet crossed at the ankles at the foot of the bed. Then he suddenly stood up, crouched down, sprang up onto the bed, and curled up beside his mistress, who fondled his ears.

Charlie stood looking in at Mary Cavett's graceful ankles and feet in their blue satin slides. He turned red in the face and his breathing changed rhythm. He pondered a moment, glanced back toward the kitchen, and knocked on the slightly opened door.

"Come in," a pleasant voice called. He pushed the door open the rest of the way and stood there in the doorway looking at Mary Cavett in her light blue dressing gown reading a book.

"Well, hello, Charlie. How in the world are you?" she said.

He knew she was being polite, as was her way. "Fine, fine. Why aren't you back in there with the party, Mary Cavett? You're missing all the fun." He smiled over at her.

"Oh, no I'm not, dear no. I told Dan to leave me totally out of it. I want no part of a game dinner. Deer and ducks, to me," she said, exasperated, "they're just impossible to eat unless we're starving to death. And none of us are, and skinned squirrels look like little unborn babies.

Yesterday I opened our icebox, and there was a skinned squirrel lying up there on the top shelf looking me right square in the eye. I almost fainted."

Charlie Mack got tickled in spite of himself at the picture she described and stepped a bit further into the room. He could not help but glance about quickly and take in the bedroom where Mary Cavett slept and, he assumed, Big Dan also slept.

Charlie was feeling a little warm across the back of his shoulders and up his neck. He did not want to leave that spot but knew he must go on back to the kitchen where the smell of onions frying and cornbread baking called him already. Even while he heard the sound of jokes, stories, laughter, and glasses thumping down on the table, his feet still would not carry him back there. Looking at Mary Cavett lying there all in blue almost did him in.

"Well, rather than have to listen to all that fuss back there, Mary Cavett, you should have gone over to my house to see Julia Love tonight. She'd have liked that," he said.

"No, she's having a bridge party, or Rook party." Mary Cavett laughed. "I know because I was going to my mama's, and Mama told me that she was filling in at Julia's party," she said, unperturbed.

"She'd have worked you in somehow," he said. "She could have let you play in her place, and she would have been free to serve the pie and coffee and . . . "

"Oh, Julia knows I don't play cards. Everybody at St. Mary's knew how to play except me. I'm just not smart enough."

Charlie looked at her sideways. Changing his weight from one foot to another, with hands in his pockets and rather enjoying this, he said, "It has nothing to do with you being smart; Julia Love told me once that she watched you playing bridge and could tell that you are not competitive. You just do not care, she said, what card is played or who wins."

Mary Cavett could not imagine in her wildest dreams why anyone would notice how she played card games or would think to share it, but she only said, "It's hard to get excited about a two of clubs, which is what I was usually left holding."

Mary Cavett knew it was coming. She knew he could not help saying it, and she forgave it even before he said it. It just had to be said, so Charlie dutifully said it.

"Unlucky at cards, lucky in love, they always say." He smiled a devilish grin, winking and raising one eyebrow. Not everybody could do that last little trick.

She smiled sweetly back at him and asked, "Who always says it?" Charlie Mack could sometimes be pretty predictable.

"What are you reading?" he ventured, hoping she would ask him to come over and look.

She just held the book up a bit and waggled it as if to suggest nothing too serious and said, "It's a collection of short stories by a British woman named Victoria Sackville-West." She glanced at him pleasantly, kindly, knowing perfectly well that he had not the vaguest notion this side of London or hell who Sackville-West was.

He would not be undone. "That's a right long name for a lady author. I mean, they usually use short pen names so they will be easier to remember, don't they?" he said. He thought that Mary Cavett's clear, brown eyes flickered with just the tiniest spark of real interest directed toward this lump standing in her bedroom.

Then she asked him, "Like who?"

Boy, he had to think fast. Maybe something from a UNC lit class at least eight years ago. "Well, like George Sand or Mary Shelley, for instance."

"Why, yes, that's true. I'd never thought about that before," she said, beginning to smile. Then a slight frown followed as she remembered, "But then there's Harriet Beecher Stowe and Mary Wallstonecraft Shelley. That was Mary Shelley's real name. She was Percy Shelley's wife."

"Hey, Hizzoner, is that you? Whatcha doin'? Come on back here," Charlie heard. He nodded at her quickly and started on back to the kitchen, walking about two inches above the squeaky old floorboards.

Just as he was three feet outside her door, Mary Cavett called him back. His heart skipped a beat. Yes, it did. Missed a beat. Dry-mouthed, he stepped back into her room.

"Charlie, would you ask Ben-Olive to make me a cup of tea, hot chocolate, something for the soul?" she asked sweetly.

"Sure thing," he managed as he floated back to the steamy kitchen.

Big Dan slapped him on the shoulder and shoved a fruit jar of high-class corn likker into his slightly shaking hand and a soda cracker with a nice slab of rat cheese on it into the other hand.

"Uh, Ben-Olive," Charlie said as he turned to Ben at the stove. "As I passed her room, Miz' Mer' Cavett asked if you'd send her back a cup of tea or chocolate, something for the soul." Ben nodded.

Butterball Jones, the skinniest man in the kitchen, volunteered, "Why don't you send her some of Skeeter's homemade white lightnin'? I've found that to be very reasonable for my soul." A few laughs and a "hey, yeah" followed.

"Somehow my wife has never been attracted to the charms of Skeeter's special recipe," said Big Dan, Mary Cavett's husband and host to this gathering. "Make her some hot chocolate, Ben, with lots of cinnamon." More laughs.

These men were accustomed to taking their ease in Dan's kitchen, lolling against the sink, their chairs turned backwards. They were in Ben-Olive's way every which way he turned. He pretended not to mind, as he knew each of them wanted to be closest to the middle to check the pots, and sniff the cornbread in the oven.

"Do you put any sugar in your cornbread, Ben-Olive?" asked Butterball.

"Sometimes. I don't ever tell," Ben answered good-naturedly.

"Do you use ham bone, fatback, or bacon in your collards?" asked Dr. Rascoe from Bertie County.

"Again, whatever we has handy. My preference is old ham hocks, first. Next, streak-o-lean, streak-o-fat. And I hardly ever use bacon. That gives the greens a whole different flavor. The smoke, I guess, is different. Also, I put some cabbage into the collards." They were aware they were in the presence of genius.

After awhile when Ben-Olive turned from the stove, he held a small, sterling tray with shapes of monkeys on top of banana trees in a rare and original design etched around the edges. Placed on the tray was hot chocolate in a fine Wedgewood China cup and saucer, with extra cream, cinnamon, a napkin, and several teacakes. Ben-Olive had placed a piece of folded paper on the tray. Mary Cavett's name was neatly printed on the outside.

"Please, Your Honor, if you would, take this to Mrs. Hardison for me," he said. This use of "Your Honor" was not even noticed anymore; it was just a nickname.

Charlie Mack hoped he wasn't blushing, and certainly he did not look up and about to see if anyone had recognized his extreme pleasure at performing this small service for his host's wife.

As he was leaving the kitchen, Big Dan was filling two fruit-jar glasses with his neighbor, Skeeter's, preparation and saying to one and all that it was guaranteed to put hair on your chest or remove the fillings from your teeth, whichever.

Stepping down the hall, Charlie kept his eye carefully on the bubbly, rich, hot chocolate, his heart hanging on his Adam's apple. He was moving toward his third entry of the evening to HER bedroom in anticipation of what she might say to him and what fool thing he might say to her.

However, he did pause long enough to put the tray down on a side table and read what was written in the note with unabashed abandon. He was disappointed to discover it was merely a recipe—a recipe for rock muddle:

Rock Fish Muddle

1 pound. white potatoes, sliced
1 pound. spring onions, w/green tops included
1/2 pound. rockfish, cut in chunks
Bacon drippings or streak-o-lean, rendered
Salt and pepper
Corn meal dumplings, if desired

Layer in pot, fish on top, cover with water, salt and pepper, cook over medium heat until mushy and done. Feeds six.

He folded the note back carefully, picked up the tray, sucked in his stomach, tapped on the door, and stepped in.

"Why, thank you, Charlie Mack. You're all too good to me. I was hoping it would be hot chocolate. What are you staring at?" she asked.

"That quilt on your bed. I hadn't noticed it," Charlie said. "Isn't it that old Pine Tree pattern? Like the one my mother gave me, called Bear Track? Close to it. Mine is all brown on a, uh, white background. She bought it from the Methodist church ladies' auction last year."

"You amaze me, Charlie. All the things you know about. That is exactly the name, Pine Tree. Mama got this for me at the same auction two years ago. We all went a little crazy over their quilts, didn't we?" Mary Cavett's eyes glowed over the memory. "Mama picked this one for me. Sky blue pine tree symbols on the off-white—we girls call it—background, and I love it. It's supposed to represent all the pine trees out here on the farm. In fact, you may not know, but on the books this farm is referred to as The Pines, and the other one is known as The Cedars because of the long cedar drive that led up to Grandmama's house, Monkey Top. That's where Mama grew up, you know—out on her daddy's farm near Hamilton."

"Oh, everybody knows where Monkey Top is, Mary Cavett, but I'm not sure I know where it got its name," he laughed.

"Sure, you must know. When hurricanes destroyed my grandfather's house in Jamaica, he sold the banana and coconut plantations down there and moved back out here in the country where he still had some land. He built the same cupola house again and named it Monkey Top II," she explained.

"One more time. How does a cupola cool a house?" he asked.

"You know how heat rises. And if you open the windows up in the belvedere or cupola, a wonderful cooling draft flows up the stairs and keeps the whole house cool, even in hot weather," she said.

"Is that why it's called Monkey Top?" he asked, still confused. "Because it has a belvedere on top?"

"Oh, no," she laughed. "Granddaddy said he planted all those banana trees in Jamaica after the Civil War, and every time he looked out the window he saw a monkey 'top every tree eating his profits. When he finally made enough money to build a house, he named that house in Jamaica for those monkeys. So, his second house in the country is a copy of the first in Jamaica, and the third house here in Williamston is a copy of the first house in Jamaica and the second house in the country. Mama and Daddy named their house here in town Monkey Top III.

"Grandmother had an artistic streak in her. Her fancy was to commission two dozen silver trays made for granddaddy, rather as a joke, each with a monkey 'top a banana tree design. This tray here is one of those twenty-four trays my grandmother had ordered to commemorate the banana plantation in Jamaica. Then granddaddy started giving them away to house party guests as mementos, and she had to hide the rest to keep him from giving them all away. Aren't you glad you didn't marry into a crazy family like Dan did?" She smiled prettily at him to apologize for her lengthy chitter-chat.

Charlie was not inclined to answer that last question, so he went back to the quilts. He leaned against the doorjamb. "Have you ever seen the quilt Julia Love's mother gave us? It's called Wedding Ring. It has too many colors. Too busy for me." He wanted to stop this stupid conversation and talk about something else with her, but he didn't know how to change the subject. Finally he just waved bye at his good friend's wife, backed out, and closed the door. In the few, rare moments he ever found to converse with her, why'n hell, he thought, couldn't he find something else more interesting to discuss—like her favorite flower, her favorite perfume, or why she had no children? Well, maybe not.

Upon arriving back in the kitchen, he said to Ben-Olive, "Ben, I noticed the really nice printing on that note, Mary Cavett's name. Neat, like an architect's printing. Is that Biddy's writing or yours?"

If a black man could blush, Ben did and said, "Oh, um, it's mine, Mr. Charlie."

"Where in the world did you learn to write like that? I bet nobody in this room can print like you do," said the mayor.

"Oh, my grandma, Meemaw, taught my sister, Beulah, and me both to print like that. She'd settle for nothing else. She said learning to write is a privilege, especially for black folks. And we should do it the absolute best way we can, every time, an' all that grandmama stuff. In fack, she 'bout got me into St. Augustine's 'Pistopal College up in Raleigh. Got up the money and all. But I couldn't go."

"Why not?" Dan asked.

"You know how it is," said Ben-Olive, shrugging his shoulders. "Biddy got expecting and we had to get married."

There was a pause before Endicott Brown, the lawyer from nearby Windsor, asked, "Who said you had to get married? Who knew who the father was?"

Big Dan, the host, broke another pause with, "He did, you bastard. Now shut up." He hit Endicott a friendly whap on the shoulder to lighten the content of his words to his guest.

The subject would have been closed except for the fact that Endicott had to have the last word, as some lawyers and many judges feel required to do. "Ben-Olive, you screwed yourself out of a college education, didn't you?"

Not many found this particularly amusing, but Ben-Olive smiled and turned back to the stove and the deer-meat stew.

Standing around in Dan's kitchen with the boys, laughing at their old jokes, they "sought for amiable insults" and "fought for friendly retaliation." While the others talked county politics, a picture kept returning in the back of the mayor's mind. Before the dinner they grazed on boiled peanuts, rat cheese on crackers, and sliced liver pudding—the poor man's pâté, Dan called it. A large bowl of coleslaw sat on the sink, and a pot of cheese grits still simmered on the stove.

As Charlie Mack sat in a chair in the corner, the flash of a picture in his mind became clearer, and he thought he recognized what it meant. He saw and felt the image of a graceful yellow cat walking along while innocently carrying a small live mouse by the tail in her mouth as if she were not aware of the mouse. The poor, helpless mouse tried to jerk itself up to catch the cat's whiskers but could not reach them. If you asked, "What are you doing with that mouse in your mouth?" she would casually drop it, place her paw on it to hold it, and answer, "What mouse?" The image reappeared to him for the briefest moment, and he knew how the mouse felt. He could not leap down and dash away to freedom, and he could not jerk himself up by the tail to snatch the beautiful cat's whiskers to make her let him go—a most helpless feeling. He also wondered in an honest moment if Mary Cavett was deliberately keeping him dangling, or if she even knew he was alive.

The sheriff, Timothy McKinnon, brought him back from his cat-and-mouse reveries.

Tim was the Presbyterian preacher's son, the sheriff who refused to wear a gun, telling the same old joke about the tobacco warehouse fire over in Wilson. For a minister's son, he told a pretty good story. He often told it by popular demand, and they always laughed, every time. They never tired of it. Each man had certain stories in his repertoire that they all delighted in hearing over and over again in fond repetition rather like the liturgy over at the 'pistopal church. It gave one a sense of continuity and security, of bonding with the Lord in one sense and with trusting friends in the other.

3

Who caught his blood?
I said the Fish
With my little dish
I caught his blood.

MEANWHILE, back on the *Swamp Monkey* on 9 April 1927, the dancin' man finished his fond reverie as to how he came by his dancing shoes, looked at himself one more time in the mirror, and saluted himself smartly, clicking the heels of his black and white wingtipped shoes.

"You g . . . g . . . g. . . g, gotta' get back to work, boy." His old stutter would come back on him every now and then. His grandmother, Meemaw, who raised him and his sister, Beulah, always said it was just a nervous tick of his speaking mechanism, when his nerves got too stretched from worrying about so many responsibilities. She also said more bright people who were sensitive and, how did she say it, conscientious, had a stutter. More than slow, dumb people. Right or wrong, she made it almost a compliment that he should have been a stutterer as a little boy. She said it would most likely go away as he grew up, and it did. Just occasionally, it would pop up like a warning, Meemaw said, telling him to slow down and let off steam. Stutterers had a lot of ideas they wanted to say, fast, while they had the attention of their listeners. They were afraid they would not get it all out before the listener, parent, or teacher, would turn away to something more important. Meemaw also said stutterers did not stutter when they sang!

Meemaw must have known what she was talking about, because under his favorite teachers, the ones he liked the most, he stuttered very little. Under the impatient, not-so-kind teachers, he stuttered a great deal more. This, in turn, embarrassed him, and then he stuttered even more. He would finally shut up and try not to say anything at all. Then the not-so-sensitive teacher thought he was just a dumb little kid and treated him thusly, like pretty well ignoring him and hoping he would just go away. He pretty much just did, for all practical purposes. Only Meemaw seemed to really understand the whole rigmarole, or cycle, as she called it. Meemaw had a good vocabulary, he always thought, for a black woman who had very little schooling. He used to wonder what she would have been if she had a college education. Certainly a teacher, or maybe even a writer.

He removed his beautiful shoes and placed them neatly side-by-side on the top shelf by a bag of rice. Then he pulled on his regular "working" shoes, headed out the door, and stepped along the deck to a board that he crossed to the swamp side of the river. He walked down the bank through the weeds along a path to the fishing machine moored to a large cypress tree. He walked another ten-foot board out to the "machine," carrying a tow sack to bring back his pick of the fish to make rock muddle that night for their supper.

This fishing machine consisted of a sturdy rowboat about the length of three men laid out, with a large paddle wheel on the deeper side toward the center of the river. The swift current of the spring, rain-swollen river turned the paddles. At the end of each paddle was a long "cup." While the spring run of herring, blues, and rock was at its peak, the "cups" would, upon dipping down into the rushing water, scoop up fish—sometimes one or two, sometimes none. As the cup-paddle rolled on up to the top of the turn, the fish would slide down the sluice-shaped paddle into the boat and remain there in a growing pile until the boat owner, or a friend or relative, came. They'd empty the fish into a bag, go sell it, and eat what they could or when it was herring, salt it down in barrels.

The Roanoke River valley was and still is famous for its salt herring, fried plain or with scrambled or fried eggs at any meal of the day. The locals referred to the river as the "storehouse." The *Enterprise* in Williamston and in Plymouth wrote up the first person who caught a herring in the early spring for having found the "key" to the storehouse, signaling the grand opening of the herring run.

Ben-Olive selected eight of the freshest rockfish in the pile. He judged the freshness by looking at their eyes. If they were even a bit cloudy, he'd leave those in the boat and remove only those with the clearest eyeballs. Clear eyeballs indicated that they were among the rockfish that the big turning paddles on the side of the fishing machine had scooped up most recently.

He returned to the *Swamp Monkey* and laid the eight rockfish on the deck of the barge, where he would return to clean them and throw the heads, tails, and innards into the river to feed the other fish. He paused a moment, admiring his rushing river. It was the color, he thought, of hoecake batter in the spring because of all the topsoil it was carrying to the ocean. The tea-colored swamp water (tea-colored because of tannin in the tree roots) turned muddy when it joined the swollen river.

He stepped on inside to the coffin-shaped wooden box, opened it, and pulled out eight nice, dry logs and some lightwood sticks to start the fire in the old iron stove. He balled up pieces of newspaper from a pile in the corner and placed them into the heart of the stove through the large front door. He started to place little pieces of lightwood over the paper stacking them up like an Indian tent, the first bits as big as his little finger, just like his grandma had taught him. Then he chose sticks the size of his thumb, then his wrist, then his elbow, then his shoulders, so the larger logs would catch fire from the smaller ones. Otherwise, it might all go out and he'd have to sit back on his heels and start the whole process over again.

Just as he was reaching in to stack his thumb-sized fatwood, a large granddaddy long-legs spider leaped out of the stove onto his arm and ran up toward his shoulder.

"Run ol' girl! I'd barrel myself outta' there too, faster'n you," he said. He wondered briefly if females of this breed were also referred to as "Granddaddy Long-legs" spiders. When the spider hesitated a moment, he grabbed her gently by one leg and carried her outside to the river on the swamp side, flicked her over the water, and watched her float to shore in the eddies. There she climbed up a reed, leaped over to the ground, and climbed up onto a leaf of poison ivy, turning around to look back at him, it appeared.

As Ben-Olive stepped back in from the swamp side, he glanced out a window on the river side. Something shining caught his eye. He moved toward the window and saw, perched lightly on the railing of the houseboat, the largest, most glorious dragonfly he had ever seen—and he had seen many. This girl appeared to be four inches long in the body, and her gossamer wings spanned four inches. The long body was glinting, metallic, and colored blue-green, yellow-green, and black.

He watched in quiet awe. Ben-Olive had read in the nature book at the lobby library of the Tar Heel Hotel that dragonflies were capable of long and sustained flights,soaring, hovering, and darting. Some species had been clocked at speeds as high as sixty miles an hour. So wedded to the air are dragonflies that some mate on the wing, and others lay their eggs while skimming the surface of the water. This glowing girl modeled dots of spring-grass green and early-dawn aquamarine on her slender body, just like the drawing in the book. The book said there was one species that remained as a slug in the mud of a pond or swamp for up to eleven years, enduring several underwater molts before it finally emerged as an adult to breathe oxygen and fly away.

More interesting to Ben-Olive than this was what Meemaw told him about dragonflies— that they were messenger angels. When one appeared to you as this one had, you could be assured that something special was about to happen, she said. Start getting prepared because some changes were imminent. Good or bad would not be indicated—just a difference. "Whoa," he thought. "I hope this don't mean Biddy is going to have another baby. We 'bout got enough." He tiptoed out through the door to get a closer look at her, and she seemed to watch him. The dragonfly honestly appeared to look back at him. But as he drew within two feet of her, close enough to reach out and touch her, she lifted off and headed toward the swamp, sparkling in the golden four o'clock sunshine.

Well knowing he had to go back inside and start that fire in the stove, come back on deck to clean the rockfish, go back inside to start the cornbread, chop the cabbage for coleslaw, slice the cucumbers and tomatoes, peel the apples, and make the crust for a cobbler, he leaned a few moments over the side of the deck looking at his reflection in the river. He thought of the wonders of nature Meemaw had shown him and Beulah as children. How the birds talked to you if you just listened. How foxes were loyal to one mate for life, all their lives, unlike some people. She told him that black snakes were their friends because they ate the poisonous snakes' eggs or their babies. They also ate rats, mice, and other rodents that would otherwise get into the barn and eat the corn, wheat, mule feed, and chicken feed. Brown and green snakes were harmless, she said. Just leave 'em be. Well, he tried, sort of, but he didn't really take the time required to decipher markings or colors in order to be able to recognize absolutely for sure whether this snake was a friend or not.

Meemaw told them about the Roanoke River, how it started up in the Blue Ridge Mountains of Virginia on a mountaintop so sharp it would split a raindrop. One half of that raindrop would go down westward through creeks, streams, and little rivers 'til it reached the great Mississippi and rolled on down to the Gulf of Mexico. The other half of the raindrop headed eastward, down through North Carolina, right by this ol' boat helping her float, and ran on down to the Atlantic Ocean. He had always liked Meemaw's raindrop idea. She seemed to have learned a lot to have been in school just six years. She stopped school to help with the younger babies. However, she had a good teacher in the neighborhood in Mrs. Johnsie Jennings, who would read with her during summers on the back porch while they shucked corn or shelled field peas. Meemaw was always asking Ben-Olive the question, "Ben-Ollie, why would you want to stop learning?"

"Lord a'mighty," he spoke to the river. "I come out here wid' that spider and I ain't built that fire yet." He rumbled on back to his fire-laying and struck a match off on the side of the stove, stuck it to the paper, and blew on it until it caught up.

He remembered his ride down earlier this afternoon with Big Dan Hardison, the former football star at N.C. State. That's how everybody in Martin County referred to Dan. They bumped down the corduroy road together that ran from the main highway out here to the dock at the river, where they kept the rowboats. Dan drove a 1926 Ford pickup truck. All of a sudden, he slammed on the brakes, sending the truck skewing all over that dirt road. They almost skidded into the ditch. When he screeched to a stop, Dan leaned up over the steering wheel to watch a little baby gray rabbit scurry off down into the ditch, up out of it, and out into the field, with his white cottontail vanishing behind him.

"Run, little wabbit. Run away home." This came from Big Dan Hardison, the former football star at N.C. State.

Ben-Olive's heart had stopped, and he could hardly speak. As Dan restarted the motor, Ben-Olive put his hat back on his head and got his wits together enough to ask, "Mr. Dan, would you explain something to me?"

"I'll try. What is it?" asked the driver.

"Uh, and I'll try to figger how to ask," said Ben.

"Ask what?" said the former football player-now-farmer.

"How in the world do you explain how you fling us all over the road, almost into the ditch, puttin' our lives in danger, me with three chirrun dependin' on me, to save that rabbit's life, when anytime in hunting season you'll grab up a gun and shoot her 'blam, blam' right between the eyes without skipping a beat? Can you answer me that?" Ben asked, leaning over toward him and looking directly at his boss.

Big Dan drove on awhile, looking straight ahead, and finally said, "I don't know. I don't know the answer to that. Sometimes I almost think a man, this one at least, is two, at least two different people. Maybe even three, maybe four."

"How' you come by that?" asked Ben-Olive.

"Well, think how a fella acts, say 'round his mother and grandmama. Then how he is 'round his wife and children, not to mention how he is in private times with his wife. Then how he acts, say at work with his business face on, dealing with customers, tenants, whoever, and . . . "

"Yeah, I'm listening," said Ben.

"And then how he is with the boys off fishing or cross town at Mrs. Alice's house. That's four different people right there," said Big Dan.

Ben-Olive showed a crooked smile as he changed the subject. "How come you leave any money over there at Mrs. Alice's house, Mr. Dan? You don't take nothing away."

"How do you know I don't, an' what business is it of yours?" Dan laughed.

"Ain't none of my business, but my cousin Melissa Bazemore works over there. Helps out at Mrs. Alice's big parties, cooking and serving. All the regular help tells her everything going on, who comes by, how often, and whose wife calls over there telling them to get their backside home. What do you think the help talks about? The weather?"

Dan's eyes got a little wider as he watched a hawk perched on the tip top of a tall pine tree by the road. The hawk was watching, seriously watching, her supper of an innocent raccoon who was going about her affairs seventy feet below looking for her own supper. Dan said, "Well, why don't you just write a column for the society page in the *Enterprise* every week, Ben-Olive? You would pick up a little extra change that way."

"Actually, I could, I could. We could call it 'Happenings at Alice's Palace' couldn't we?"

"Don't say 'we' to me. I'm having no part of it—your little gossip sessions. Somebody ain't got much to do if they have time and the interest to talk about what goes on out there. I'll be dam'. Everybody lives in glass houses, don't they?" Dan said, shaking his head.

"Naw, not everybody. Just the mens that goes out there to Mrs. Alice's house. When folks stay home, there's not so much discussion of their activities," said Ben-Olive with a straight face. "The people that comes in and helps during the week just mention sometime what they observes." He was very matter-of-fact, like business as usual.

Later, aboard the houseboat, the Chevrolet dealer and the Ford dealer sipped their hootch and branch water and cracked open boiled peanuts. One called attention to Sheriff McKinnon.

Charlie Mack said, "Sheriff, since you're so famous for being a poet, how come you don't ever make up any poems for your old buddies here? Tonight's the night. Let's have one."

A bit shy, the quiet sheriff who refused to wear a gun said, "Well, now, I don't really do poetry. Where'd you get that from?"

"Oh, I have my sources. Let's have one, right off the cuff. I bet you have one in your pocket right now."

The others joined in, "Yeah, let's have a poem. Do us a poem."

"Okay, you asked for it," he said.

Boys, you're way out in a fog.
See, here, I ain't no circus dog.

"Aw, shoot," said Bill-John, the Ford dealer. "Fog and dog don't even rhyme."

"Sure they do. Can't you see it on paper? I like how it looks on paper. I'm a visual poet."

Somebody commented, "And not a very good one."

At the same time someone else asked, "What's a visual poet?"

"I knew you wouldn't like it," said the sheriff, not apologizing.

"You're not really trying," said Dr. Rascoe from Windsor. "Do us another one."

Mayor Charlie Mack said, "You come down here and drink our spirits . . ."

But Doc Haughton interrupted him and reminded them, "He doesn't drink much of your spirits, now, fellas, even when he's off duty."

Big Dan defended the sheriff. "We certainly don't expect the high sheriff to have to pay us off for sharing our good company. He comes because we invite him, we invite him because we like him—and 'cause he don't arrest us," he said.

"Hey, you did a rhyme right there, Dan," said Dr. Rascoe. "He comes because we invite him, we invite him because we like him—and 'cause he don't arrest us."

"One reason he don't arrest us is because we're over the county line into Bertie County," said Bill-John Bellamy.

"And I have no jurisdiction over here. The county line runs right down the Martin County side of the river," commented the sheriff.

The mayor-Chevrolet dealer continued, unperturbed. "And our high sheriff can use big fancy words like 'jurisdiction,' and we love it. But don't let him catch us drinking booze in our home county or he might take us in to his friendly jail, and Mrs. Carpenter's good cooking." Looking suddenly at the handsome sheriff, Timothy McKinnon, he asked, "How in the world did you get that pretty Sally Carpenter to cook and carry her good meals to your jail, Sheriff?"

Big Dan said, "I think she's sweet on him."

"No," insisted the sheriff. "She's in my church, and I always preferred her cooking at our dinners on the grounds of the church. Why should we have bad food at the jail?"

"Why, indeed? Well, we're waiting for another rhyme. A rhyme every time," said the mayor.

Ben-Olive stopped his stirring. He wanted to hear this too.

"All right," said the sheriff. "This one is about money."

Money . . . makes jokes funny.

"And is that all?" asked Dr. Rascoe from Windsor.

"Isn't that enough?" asked the sheriff. "You wanted it to rhyme, and that says it all. It's a one-liner," the sheriff explained patiently. "It's like Japanese Haiku. The fewer words, the better. Less is more. Beauty in simplicity. You're not too dense for that, now are you, boys?"

"Well, we might be too dense to understand that Haiku stuff. What did you say? Less is more better? That was incorrect grammar last time I heard," said the lord mayor.

"Don't you see how profound that line is?" asked the sheriff. "It is really heavy with meaning. The fact that none of you laughed clearly proves that sheriffs are not paid enough money. If we were paid more, you would laugh at all my jokes. That's the long and short of it, right there, see?" The sheriff's kind eyes were smiling.

"Well, they might have to pay you a whole lot more," said Big Dan in spite of himself.

"That's right, boys," said Doc Haughton. "Everybody knows a rich man sings well and tells the funniest jokes. But we didn't ask him for a long poem, just a rhyme . . ."

Charlie Mack interrupted him. He had pulled a paper out of his pocket. "Well, here's why I brought it up. You know that our friend, the sheriff here, sometimes goes out, or stays home rocking in the porch swing with my smart sister, Dr. Dorothy, right? So, I discovered this stuck in the pages of a book at home and felt it deserved to be shared."

The sheriff grabbed for the paper, but his friends held back his arms. The sheriff blushed as Charlie Mack read:

To Dorothy:

Dorothy, why do I feel a thrill
Each time I see a daffodil?
Like when I gaze into your eye
I wonder, always wonder why
God helped us find each other,
Soulmates,
Soulmates,
One to another.

The young sheriff, deeply embarrassed said, "Charlie Mack, I thought you were my friend."

"Oh, I am, Tim. And I'll be very kind in my critique," said Charlie, solicitously. "But it is my opinion that you still have a ways to go yet."

Big Dan, of all people, threw in his bit. "The biggest problem with that one is that Wordsworth has already been there, to the host of golden daffodils." Before the others could josh him for admitting he remembered a poet's name from high school, he pressed on, "I mean, you could have chosen another flower, maybe not so famous."

"But," insisted the sheriff, nonplussed, "I'm just like William Wordsworth. No other flower affects me quite the same way. Not even roses."

Dr. Rascoe from Windsor broke in laughing. "I can't wait 'til I get home and tell my fishing buddies what you fellas over here really talk about," he said. "They won't believe me, of course."

"Hey, Doc, we're no different from ol' boys anywhere," said Mayor Griffin. "As little boys, we came down to the river to fish and swim. We built treehouses and camps to get away from our mamas. We still have to come back for sustenance, nurturing, as my grandmama says. To help us stay little boys and live longer, she says. She tells my wife, Julia Love, not to fuss with me 'bout it cause she's observed that ol' boys that have a chance to get away and talk stupid an' all live longer than the types that don't. Don't you know?"

Doc Haughton broke in, "Okay now, Dr./Mayor, now tell me where the women get away to for nurturing, to talk stupid and live longer?"

All those men just stood there staring into their booze with no answers. Before anyone could mention "church, beauty parlor, bridge table, or quilting party," Dan, feeling a need to slide the conversation to a different course, picked up the booze bottle and offered it around.

"Hey, Rascoe," he said as he knocked the doctor 'side the head. "Tell us that story you heard at Nags Head at the medical convention, about the traveling Bible salesman."

4

Who'll make his shroud?
I said the Beetle
With my thread and needle
I'll make his shroud.

IN the front porch swing, Dwight was laughing at something Mary Cavett was telling him about old man Caviness out in the country who, after his wife, Eileen, died, seemed to slip over the edge somewhat. One day his grown children discovered him beside a bonfire he had started in the back yard, burning up all of his furniture. They were not just upset, but fightin' furious about it and demanded to know what in hell's name he was doing. He informed them he was so darn tired of hearing all of them argue about who was going to get what of his and their mother's things when he died that he decided to set this fire and settle it once and for all.

"He was sure right about that," said Dwight, laughing. "You people are so funny down here. I believe you really are different from the outside world."

"Sure we are," she said. "Your old Governor Byrd back in the early 1700s made a trip down into northeastern Carolina and went back up into Virginia to declare two things about North Carolinians."

"What was that?" He couldn't resist.

"He said we were the laziest and also the heaviest consumers of alcohol of any people he had ever seen," she said.

"What a terrible thing to say," Dwight laughed again.

"He even wrote about how the Episcopal church sent out a retriever, a person to search out and recover a priest from Edenton who had vanished. They found him, but he was quite inebriated, awash with alcohol, and had long since stopped holding services or communicating with his bishop." She went on to explain, "But the reasons given for our laziness and the boozing were the extreme heat near our breezeless swamps and the malaria, which struck most of the population. They didn't know that mosquitoes carried it, and certainly nobody had discovered quinine. The only way they could survive it was to become, as the fellas say, skunk drunk, and try to live through it. So the laziness, you see, was probably illness."

"Excuses, excuses." He wouldn't let her off that easily.

A cool spring breeze smelling of rain rolled in off the fields, and they stood up and moved back inside the house. She arranged herself at one end of the green sofa.

Dwight stretched out with his feet hanging off the other end and his head in Mary Cavett's lap while he placed her right hand on his cheek to tell her, "I wish I had grown up with you."

"Mercy, why?" she asked.

"Because," he said, "I want to know every little thing about you, how you think, what you dream about, what you like to eat."

"You already know how I think." She tweaked his nose.

"Oh, you think so? What makes you say that?"

"You read my mind and finish my sentences . . . or we do it together. No one has ever read me like you do."

"Not even your husband?"

"Dear, no." She looked away.

"Well, for instance," he said, "I don't know why you stopped teaching. You said you loved teaching. Why did you quit? I guess you just got bored with it?" He seemed curious.

Running her fingers through his hair, she told him, "Well, you are wrong about that. I loved it most days. I miss it. That is what I am, a teacher. If I am not a teacher of English and composition, then I am nothing. But the Martin County School Board has a rule that only maiden ladies can teach our children, so when we marry, we have to stop teaching."

"You don't mean it." He sat up and looked at her. "Why?" he asked.

"I guess they assume the married ladies are too involved with their husbands, homes, and children to give enough energy to teaching classrooms. I don't know."

"How about married men teachers?"

"Oh, that's all right. They would rather have a male teacher who is married and settled, because they are usually the principals, coaches, and math and science teachers. The board assumes they have a family to support, and male principals and teachers also make more money than women. Anyway, I can't teach now that I am married unless they change the rules, which I think are merely based on the customs around here. But with the good memories, I do have a couple of sad memories about teaching. Even painful."

"Tell me about those," he insisted.

"Oh, you don't want to hear about that, Dwight."

"Yes I do. I said I want to know everything. It helps me understand the real Mary Cavett."

She looked sideways at him and smiled as if she didn't really believe him. Nobody, especially Dan, had ever asked her questions like this before as if truly interested in her feelings. It gave her a sense of near-euphoria. Just imagine. A chance to talk about her very own self. If he'd ask her to dive through fiery hoops or swim the channel, she would certainly try to do it for him. "How little it really takes to get a girl's attention, or a fella's too," she supposed. Just ask them questions about themselves and carefully listen to the answers. Where had she been all her life not to have learned this? Too self-engrossed, probably, to learn how to really make another person her slave. Did he know what he was doing to her? Did Dwight do this to all the women in his life? Was it only a part of his charm, or was he sincerely interested in her, of all things, brief teaching career? Now that she thought of it, she suspected he was just trying to work his sweet, magic charm on her, gazing intently into her eyes as she talked and pretending to listen.

"What are you waiting for? Tell me what happened," he demanded.

She hugged him instead and suggested he'd better be leaving as it was almost eleven o'clock, and Dan's truck usually rolled around to the back yard about one o'clock. She also needed to start letting the dogs and Wishbone, the old black cat, out.

Dwight would not leave. He said they never break up this early down at the boat. Except her father might leave sooner as he had early morning patients to call on before he went to the office. Besides, he really wanted her to tell him the something that happened during her teaching that made her feel sad.

"Well," she started and then hesitated a moment. "This boy's name was Herman," she said. "Herman Gaskins. He was in junior and senior English with me and did rather well his junior year. Turned in all his assignments and even had a flair for writing expressively. He wanted to drive a school bus worse than anything in the world and received that honor his senior year, tho' the county board had only hired one other student. Well, that money in his pocket changed his whole demeanor. Mine was his first class, and he began coming in late almost every day claiming that the buses ran late for one reason or another. He chose not to do most of his homework and was failing tests. One of the boys told me that his bus wasn't late. That he got his grammar school children delivered over to Church Street School in plenty of time. That he just rode around town awhile, came to school, and wandered up and down the halls making faces through the doors at classes in session. If the principal stopped him, he claimed to be going to the restroom, and he came flopping into class whenever he felt like it. What are you smiling about, Dwight? I'm not going to tell you the rest if . . . "

"No, I'm not smiling at you. But at Herman. You tell it so well, I can just see him, stopping the whole class, drawing all that attention to himself. So full of himself, the big hotshot. Making a little money and nobody can tell him anything. Of course his grades went down."

"You do amaze me, Dwight," she said. "You really do understand people, don't you?"

"They tell me I wouldn't be a salesman if I didn't. But let me guess. Herman stopped doing his homework and writing his papers. As they always say, 'Too smart to study and too cute to care.'"

"That is exactly the case!" she exclaimed. "How did you know? He hardly lifted a pencil week after week. Just shifted around in his seat waiting for the class to get over, making faces at the girls and me behind my back. It was as if he had reverted to being twelve years old again. I think he had taken up smoking. His clothes smelled like tobacco. And he was probably drinking, too. There was something about his eyes that looked different. I spoke to the principal. They warned him that if he failed two classes, he'd lose his driving job. I was forced to give him an F.

"He wandered up to my desk after class and muttered, 'I really need this job and I'm already failing math.' I told him to speak to his math teacher. That under no circumstances was it fair to give him credit for work not done, and that all the other students were doing their work, even those who had jobs after school. Then he asked me if I knew what his mother made him do. 'She makes me pimp for her,' he told me. I couldn't look at him. I must have turned very red in the face. Quite disconcerted, I wondered to myself, 'Do I tell the principal about this too? What can they do? Call his mother in? Send the sheriff out there to arrest her for exploiting children?' And in the back of my mind was that little voice that reminded me, 'Remember, Herman can lie. Can and does. He may just be trying to get your goat, pull your leg, make you pity him, and give him a passing grade so he can keep his driving job. Make money so he can keep on buying cigarettes, booze, whatever.'"

"So what did you do?" Dwight asked.

"Nothing. I ignored him. That last comment about his mother, anyway. I told him he could do his work like everybody else. If the driving kept him from doing his schoolwork, he must report this to the principal so that the job could go to someone else who was smart enough to do both. However, I felt he was quite capable of doing both. And graduation was coming."

"So, three days before graduation, the principal comes to me and says, 'Mary Cavett, this F you have given Herman Gaskins will keep him from promenading down the aisle Friday night and graduating with his friends.'

"My bad angel on my left shoulder laughed and whispered to me to ask the principal, 'Herman has friends?' But my good angel on my right shoulder whispered to me to stick to the subject, so I just told him that he needed to inform Herman of that fact, as he didn't seem to understand it from me: that study and work equals graduation. That little or no preparation or study equals no graduation and few decent jobs in the future. That graduation is something he earns, not just a present we give him. "And sir," I said, "I did not give Herman that F. He earned it, every bit of it, fair and square. In fact, he worked harder at earning that failing grade than any student I've ever had that worked for an A."

"'You can give him credit over my grade,' I told him, 'if you and the school board choose. I assume that is your decision and your privilege. But there is no possible way I can lie and give him a passing grade for work absolutely not performed. Of course, your crediting him for work undone will make my teaching here a joke—all our teaching a joke. The other students in his class or any other class will never have a need to study again. They can always throw Herman Gaskins at us. We graduated Herman, why not everyone else? But I have no choice. He performed well for me his junior year, so I know he is a capable student. I'd be happy to help him, but my lying for him would not help him in the long run, do you think?' Or so it went. I was just short of crying." She looked at Dwight. "Are you tired of this?"

"Dear, no. I want to know what happened to Herman."

"Well, the next afternoon, two days before school was out . . . "

"Wait a minute," Dwight interrupted. "Did they give him a passing grade in math or English to graduate?"

"I don't know. I never asked. I didn't want to put my superiors on the spot. Besides, the next afternoon, Herman, after he let the grammar school children off the bus, decided with the other student bus driver to run a race, side by side, down a country road to see who could reach Bear Grass Crossroads the fastest. All this in county-owned school buses."

"Good Lord! Was anyone hurt?" Dwight exclaimed.

"Fortunately, no. But they got caught. Question was, how many times had they done this before when they had not gotten caught. Of course, once was once too many. The next day, one day before graduation, when the principal passed me in the hall, he stopped. I stopped. What could I say? Not, 'I told you so.' So I mumbled something about being glad no one was hurt. Then he asked me if I wasn't planning to ask him if Herman Gaskins was going to graduate and walk down the aisle and up on the stage with his friends. I told him I was glad I was not a principal."

Dwight said, "There should have been some sort of test for those boys to measure their maturity and decision-making abilities before they were granted so much responsibility."

"You're exactly right, of course, Dwight. But you know, the state grants driver's licenses to anyone over sixteen, even mentally deranged people, without any intelligence tests or maturity tests. And did you know this? A child of eight or nine can drive a tractor down any highway in North Carolina without a jot of training, tests, or a license at all? Can you imagine?"

"Dear heart, that's because you good farm people are in control of the legislature in this state, and the farmers need their children to help out on the farms way before they are sixteen. I pick up that sort of information when I call on drugstores down here in the east. What else would you like to know?" asked Dwight, smiling.

"My gracious, I'd never thought about it that way before," Mary Cavett exclaimed.

"No one ever does, Mary Cavett, not when it's their ox that's being gored," he reminded her.

She looked at him admiringly. "You are just so interesting to talk to, Dwight. How do you know so much?"

"Honey, I'm just a listener. If I know anything, it's from listening. Salesmen, they say, do better when they mostly listen, we've been told. But the truth is, I really like to hear you talk—about your students, the things that interest you, your family. God knows I wish the circumstances were such that I could know Doc and Serena better, see them more often. Doc is such good company. They remind me of my parents. I enjoy calling on your father at his drugstore."

He looked at her with a sad, sweet look and asked her, "Why do our lives have to be the way they are? Why couldn't I have met you years ago instead of getting involved with Marietta. She and her mother are not like me. They are the two women, except for my mother, that I'm supposedly closest to. And we aren't, any of us, even in the same country. We have none of the same interests or hobbies. All we share is Heidi, my daughter. But look here, back to Herman. I guess he didn't graduate. I can see why you would like to forget about him."

"Oh, my dear, that isn't all. When I returned to my classroom after seeing the principal in the hall, the students had left for the day. I noticed the empty wastebasket from the right side of my desk was sitting out in the middle of the floor. When I reached down to move it back in place, I found that somebody had urinated in it."

Dwight couldn't believe it. "What did you say?" he asked.

"You heard what I said."

"As fine a person as you are, a lady! Damnation."

"Apparently Herman did not think I was a lady, and," smiling at Dwight, she continued, "maybe, I'm not."

Dwight couldn't get enough of her—her talk, her smile, her dimples, and her intelligent eyes looking right square back at him when he spoke.

Dwight could listen to Mary Cavett talk all night long and she, him, but he pulled himself away to his car down in the pine thicket and went back to the Tar Heel Hotel until his next trip through Williamston, one month later.

5

Who'll dig his grave?
I said the Owl
With my pick and shovel
I'll dig his grave.

ONE month later, Ben-Olive and Big Dan were headed along the steep last eighth of a mile on the dirt road that led down to the dock where two motorboats were tied. The two boats were named the *Hot Shot* and the *Big Shot* and were employed to carry men and supplies over to the *Monkey*. Big Dan pulled to a stop, but before climbing out he asked Ben who was he expecting to come down that night. Fellas from miles around and even from other counties really liked to be asked aboard the *Monkey* for Ben-Olive's good cooking, the cards, the stories, and the all-roun' hell raizin'. Furthermore, these men were disappointed if they were asked once and not invited back at least once a year. They were known to make gifts of fine hunting dogs or take one of these members up to Chapel Hill or to N.C. State to see football games in hopes of getting a reciprocal invitation back aboard this regal old girl, the *Swamp Monkey*.

"Well, yes, we got a little of everything tonight," said Ben. He was in his element, putting on a supper. He didn't just know everything, he knew everybody. "We have you and the mayor, Mr. Charlie Mack. That's two. Also Sheriff McKinnon and Bill-John Bellamy, the Ford dealer, and your daddy-in-law, Doc Haughton, is bringing some man. I think he tol' me he was a drug salesman from Nawfolk. Nawfolk, Virginia. And two or three others."

"A drug salesman?" Dan asked.

"You know, drugstore stuff. He calls on your daddy-in-law's drugstore and takes orders from Dr. Bennett, the pharmacist, 'bout once a month. Doc Haughton said he's been asking him every month for a year or so to come down here on the first Tuesday. That's when his sales route brings him to Williamston, but the fella always had something else to do. I can't think what, in Williamston," said Ben. Dan rowed Ben across, then brought the boat back to run an errand out at the farm.

Ben started making dumplings for his famous rockfish stew. Ben-Olive never tired of this old boat. It felt more like "home" to him than his own house, where he sometimes felt in the way and underfoot. Here, however, he felt like king of the castle, and captain of this here ship, all alone every Tuesday afternoon on the swamp side of the river. In the early part of the twentieth century, the boat was tied over there, far from any curious communities so that the "respectable" owners could indulge in booze, which was later outlawed. By 1927, the original owners' sons were still keeping the houseboat on the swamp side of the river to continue to enjoy the same pleasures as their fathers did, especially during rock and herring season.

A loosely organized "club" of local brethren from in and around Williamston owned the *Swamp Monkey*. Every Tuesday night in season, Ben-Olive prepared rock muddle or another of his fish or game dishes, always cooked without a recipe. The men enjoyed any of his dishes with B & B (Bourbon and Branchwater), coleslaw, cornbread or cheese grits, and collards. They played card games of the gambling variety. The old, recycled barge was ninety-eight feet from stem to stern and thirty-six feet across. Taking up most of the area once used to carry logs from upriver lumber mills was a crudely built "house" centered in the middle of the deck. It made the whole boat resemble Noah's ark pictured in Sunday school lessons.

One entered the house on the boat through either of two simple doors, one on either side near the middle of the one large room. Sixteen windows offered views of the swamp and the river, both upstream and down. Four windows appeared across the front, enabling the captain to see where he was going. The four at the rear were for him to see where he had been, and whether something was gaining on him. The four on either side let him decide where he was at the moment. Two crude doors, one on either side, had a small window at eye level, all built, apparently, by nonprofessionals.

The house was designed in the simplest form. A group of grown-up little boys had constructed it for a few weekends of fishing, gambling, nipping from various bottles.

They hammered away with donated boards, nails, roofing, and preused doors and windows from somebody's tenant house. These grown-up little boys were still building their "tree house"—but building it on a barge. The sixteen windows resembled old Nags Head beach cottage windows. One shutter over the window was made of three, ten-inch wide planks attached together and painted dark green. The boys nailed the planks above the windows in order to hang down over the window and be hooked to the rough "sill" by the simplest johnny-house hook. To let in light and air, they were pushed out away from the sill and propped up by a tobacco stick about three feet long. These were the same sticks the man used to prop up tomato plants, such as those growing on the deck in low, wooden barrels cut in half and filled with loam from the swamp.

The simplest form of "slide back and forth" wire screens let in the light and air but kept out flies, mosquitoes, and and particularly the birds. These men all believed what the black folks had told them when they were little boys—that if a bird got in the house, somebody was going to die. The simple screening usually kept birds, flies, and mosquitoes outside until it became too rusty to use. The tin roof rose up over beams in the center with lines similar to "bungalow" houses or California "craft" houses, built plentifully after World War I and in the 1920s. The boys hung a "girly" calendar on the river side of the wall in the houseboat, which noted the year and month but also showed a pretty blonde with big smile, dimples, and short, permanent-waved hair. She leaned against a Ford automobile as if she owned it. Next to this calendar was an equally pretty brunette leaning over the hood of a shiny new Chevrolet as if she owned it. Why did a poker room on a houseboat need two new calendars?

Stepping through either side door from the deck, the visitor beheld a large, dully furnished room with a homemade poker table at the back, where as many as six to eight might play. A big eating table sat at the front end of the room with eight or ten unmatched chairs or benches scattered about. One or two of them were cracked or broken. On the swamp side of the room, a few feet removed from the wall and resting tiredly on a heavy tin sheet, was an elderly wood-burning cook stove, big and black, standing on six fat metal legs. There were four large holes on the upper left top, each with a round cover. The oven was on the lower right side, suitable for right-handed cooks. A long, wooden box as large as a coffin for a tall man held dry wood for cooking. The stove's pipe ran up and out through the roof.

A window seat had been created across the front under four windows, with storage underneath but no pillow on top. At the sixteen windows, four on each side, there were no curtains. Comfort was not an issue in this place. However, the things that were important to the owners were here. Besides the stark tables and unmatched chairs, the wood-burning stove and coffin-shaped wooden box, and the two girly calendars, somebody's wife had sent down a long, cracked mirror. She was happy to see it go. It hung on the river side between the door and the second pair of windows.

On shelves near the stove, there were bowls for crisp coleslaw and creamy, buttery mashed potatoes. There were also bowls for butterbeans, corn on the cob, fresh cucumbers, and tomatoes in season, as well as stacks of unmatched plates, glasses, jelly glasses for quick "shots" of bootleg whiskey, and mugs for coffee and beer. Bent-up pots gave birth to lovely odors that smelled like we hope heaven do. Fish stews and turnip greens. Cabbage or green beans cooked with ham bone, heavy with rich, salty meat. Dried beans cooked with streak-o-lean, streak-o-fat. Frying pans that promised crunchy fried fish, steaks, pork chops, fried green tomatoes, okra, or crispy fried lace cornbread hung on the wall. And the dessert pan! Dessert, a word used loosely as the word "pudding" in England, represents the last sweet course, whatever it might be.

On this floating kitchen, every Tuesday night, the "dessert" might consist (in these bent, beat-up old pans) of cobblers (peach or blackberry), or apple, blueberry, lemon, pumpkin, pecan, or sweet potato pies. Or puddings, tapioca, rice with raisins and custard sauce, or Brown Betty. But not layer cakes or desserts with fancy icings. When the ladies were invited down, only once a year, Ben might make homemade banana, strawberry or peach ice cream, served with pound cake. A pound of butter, a pound of flour, a pound of sugar, a dozen eggs—a man's cake served with ice cream. But only when the ladies came.

◆ ◆ ◆

About seven o'clock that evening, the boys began to arrive aboard Ben's boat, puttering the two motorboats back and forth across the river to get everyone aboard. This was part of the pleasure, of course, and not always so simple to accomplish when the river was swollen and swift from the spring snow thaw in the Virginia mountains and the recent rains. There was a lot of joking about how often they had to row like heck with their paddles to help the old motor chug them across. Climbing aboard the *Swamp Monkey* from the boats was always a challenge, also, but not nearly the challenge they met later those nights after boozing it up and trying to get back down into the rock ing boats and across the river to the dock. It was a never-ceasing miracle that none of them had drowned.

First, Bill-John Bellamy, the Ford dealer, came putt-putting over with the sheriff who refused to wear a gun, Timothy McKinnon. Next came the mayor and Big Dan Hardison. Upon the arrival of two cars over at the dock, Bill-John and Ben-Olive rowed and putt-putted back across to bring over the final two, Doc Chase Haughton and his guest, the pharmaceutical representative from Norfolk. After they had all climbed aboard and had been introduced around, they poured themselves the first obligatory B & B.

"But you will play cards with us, won't you?" Dan went on.

"No, that's why I had to follow Doc, here, down with my car. Got to leave after supper. Have to be in Plymouth early tomorrow morning and Little Washington in the afternoon. Need to turn in early before you fellas get a good start," he apologized.

"Dam', a traveling salesman's 'sposed to have more fun than that, I always heard," Dan pushed on.

"Shut up," said Doc. "I had a hard enough time getting him to come down here at all. Leave him alone."

"Well," continued Dan, "usually a grown man that refuses a hospitable drink of alcohol . . . it just means he's had a problem with it and had to quit. Ain't nothing wrong with that, is it? Or admitting it, right, fella?"

Doc interrupted again. "Except it might not be any of your business, okay?"

"Oh, well, I wasn't trying to be nosy or nothing," Dan laughed and turned away.

Timothy, the sheriff, quickly added, "No, mostly curious, and maybe, uh, out of line?" Timothy smiled pleasantly as he suggested it.

"Well, preacher, when did you start setting our manners standards, huh?" They just laughed, ignoring Dan, which did not happen often. Matter of fact, Timothy McKinnon, the sheriff, was an odd number. His father had been the Presbyterian minister in Williamston all Tim's growing up years. After Tim had graduated from Davidson, a Presbyterian men's school near Charlotte, he had come back home, maybe to teach. His father had accepted a church call in Laurinburg, and Timothy didn't want to leave Martin County. There were no teaching, principal, or coaching jobs available, however, so Sheriff Gurganus asked him to help out as a deputy awhile until he made up his mind where to go and what to do. Jobs were short down there, so Tim accepted it. Soon afterward, Gurganus had a stroke, which explains how Martin

County boasted a Davidson College graduate as sheriff, though he majored in English.

Meantime, Doc was wondering why his sometimes obstreperous son-in-law seemed even more bothered than usual and noticed him grabbing his stomach a time or two. "Are you feeling okay, boy?" he asked. "Anything wrong?"

"No," whispered Dan, as if embarrassed. To change the subject, Dan called attention to a pot simmering away on the back burner of the stove. "What the dickens is this?" He demanded of Ben-Olive. "Do we get some of this, too?"

"No, suh," said Ben-Olive, smiling broadly. "That's just for me. White folks ain't supposed to like it, so that means more for me, all to myself." Of course, everybody crowded over to look into the pot. Ben-Olive said, "Them's eels, eel stew, cooked up with spring onions, dumplings, lots of salt and pepper."

"They look like chopped up snakes to me," said Big Dan, screwing up his nose.

"Oh, Americans don't care for 'em, but the French love 'em," explained Ben. "They sell 'em at high prices in fancy restaurants in Paris and call them a del-i-ca-cy."

"How come you know so much about eels?" asked Hizzoner.

"Well, it's like this," said Ben, warming to his subject and punctuating with his stew spoon. "My Grandma, Meemaw, who raised me, thought I'd find eels interesting or somethin' and made me look them up in a book and make a report on it in school in the fifth grade. And she was right. They is amazing creatures. They all, in this part of the world, spawn right out there," he said, pointing with his spoon to the Atlantic Ocean down at the mouth of the Roanoke River. "In the Sargasso Sea, where all that seaweed grows. You sort of fancy a sea within a sea, the book says. Like the Gulf Stream is a river within an ocean."

Bill-John interrupted, "What the heck does 'spawn' mean, anyway? How do they do it?"

"I don't know about other fish, but eels go down this river and a few others on the East Coast. The boys and girls they swim 'way out there, kinda move around together, like a big church dinner on the grounds."

"Or," interjected Doc Haughton to Dwight Carter, the handsome pharmaceutical salesman from Norfolk, "one of those big cocktail parties you have up in Norfolk that Serena loves to go to."

Dwight nodded and smiled. "My mother and my wife also," he said.

"And somehow," Ben continued, "the females let loose the eggs and the males swim over them and, uh, impregnate the eggs. And then, then the females all die. Die and drift to the bottom of the ocean. Then, when the babies hatch—now hear this, little bitty things—the American babies start swimming toward our coast and go up our rivers. It takes about a year for them to get here if big fish don't eat them on their trip. And the French eels know, just by nature somehow, to start swimming toward the coast of France and go up those rivers. Course most of them get eaten on the way. Besides, their trip takes up to three years before they arrive."

"How do they know if they're a French or an American eel?" asked Doc, fascinated.

"God only knows," said Ben, "how they know, but they is a difference. One of 'em has one more, uh, vertebra in his backbone (which is very long as you know) than the other. That's how scientists can tell the difference. Don't ask me how a eel knows the difference. In fact, how do a eel even know if she or he is a boy or girl? Anyway, funny thing, sometimes an old female eel will get stuck up here near the Roanoke River. She might've flopped and flipped through the swamp to some ol' back pond, and she could live to be up to eighty years old! Ain't that something? This ol' girl in here might be one of those. I caught her in a dip net today. Mr. Dan, don't you want some eels?"

"I'd as soon pick a pocket as eat that stuff, Ben," he retorted. "Rather, in fact," with a snort.

"Go on, Mr. Carter, whyn't you try some?" Ben said, handing the spoon to the newcomer. Dwight nodded, saying hesitantly, "Uh, well, since I've turned down so much of your good offers, the least I can do is try this." He dipped down and got a bit of the flesh, the onions, and the dumpling and tasted it. They all stared at the spoon suspended in the air as he swallowed.

6

Who'll be the parson?
I said the Rook
With my little book
I'll be the parson.

WHAT an interesting thing for you to bring to me, Dwight. The original *Oxford Book of English Nursery Rhymes*. You are full of surprises," said Mary Cavett, smiling up at him and looking delicious in her blue velvet robe.

"Oh, I'm not giving it to you, Lady-Girl," said Dwight. "It belongs to Heidi. Her grandmother gave it to her. Brought it from London. I just wanted to read you something from it. Sort of an unusual nursery rhyme. See what you think." He leaned back on the sofa, her head in his lap, with his right hand holding hers and the other holding the book.

Key to the Kingdom

This is the key to the kingdom:
In that kingdom is a city,

In that city is a town,
In that town there is a street,
In that street there winds a lane,
In that lane there is a yard,
In that yard there is a house,
In that house there waits a room,
In that room there is a bed,
On that bed there is a basket,
A basket of flowers.
Flowers in the basket,
Basket on the bed,
Bed in the chamber,
Chamber in the house,
House in the weedy yard,
Yard in the winding lane,
Lane in the broad street,
Street in the high town,
Town in the city,
City in the kingdom:
This is the key to the kingdom.

When he finished, she lay quiet a moment before she said, "Oh, my goodness, just the way a real marriage should be. But there're no weeds in my yard." She sat up looking at him defensively.

"Lord, no, not in your yard. Your yard is raked dirt. I never saw such a thing 'til I came down here. No weeds, no grass, no nothing," he laughed.

"Well, now," she said. "There are some shrubs, flowers, and azaleas. And in the summer we have sweet peas, chrysanthemums, and Daddy's dahlias he loves. He gave us some plants, black-eyed Susans, and daisies. You've never seen it in the summer. Besides, raking the yard beats cutting grass. Help is hard to come by."

"Mary Cavett, you have all that help out here on the farm. Surely some of them could cut your grass."

"Daddy says we need them on the farm. Actually, the tenant we had living here before we moved in started raking the dirt, and it was easier to just keep it up. Why were you late tonight?—not to change the subject."

"Oh, I thought you might have heard. Your daddy finally got me to go to that crazy ol' houseboat. You know I can't drink. I told you, and I sort of tried to tell him, but he was bound to get me down there. Obviously, I didn't stay for cards, as you can plainly see."

"Where did you park your car?" she asked. She looked nervous.

"Over in the pine thicket, away from the road, like always. Are you worried?" She admired his sun-streaked blonde hair, his face tanned from tennis, and his white, even teeth.

"I always worry. This whole thing is just so confusing and wonderful. I'll never figure it out. Look at Cotton, even he likes you. He's never barked at you once. You don't know how truly amazing that is. He's always been suspicious of anybody that comes near me."

"That's because Cotton knows the real thing when he sees it." He smiled, showing his perfect teeth and a dimple to the right of his mouth. "Dogs are smarter than we are. He knows I'm good for you, even if you're still not so sure, Mary Cavett. Trust Cotton. I am here to tell you, trust your dog."

Mary Cavett forced a smile.

"Do I have to ask? Did you meet Big Dan?"

"Uh huh. I met everybody."

"I don't care about everybody. What did you think of Dan?"

Dwight was quiet a moment. "Is he always so abrasive? Does he talk to you like that?"

"Actually, Dan never really talks to me, which makes it hard for me to talk to him." Mary Cavett seemed to be thinking out loud. "Does that make sense?"

"Of course it does," he said.

"And he doesn't seem to even know how to show affection—you know, no pats, no hugs. I might as well be a footstool in the room."

"Is he mean to you? Rude? Hurtful?"

"No. Probably not deliberately. Unless somebody's hurt by being ignored."

"Well, look here, Mary Cavett. I don't know why the hell I'm trying to take up for him or explain him. But it is rather like a puzzle—what makes people do, or not do, what they do—how they treat people! Didn't you say his father died when he was young? So he never saw how husbands treat wives. He never saw any affection." Dwight was playing psychiatrist, she thought, and she smiled at his concern for her, unusual as it was in this peculiar situation.

"That's probably a large part of it," she agreed, nodding and tickling the cleft in Dwight's chin. "But so many farmer-type daddies around here," she went on, "are not the types to express affection anyway. It's just jokingly in a low masculine growl, 'Got to get the corn on in tomorrow, Betsy. Need you out there, too—at seven o'clock in the morning.'

"'All right, Howard,' she'd say." Mary Cavett was speaking in a high-pitched voice. "Then she'd add, 'soon's I feed and wash the children, finish canning this okra, washing your rags, making your shirts, milking the cows . . . ' How do the women do it?"

"They get up early, for starters," he teased her. "And they have no choice."

"And, too," she mumbled, "the men probably associate sweetness with weakness." Dwight loved that.

"And they're right," he said. "Cause I'm sweet on you, baby, and I'm weak as a kitten when I'm near you."

He reached over and hugged her tightly but ever so gently, if that's possible. She sat up and asked, "What did he say to you? Dan, I mean."

"Well, he seemed to want to embarrass me right off the bat by bringing up my not drinking and then making jokes about traveling salesmen." At that they both stared at Cotton lying over near the door with his nose on his paws looking back at them.

Mary Cavett put her head on Dwight's shoulder. "I still remember the day Cotton and I first saw you down at the drugstore. You were sitting on one of the end stools waiting for Daddy, and I was looking in that big mirror behind the soda fountain. We looked at each other in the mirror. I was at the other end, and I couldn't stop looking."

"You were wearing," he said with his eyes twinkling as he teased her, "an out-of-season, delicious, grass-green linen dress with a white collar and white sandals. There were yellow spring daffodils on the dress, and you had a silly daffodil clip holding back your hair on one side. In Norfolk, ladies don't wear white shoes after Labor Day. My mother always said so."

"They don't in Williamston either, thank you. Except me."

"You know, the image of you in that dress actually keeps me going. When I'm driving from town to town in the heat, it gives me something cool and beautiful to dream about. I can't seem to imagine my life if the Lord hadn't put you in my path." He looked straight at her.

Mary Cavett rolled her eyes. "Oh, Lord, where did you learn that line?" she asked.

"Look, little girl, we're ignoring the elephant in the living room while we sit here sipping tea. All I can think about is how in the world did you marry that man? Where did you find him?"

"I thought I told you," she said. "He can be a right okay person. He does favors for his friends and people with problems. You're right, he and I don't have much to talk about or anything else in common. As I told you." She paused. "He had came home from State when I'd finished two years at St. Mary's in Raleigh, and he was available to run Daddy's farms."

"Oh, I do remember. You had been pinned, as they called it, to your roommate's brother in Atlanta? Then he suddenly married his old girlfriend. Was she pregnant?" he asked.

"Apparently so, but that was never mentioned. Her family had sent her to Wellesley, and next thing we knew, they brought her home, married her to Grainger, and put on a big wedding reception at the Piedmont Driving Club. He never explained anything to me. And his sister, Sally—my roommate—refused to talk about it. She just shook her head and changed the subject."

"Could the father have been a Harvard guy? You say she was at Wellesley?"

She shook her head and shrugged as she said, "Who knows?"

"Sounds fishy to me," Dwight said. "So you came home and married the first thing that came along wearing pants?"

"Oh, he's not so bad as all that. Dan's grandfather was a Civil War hero, and his father was a leader in the county, in the legislature and all. But he later lost their farms with floods and bad weather, then killed himself. Dan's mother tried to raise him best she could. They moved to town. You've always heard 'from shirtsleeves to shirtsleeves in three generations?' Well, then, he went on to State with a football scholarship."

"So I heard."

"But he did very well. President of his fraternity."

"Not president of Phi Beta Kappa?"

"Well, no. Were you?"

"You know perfectly well, as I told you, that I flunked out."

"Of medical school, not undergrad. You said you didn't want to be a doctor anyway. You were just doing it for your father."

"I think I'd have made it, however, if I'd stayed single and concentrated. I try not to blame it on Marietta. I do try not to. Maybe I should have gone to court or something. I don't know if I explained it to you very well."

"Oh, I got the picture clearly," she said. "They asked you, the handsome Carter family medical student, to be her escort at a debutante ball. Kept you for a late party at their house and plied you with alcohol, to which you happily applied yourself. You passed out, and the next morning, they informed you that you had, in effect, compromised their darling." She hesitated. "That you needed to make an honest woman of their daughter. And you actually agreed. What did your family say?"

"They didn't believe it either. They knew Marietta was not my type. They might have let me go to court, except they were all old family friends, same golf foursome. They finally decided the Scott family might help us get started when I finished medical school.— considering the Scotts seemed so anxious to get us "going" in the first place. I felt like a prized bull. A not very smart prized bull," he recalled sadly.

"So who was most disappointed when you didn't graduate? Your mother or hers?"

"Oh, hers, absolutely. Their little plan backfired. Marietta later—later you understand—found herself with child, and I was trying to study with a throwing-up wife gagging around the apartment."

"Down here, we call it 'expecting.' "

"Well, she got 'expecting.' What? Anyway, she delivered little Heidi. Actually, Heidi is the only reason I go home at all. However, she did cry a lot when I was trying to study. Sometimes all night long. Colic I think."

"What a sad life, for all of you. Heidi with no daddy around all week. Surely Marietta must need you. "

"No, she doesn't. They stay over at her mother's big house in her old room most of the time. She has help there with the baby, so Marietta and her mama play tennis and bridge and do Garden Club. When I get home on weekends, they treat me like I'm an embarrassment and sort of in the way."

"Dwight, why do you do this job? You can do many things. You don't have to travel around to drug stores."

"To get away from there To be able to breathe."

"Does your family give you a hard time about the money they wasted, I mean, spent on medical school, or should I ask?"

"No, they're pretty good sports. They found me this job, just as something to tide me over until I decide what I want to do."

She looked into his sad, slate-blue eyes, smoothed his eyebrows, rubbed the worry line away from between his eyes, massaged his temples, and asked, "What would you really like to do?"

"You mean, right now?"

"No, silly. I mean with your life, if you had your way."

He looked at her, incredulous. He shook his head, staring at his hands.

She urged him, "Haven't you ever thought about it?"

"Sure, as a little boy. I was going to be a fireman, an Indian, a policeman, a sailor, in that order. But all I ever heard I was going to be was Dr. Dwight Edmonton Carter, Jr., M.D."

"That's redundant."

"It sure was, baby, it sure was."

Turning to him and settling up beside him a bit, she said, "But now, Dwight, look here at me. What do you dream of, imagine, see yourself doing that you feel—you know—fulfilled doing? I'm serious. Tell me what?"

"What are you going to do about it?"

"Probably nothing. Who knows. But, Angel, I really want to know more about the person you are, your dreams, how you see yourself. We're kind of acting like crazy people here. Once a month . . . but you're the only person in this whole world I feel like I can say anything to, and you understand it. So why shouldn't you tell me your dreams? Didn't you say, months ago, that we're soul-mates? Or was that just silly talk—a line you hand all the girls you meet on your monthly rounds? Hmm?"

He jerked himself around away from her angrily. "You keep going on about 'all the girls on the road' and my 'lines.' That hurts me. Please don't suggest that kind of thing ever again. It makes me feel like some kind of traveling clown. If you don't trust me, then I might as well jump in that river down there."

"Jump in the river? You said you loved your daughter, Heidi."

"Of course I do. I'm not going to do anything stupid. It's just that when my parents look at me so, you know, kindly, I still feel guilty that they really expected me to keep up the family name, heritage kinda' thing. Not just learn how to spend Granddaddy's money—how to dress and who to pal around with. They wanted me to really make something of myself on my own, like my father, as if I would never inherit anything from my grandfather. They wanted me to be totally dependent on myself alone and not to be one of those playboys. Virginia has plenty of them—they think they have it all, just because they inherited an old name, and may someday receive some money to come along with it. I've always admired my parents for their independence. I've tried to tell them I don't want any of my grandfather's money to dispel the feeling I have that they think I'm just waiting around for my inheritance."

"Poor baby. I'm so sorry you have to worry about how you appear to your family. Family feelings get so mixed up, so confused. But you still haven't told me what you'd really like to do. Why am I having to beg you? Why don't you tell me?"

"Because you'll laugh."

"Swear to God. Cross my heart. I'd never laugh."

"Okay, uh, I tried to major in history at the University of Virginia. I could read history for hours. They made me change to chemistry. I thought then—and still sometimes think about it—that I'd like to teach history and maybe write history at a small college somewhere in the South. I wouldn't want to get caught up in the academic politics that exist at the large universities."

Interrupting, while her eyes brightened, Mary Cavett said, "Oh, you could teach history at Davidson. That's where my little brother, Chase Jr., and Sheriff McKinnon finished. It's small, like family. Everybody knows everybody. And the fellas really do study there. The library is even open on Sunday afternoons, which is more than I could say for St. Mary's."

"St. Mary's wasn't turning out future doctors, lawyers, and American presidents, either," Dwight reminded her.

"Ouch," said Mary Cavett.

"Yeah, ouch. We keep coming back to it," Dwight observed. "Just like at home. At both my house and Marietta's mama's house. Do you see why I stay away from home?"

"I hate for you to hurt so. Let's change the subject. Look at this nursery rhyme in Heidi's book. I never heard it before."

Lord Randal

Nephew to Robert Randal, Governor of Scotland,
Sixth Earl of Chester, died 1232

Where hae ye been, Lord Randal, my son.
Where hae ye been, my handsome young man,
I have been to the wild wood . . . mother,
make my bed soon for I'm weary wi' hunting and fain
wald lie doon.

Where gat ye your dinner, Lord Randal, my son.
Where gat ye your dinner, my handsome young man,
I din'd wi' my true love . . . mother,
make my bed soon for I'm weary wi' hunting and fain
wald lie doon.

What gat ye to dinner, Lord Randal, my son.
What gat ye to dinner, my handsome young man,
I gat eels boi'd in broo . . . mother,
make my bed soon for I'm weary wi' hunting and fain
wald lie doon.

When she finished, she looked up at him and wondered at his expression, a strange smile. "What is it? What's so funny? It didn't strike me as amusing, exactly," she said.

"Me neither. But wait'll you hear . . . hear something ironic. Have you ever eaten stewed eels before?"

"Lord, no, and I hope I never have to."

"Well, guess what?"

"What?"

"I have."

"Have what?"

"Eaten eel stew."

"I don't believe it."

"Well, believe it. I have."

"When? Where?"

"Tonight on that dam' houseboat, the *Swamp Monkey*. With your father and your husband Dan. Ben-Olive cooked them for himself."

"Did anybody else eat any?"

"I don't know. I didn't notice. I only know that yours truly, Dwight Edmonton Carter, ate eel stew for the first time in his life, tonight, on an old logging barge on the Roanoke River. And he came over here and you read him that old. . . . You don't think it's a bad omen or something?"

Her eyes grew wide. "Well, it apparently killed Lord Randal in 1232, but of course not you," she said. "You brought the book in here, I didn't. Oh, did Dan eat any?"

He laughed. "No, he said he'd as soon pick a pocket as eat that stuff. Rather, in fact. He can be right amusing sometime. Here," he said. "I want to change the subject to something more cheery. I want to read you one. It's Heidi's favorite. She cries every time I read it and then wants me to read it again, so now I just read it to her once a month."

"Just like you come here."

"Yeah, here goes. I won't read it all. It's rather long."

Who Killed Cock Robin?

Who killed Cock Robin?
I said the Sparrow
With my bow and arrow
I killed Cock Robin.

Who saw him die?
I said the Fly
With my little eye
I saw him die.

Who caught his blood?
I said the Fish
With my little dish
I caught his blood.

Who'll make his shroud?
I said the Beetle

With my thread and needle
I'll make his shroud

Who'll dig his grave?
I said the Owl
With my spade and trowel
I'll dig his grave.

Who'll be the parson?
I said the Rook
With my little book
I'll be the parson.

Who'll be chief mourner?
I said the Dove
I mourn for my love
I'll be chief mourner.

Who'll sing the psalm?
I, said the Thrush
As I sit in a rush
I'll sing the psalm

Who'll carry the coffin?
I said the Kite
If it's not in the night
I'll carry the coffin.

Who'll toll the bell?
I, said the Bull
Because I can pull
I'll toll the bell.

All the birds of the air
Fell sighing and sobbing
When they heard the bell toll
For poor Cock Robin.

"Oh, my," said Mary Cavett. "You call that cheery? Well, I'd like to hear a sad one. It makes me want to cry just like Heidi. That is so haunting—for a nursery rhyme. I believe Sarah read "Cock Robin" to me when I was a little girl."

"Is Sarah the nurse who raised you?"

"Yes, and also my mama. They brought her in from the farm when she was about twelve to help around the house because she was too frail to do farm work. She had asthma. But she was smart and could do everything else. Her room was up on the third floor. I loved to go up there. She always kept a clean bath towel across her pillow. The room had a wonderful smell like medicine, like mustarole. Besides nursing Mama and later me, she could also curl and style all the girls' hair and arrange flowers for bridge parties and wedding receptions. She was not one bit happy when I married Big Dan. She wouldn't even look at me. She just didn't think he was right for me, or me for him."

"Why did she feel she should have any say-so at all in whom you married?"

"Well, I was her baby. She knew me better than anybody. She knew I would expect lovemaking to be something like a religious experience, glowing stained glass windows, organ music—no pun intended." Dwight smiled.

"Church bells, the whole sentimental, Cinderella thing. And she felt Dan was not qualified to bring it all to pass."

"Was he not?" Dwight couldn't resist. Mary Cavett ignored his question.

She winked up at him and said, "By the way, she would have loved you."

"You really think so? You think she would've thought I qualified?" He loved it.

"Um-hmm. And, besides, she also saved my life."

"So that means she should select your husband? And how did she save your life?"

"Have you ever seen the goldfish pond in Mama's side yard? I guess not. Well, Sarah had given me my afternoon bath. I was about four years old. She had dressed me in a white starched dress with a blue sash that tied in the back, and another one in my hair, and told me to wait in the yard while she dressed before walking me down to the drugstore to get an ice cream soda. Bymanishus, the yardman, was working over in the shrubbery, but he didn't pay me any mind. A little girl who lived next door on the other side of the privy bushes had snuck over to play. She was older than I and took me over to the fish pond. We were stooped down on the edge, on the wall around it, holding hands and swinging. The next thing I knew, I was in the pond, blubbering around with those big old goldfish. I couldn't swim, Dwight. I couldn't even scream, 'cause water was in my mouth. That little girl from next door had run fast through the shrubs on home, scared to death. I'd grab hold to—oh, I remember it still—a water lily, and it would go down too. I had nightmares about it for years. The sides of the pond were black and green, shiny and slick with algae and moss. It was deeper than I was tall. My fingers couldn't catch hold to anything."

"I haven't seen Sarah saving your life yet!"

"Sarah told us later that she felt something grab her chest and she couldn't breathe, like a sudden asthma attack. She glanced down from her window and saw me flapping around down there and going under and making no noise, or not enough to raise a fuss. She screamed down at Bymanishus to take the rake to the fish pond, fast, and get me out. She ran down all those flights of stairs when she could hardly even breathe anyway and pulled me out with his rake. He was frozen with fear. So you see? Sarah saved me."

"Amazing."

"Furthermore, she slept with me when I was sick and had a fever or the croup, or when Mama and Daddy went to medical conventions or to Nags Head on house parties with their friends. She helped me breathe when I had croup, holding me over the steam from the croup kettle smelling like melted Vick's salve. She would often sleep with me so I wouldn't be scared. Oh, you should've seen her. She was about five-foot-ten and always wore white dresses and a white turban 'round her head. She had long, skinny arms and legs and a soft voice and never had to yell at me but a time or two. Up in her room, I remember her bed and dresser and washstand with a marble top. The room smelled like argyrol and Ben-Gay, and she always had unguentine handy for scrapes and burned fingers. She had a fabric picture her mama had sewn. Sarah had framed it and it said, 'As for me and my house, we shall serve the Lord.' She kept a croup kettle just for me. In fact, I could always breathe better around Sarah."

He nodded, entranced. "What did she yell at you for?"

"There were two times Mama described to me, or I heard her telling other people. I don't really remember them. Once she called down from the second floor when I was playing over at the edge of the yard. 'Mary Cavett! Mary Cavett!' she said. 'Get yourself outten them scrubs! Snake get you!' She was like God watching me. She knew where I was every minute.

"The other time, she didn't actually yell at me. She just told Mama about it when she came home from her church circle meeting. Sarah told her that a little boy—you met him, Charlie Mack Griffin, the Chevrolet dealer, grew up across the street—called over to me and said, 'Mary Cavett, Mary Cavett come over here and let's play cowboys.' Sarah told Mama I looked up at our house and said, 'I cain't. Sarah's looking.' Even though I couldn't actually see her looking out the window on the upper floor, I always knew that she knew exactly where I was. Sarah and Mama had a big laugh at that."

"Your mother was lucky to have her. Where is Sarah now?"

"Oh, I never told you about that? The summer after Dan and I married, Mama and I were down at Nags Head visiting some people when Daddy phoned down there and said that Sarah had taken really sick with her asthma and he was sending a car down with one of the tenants driving it to get us. When we got home, she had already passed away, and I was so upset that I hadn't been there with her. I asked to see her. First, Daddy wanted to take me upstairs to his little sitting room and talk to me. Everybody was acting so strange. The help would look at me and kind of vanish out into the back of the house. I asked Daddy, 'Whatever is going on?' So he took me upstairs with Mama and sat us down and told us. Something he didn't want us to hear uptown or at the drugstore or church."

"What in the world was it?"

"Sarah was a man."

◆ ◆ ◆

Dwight couldn't speak. He turned red in the face. "Damnation," he whispered. "How did you never know?"

"She was a very private person."

"He."

"She."

Dwight sat up and exploded, "How in the hell did she/he get by with that—fooling all your people all those years?"

Mary Cavett smiled kindly at him. "We were shocked. But when we found out, we didn't consider he was trying to fool us. He was trying to survive, to have a place in life, to live, to eat, to get along, to do what he could do best—nurse people, look after children, and teach. First it was mother, then me. The whole family in a sense. Besides, he was artistic and creative. People from far and wide sought after his flower arrangements for weddings and luncheons. Mother let him accept pay for them even when he used flowers from her garden. Sometimes people would collect their own flowers and tree branches, and he'd go to their houses and arrange them in their family containers. She'd—he'd—I get confused . . . would take me with her when I was little and let me help with the little arrangements she'd make in sterling water goblets. There was one for each luncheon table, with boxwood, daisies . . ."

"Mary Cavett, shut up! Flower arranging! Fuh Lord' sake, he was in your bed nursing you, yeah, and you claim you never had any idea."

"Dwight, just relax. Sarah was a wonderful, special human being. She was more of a real Christian than just about . . ."

Before Dwight could take it in or quite figure it out, Mary Cavett had jumped up off the sofa wide eyed. "Big Dan's coming!" she exclaimed.

"You're crazy. It's only eleven-thirty. They're out there another two, three hours."

"That's his car. He's about a mile away."

"Mary Cavett, darling sweet. I know you're rare and unusual, but you can't hear a motor that far away."

"Of course I can't, but Cotton can. Look at him. Cotton had jumped up at the door and stood with his tail wagging and was making little whimpering sounds. "Cotton never misses. *He* recognizes both our cars a mile or more away. Get out, quick."

Dwight started toward the back door.

"No, no. He parks out back—go out the front door!"

He stopped at the front door, trying to say something. "Things have got to change. We don't have to live like this. Surely to God . . . "

"Hurry. Just hurry. Get to the pine trees. No, wait 'til he gets out back. He may see you if you go out the front now. I'll cut out the light. Oh, I'm so sorry. This is so cheap, for you, for . . . "

He slipped through the door quietly, closed it, and ran into the dark as Dan's car pulled around to the back yard.

Mary Cavett hurried onto her side of the bed. She pulled up the quilt and closed her eyes, facing the back wall. That was how Dan found her after he came into the kitchen, drank a glass of milk, and came into the bedroom holding his stomach and leaning over worse than a woman having labor pains.

Mary Cavett was in the bed still lying with her face to the wall.

"Are you asleep?" he asked

"Well not anymore. What time is it? What are you doing home this early?"

"I was hurting so bad. I had to get out of there," Dan said.

"What kind of hurting?" she asked, still facing the wall.

"I've been mentioning it to you. But I guess you just didn't hear, right? It's my stomach. My dam' stomach hurts after every meal."

"Sounds like ulcers." She still faced the wall.

"That's what your daddy said," said Dan. "He said to drink goat's milk, for God's sake, and to eat small, tiny servings of stuff. Can you picture me eating like that? He also asked me if anything was worrying me. Worry! Why does nobody listen to me? I've been trying to tell both you and him that this farm is driving me crazy. The help, or lack of it, the taxes, the bad crops, the losses. Mary Cavett, turn over here and listen to me. I'm afraid we're going to lose this farm, both of 'em.

With that she did slowly turn over, blinking into the overhead light bulb hanging down in the center of the room.

"We? I don't run this place. You do. Where do you get this 'we' business?" she asked.

"Okay," he said. "We all. We're all in it together. But I, we, somebody, has got to quit borrowing money against next year's crop, you hear? Your daddy won't listen. He's not interested in the farms, except the cattle. He would love for them, and the farms, to just run themselves."

"You're right, of course. If he'd been interested in farming, he wouldn't have gone to medical school." She stared at him. "But you're the one with the degree in agriculture. Not Daddy, not Mama, not me. We thought this would be a song for you. What's wrong? Don't you like it either?"

"Look, I know. Maybe everybody in town thinks you married me just to run your daddy's farms. To support you and me, him and Serena, your Mama's help, Beulah, and all those fifteen tenants and their families. And it's just more, dammit, than I can do. Nobody could do it. There won't nothing in the books at State."

"Please, that's a double negative."

"I don't give a dam' if it's a quadruple negative. There was no mention in the agriculture books about how to keep tenants, pay them a living wage, tend to their medical bills, give 'em something at Christmas, for their birthdays, and when their babies are born. And make any money left over from a farm!"

"Well, other people do it," she noted for his information.

"Do you know how they do it?"

"Of course not. But Mr. Hawkins down at the feed and seed store did give us a clue about your fine business sense." She finally sat up as if she was about to get interested in this subject. "He laughed at you and told Mama and me . . . " she paused.

"What did he tell you?" Dan asked, mildly curious.

"Well, he said he rang you up one time to bring to your attention that while most of the local farmers and landowners charged twenty percent on their loans of money to their tenants to buy their seed, feed, and fertilizer, you only charged yours—ours—ten percent. And, as he said in his wonderful choice of words, 'Big Dan ain't gon' make no money like that.' And he said your answer to that was choice. You told him, and he laughed again, that the 'Bible says to charge ten percent interest on loans and that I might go to hell, right straight to hell, but it won't be for that.'"

Big Dan looked at her helplessly, as if he'd been caught stealing chickens.

"Who's been to see you tonight?" he asked suddenly.

"Nobody. Why do you ask?" She looked straight at him then.

"Here's this nursery rhyme book, in a house where there aren't any children. Seems kinda' strange." He opened the front page and read, "To Heidi from grandmother, Christmas, 1923." "Who the hell's Heidi?"

While Mary Cavett lay there looking at the white magnolia blossoms on the wallpaper as if the answer might be there, Big Dan noticed a man's coat of blue summer cotton cord hanging on the bedpost. He walked over, picked it off, reached in the pocket, and lifted out a wallet. Putting the coat down, he studied the wallet outside and in while Mary Cavett watched transfixed. He pulled out a big pack of large bills. Dan lifted them up to his forehead, gradually released them from his hand, and seemed to admire them as they trickled through his fingers and drifted all down on the floor. Cotton watched, fascinated, then started barking at them. She jumped up trying to catch some of them in her mouth, and did. She tasted the old dirty money and spit it out. Mary Cavett watched, horrified, and could not possibly speak.

But Dan spoke, eventually. "Mary Cavett, you know that white flower that grows wild on the ditch banks, the one your mother named her Garden Club after, and the colored folks laughed at her behind her back?"

"You mean Queen Anne's Lace?" she breathed, thinking he had surely lost his mind.

"Yes, well, do you know what the black folks call it?"

"No, what?"

"Stinkweed."

7

Who'll be the clerk?
I said the Lark
If it's not in the dark
I'll be the clerk.

GET your cotton-picking paws outta' my pickled egg jar!" shouted Grey Dog Johnson through the curtain to the front of his general store out on Bear Grass Road, about four miles from Williamston. It was seven o'clock two mornings later. He had been open since six for his regulars who came in for seed, feed and fertilizer for their fields and livestock, as well as a breakfast of sorts on their way to work on their farms.

"I'm not stealing your eggs, Mr. Grey Dog. Actually, my hand was in the pickled pig's feet jar, if you'll excuse me. I had an egg yesterday." Grey Dog recognized the voice of a son of the soil. Problem was, he was a son of the mountain soil, totally different from Martin County soil. Thomas Joyner had just graduated from N.C. State University in agriculture. The state agriculture commissioner, in his wisdom, had shipped him straight down here to run the Martin County Agricultural Extension Service, wouldn't you know? This nice kid carrying a college degree in farming was down here to tell these ol' codgers how to plant their corn, collards, and tobacco, and how to raise their pigs and cows. Not to mention the cotton crops. Thomas Joyner was up early and meant well. At least he was no slug-a-bed like a lotta' these college types, Mr. Johnson thought.

Even Grey Dog's own son, Billy Grey, when he came home from four years of college and was looking for a job, made the adamant statement, "Well, I'm certainly not going to work on Saturdays! No, sir. They can just forget it." So there. Daddy Grey Dog didn't want to whine, so he stayed quiet, wondering what young Billy thought his mama and daddy did all those Saturdays for twenty-two and more years to enable him—the son—to go off to college and develop this attitude about Saturdays.

What they did was, Grey Dog opened the store at seven o'clock instead of the weekday six o'clock and kept it open beyond the weeknights' eight o'clock. Kept it open 'til ten to catch the Saturday night movie show crowd from out there in the country. They all had to stop by and get a soda, crackers, cigarettes, candy, and lots of chewing gum, which the boys liked to chew a large wad of before they took their girlfriends home and up to the front door. Then the boys went home and stuck it on the bedpost so their little brothers could borrow it and chew off it later on. This really happened.

Anyway, by the time he cleaned up and closed up, it was eleven o'clock. So he only worked on Saturdays from seven 'til eleven, and his wife did her usual cooking and cleaning. She helped in the store, took in sewing, and even made a few wedding dresses to help keep him, the son, in college so as to learn not to work on Saturdays. Well, hell.

"So, Thomas," Grey Dog began, "what does bring you in here at seven o'clock in the morning except to eat everything my wife can pickle?"

Thomas smiled broadly. "I'm really learning to love your wife's cooking. Soda crackers, Vienna sausages . . . "

"She don't make those," said Grey Dog.

"I know," said Thomas Joyner. "But that was my first introduction to the real delicacies you offer here. The pickled pig's feet, pickled hot sausages, cucumber dills—the biggest I ever saw—and of course, the pickled eggs and your rat cheese. But enough of this, man. I have a date to meet somebody here."

"A woman this early?" asked Grey Dog.

"No, Lord, no. A fella who wants me to . . . oh, I guess I shouldn't tell his business. In fact, I think I better just drop it and wait for him outside here. We've got a lot to do today. "

"Like what?" asked Grey Dog.

Thomas couldn't resist. He was so rarin' to start. "Gonna go look at some tractors and a combine, and check out a new line of rot-resistant seed. I called Raleigh about the new fertilizer they're developing at State, and we're gonna take some soil samples."

"My gracious. Who's got the money to do all that?" half-mumbled Grey Dog.

"It don't take too much money to pay down on a tractor. To go in with two or three other people on a combine, plant crops in the most suitable soil. It's really just common sense," explained Thomas Joyner, all serious.

"But the trouble with common sense," said Grey Dog, "is it takes preparation and planning. Like luck, don't you know?"

"Ah, my dear Mr. Grey Dog," Thomas beamed, putting his hand on his new friend's shoulder proudly. "I believe you are my very first convert. If all your neighbors did just exactly what you described, they and you would be making so much money that you could just sell out here and retire to Miami, Florida."

"Why in God's world would I want to do that?" said Grey Dog, crossing his arms.

"Wup, here he comes. Gotta run. Put it on my bill, hey?"

Thomas Joyner ran outside, jumped into a pickup truck like he was going to play baseball, and roared off south. Grey Dog leaned across the counter and stared as hard as he could to try to recognize who was driving, but he couldn't see through the dust the truck kicked up behind. So he went back to taking the pennies and dimes out of the bank rolls and putting them in his father's old cash register. The only music in his store was the lyrical "ping" when the cash register opened and the "whump" whenever it closed. The more often it happened, the more musical it sounded to Grey Dog's tone-deaf ear. But he could verily dance to it, particularly on Saturdays, no matter what his son Billy Grey said.

◆ ◆ ◆

One hot Sunday morning in June of 1927, Beulah Bazemore rumbled over the railroad tracks going across town to her Weeping Mary Baptist Church driving the fine old Ford Mary Cavett had given her. She parked beside the very few cars in the side yard under the oak trees by the church near the graveyard. Most walked there or rode on wagons. On the other side of the church, people set up long, narrow picnic tables for a dinner to be held on the grounds after the two-hour long service, which would last from eleven o'clock 'til one unless Preacher Spotswood got even more wound up than usual on the intoxicating sound of his own voice. With this larger-than-usual crowd today, that might indeed happen. To have a packed congregation looking up at him, nodding in agreement, and calling out, "Amen," upon his every opinion or statement was as heady an elixir as any drink or drug the gods ever concocted. It made an earthling feel lifted up, resurrected as it were, to become—if only for a while—one of the gods himself.

Even if most of the worshippers—many of them invited from other churches for the annual celebration of the church's founding—were truly there for the big spread being prepared out under the oak trees, Preacher Spotswood did not want to miss this golden opportunity to enlighten them all of the true word of God in heaven.

He hoped to convince them that he had a strong, straight telegraph line.

All he had to do, he'd have you to know, was to tap in, "We're here, Lord, we're listening. Just tell me what to say. And this, dear friends, is what he tol' me to say. Right straight off the line. So listen up."

"Amen!" the two hundred people shouted, their minds prepared to listen and not even think about the collards, sweet potato pudding, caramel pies, and coconut cakes being unpacked outside as they spoke. Occasionally, however, a stomach would growl. The person would place his hand on his chest and glance around to see if anybody was giggling.

After church, Beulah moved on out into the churchyard, trying not to stumble in her high heels over the large roots at the bottom of every oak tree. The yard had no grass, but clean white sand was packed hard over a clay base, and there were just a few patches of weeds and sandspurs here and there. She spread out her barbecued chicken, potato salad, deviled eggs, and chocolate chess pie on a flowery tablecloth with brother Ben-Olive and his wife Biddy. Together, they had invited at least seven neighbors to join them. Some of their company would go to their own churches first and then hightail it across town to have dinner. This spread was not called "lunch." In fact, these good people never had "lunch." They enjoyed breakfast, dinner, and supper in that order. Except sometimes they might also have "breakfast for supper," especially if it was old country ham. A gift of a country ham for Christmas or for a birthday was a, or rather, the, most welcome present in Martin County next to a hunting dog—among both colored and white alike.

Beulah moved slowly, rather grandly, across the yard. Many people of all ages came up to hug her, shake her hand, or give her a peck. Most of them owed her favors of one sort or another. If a woman could be the backbone of a church, Beulah was. Some might say she ran the church. She would deny that.

Absolutely. She would remind them quickly, "I ain't never been chairman of nothing. No sir. I ain't got time." However, those who were chairmen never made a move without checking with Miz' Boo first. Nobody was even nominated to a station or an office without her approval. When she did have to make an announcement or address the congregation, she called them "dear hearts." They knew she meant it.

She might say, "Now, dear hearts, we're gonna pass the collection plate one more time tonight because the Widow Jones has been burned outta her house with three children. Doc Haughton and Miz' Serena have made a big donation, and Miz' Mary Cavett and Big Dan have tuned in, as well as the Kiwanis Club and the 'pistopal church. Also the white Baptists, Methodists, and Presbyterians. But Sudie Jones is a member of our church, and we've got to do our part. You hear? So, dear hearts, go home tonight after you've made a money donation and bring out clothes and canned goods, soap and hairbrushes. She's staying with her sister 'til we can work something out. Lord love you."

Money would come from nowhere on that last passing of the plate, just like the loaves and fishes. Yes, Miz' Boo carried right much weight at the Weeping Mary Baptist Church on the corner of Crowder and Hampton Avenues, somewhat to the chagrin of Preacher Spotswood from Virginia.

Naturally, he rather resented having to check with Miz' Boo, even if it was in a subtle sort of way, before he pursued a project of any sort. If he didn't check with her, he had discovered, a project would never move forward. Who could blame a fella for resenting that?

Beulah moved over to her cousin, Easter Howard. "Cud'n Easter, I've got a nursing job for you," she said. "In about January. But you can't tell nobody because she ain't telling anybody yet, not even her husband or her own mama."

Easter's eyes lit up with dollar marks. She lived with new mothers for two or three weeks, sometimes a month, until she got them breast-feeding successfully and the baby to somewhat sleeping through the night. She nursed the mama, the baby, and even the poor, left-out daddy until they adjusted to the little new creature in their midst.

She taught the older brothers and sisters to treasure the new baby instead of feeling jealous, and to feel proud to be able to try to help mama by answering the door, drying dishes, cleaning off the table, hanging diapers out on the line, hanging up their own clothes, and talking low so as not to wake the baby. Everybody tried to get Easter to stay on forever if they could afford it. She never would. She liked new challenges, she said. Actually, the work was very hard, though she made it seem easy. She needed to rest and get some sleep for herself after a few weeks.

So she said to Cud'n Boo, "Who in the world is it? I ain't heard of nobody. It cain't be Miz' Mary Cavett, could it?"

"That's the one," Beulah whispered, winking. "You hit it right on the button."

"Did she tell you first, before her own mama?"

"Oh, no, I just know. I can tell it by they eyes, just like you can, Cuz. You ain't the only one with that gift, see."

"Well, I don't just spot it by that self-satisfied look in their eyes. I can tell it also by the way they walks, even before they start showing, don't you know?" said Easter secretively. She didn't say "Don't you know?" as a question, but as a statement of fact, like, "You'd best believe."

"She'll be callin' you in a coupla months I 'spect, and don' you let on you already know. Just act surprised. But save that month open, all right?"

"Sure, baby. Thank you for the tip. We girls gotta' look after one another, ain't we?" said the pleased Easter.

"Right," said Miz' Boo, moving toward a big oak tree over at the side. During the last conversation, a little action had caught her eye. She'd followed it with only half a mind but was curious, nevertheless.

What had caught her eye was a young, slim, fifteen year-old girl pulling gently at the sleeve of Preacher Spotswood. He pulled gently away back to his long conversation with one of the heavier donors of his flock. The nervous-looking girl's name was Felicia Adams, and her parents were trying their darndest to raise her right after her older sisters had gone astray. You'd think they would just give up. Felicia had waited a moment, then tugged at the minister's sleeve again, but he pulled away quite firmly. The third time she tried it, he almost slapped her hand away and moved on off.

The girl moved sadly over behind the big oak tree where Miz' Beulah was headed casually to check on her. She found her crying and sitting on one of the moss-covered roots of the largest oak tree in the midday heat. She put her arms around her.

"Baby, can I go get you some cold iced tea and some of my chocolate chess pie?"

"No. Thank you, ma'am," she stammered, her tears subsiding a bit. Beulah placed her hands on her shoulders and looked into her beautiful brown eyes.

"Felicia, do you want to tell Miz' Beulah about it? You're too pretty to go roun' crying. Red eyes just don't become you. The boys might not go for blurry red eyes."

Felicia cut her a sidewise look that could have sliced a turkey.

"Well, hey there, now, girl. What's going on? Boy trouble?"

Felicia sniffed again and admitted, "Well, maybe man trouble, Miz' Boo. I've tried to talk to Preacher Spotswood about it, but he won't listen to me. He's always saying in his sermons to come to the Lord with any troubles we got and He'll take our burden off us, and that he himself will pray with us and all that, but he don't seem interested in helping me none."

"How 'bout your mama and daddy?" asked Beulah.

Felicia's eyes grew wide with fear. "Oh, Lord, they'd kill me, flat out," she said.

"Can you tell me about it and we'll see what we can do—if anything can be done, hear?" Beulah suggested quietly.

"Well, Miz' Beulah, there's this man in our church who sings in the choir wi' me, and he asked me to wait for him in the choir room some time ago. Said that he had something to tell me. So I did, and we've been meeting back there for a while now, and, un, I uh . . ."

"What did he tell you?"

"Well, he just tol' me I was the prettiest thing he had ever seen and he wanted to give such a pretty little creature, he said, something nice, to make me happy 'cause I looked sad sometimes."

"And what did he give you, Felicia?" asked Beulah.

"Well, lots of things. It seemed to give him pleasure to give me things."

"What sort of things?"

"Well, he brought me candy, chocolate raisins, hard peach candy, chocolate-covered marshmallows, chocolate silver bells—you know—chocolate kisses. "

"Any other kind of kisses?"

"Well, yes, some real sweet, soft, slow kisses. Oh, and some scuppernong wine he said his mother had made. Wasn't that nice, to bring me some wine his own mama had made?"

"Why, yes," said Beulah dully. "That sounds very nice, I do say. What else did he give you?"

"Oh, just little things. Sweet, romantic things, like a cigar wrapper ring he placed on my third finger, left hand. He said he wished he'd met me years ago, as I'm his dream girl and he would have married me."

"Just a few years ago, Felicia, you were in diapers, baby. What kind of talk is that?"

"Well, nobody in my life had talked to me like that before. He said he dreamed about me every night."

Ignoring that last statement, Beulah asked, "How old is his wife and children?"

"Miz' Boo, how did you know he had a wife and chirrun?"

"Simple as that nose on your face, or that brain in your po' head. All the signs. And you don't even need to tell me who it is. It's Bransom Jenkins, our fine undertaker and one of the biggest givers to the church coffers, tryin' to buy his way outta hell."

"I still don't know how you guessed, Miz' Beulah. I didn't give no clues as to his name."

"Felicia, all I had to do was think of the men in the choir, who had a key to the church and to the choir room because he's a deacon, and who Preacher Spotswood ain't gon' get involved about because he's a big buddy of his. He helped bring ol' Spotty down here from Virginia. But I think you haven't tol' Aunt Boo everything, because nothing you've tol' me would make you go behind this tree crying and carrying on like you did. What else did he give you? Like I don't know."

"You mean, you know that, too? Miz' Beulah, how did you know that?" Felicia's eyes were big as Orphan Annie's.

"Little girl, do you think I fell off the back of a turnip truck? Besides, ol' Mama Boo here can tell when girls is pregnant by looking in they eyes, and other ways."

"Do you think my mama can tell too, like you?"

Beulah looked at her awhile and whispered, "No, and she ain't gonna know either. You're still in school, you're halfway smart. Not all the way. However, you're too young to have babies. This man has babies all over Martin County, not to mention the three by his wife that use his name. I've had enough of his mess. Listen, you meet me down at Booker's Store Tuesday night at seven o'clock. You and I are going on a short little trip, and you're gonna play sick Wednesday and Thursday and miss school. But get your homework anyway, you hear? Tell nobody nothin'. Just tell your mama you're going to my house to help me with some cooking and I'm going to pay you. Hear? And qwitcher crying. Go home and try to pass for normal. Hear me now? Go on." Beulah whapped Felicia gently on her bottom as she turned to start away.

Beulah went into the church, selected the oldest, most beat-up hymnbook she could find, got a short stubby pencil off the piano, and tore a page from the hymnal. She wrote a note in the margin, folded it carefully, and went back down the worn, wooden, unpainted steps. Strolling over to Preacher Spotswood, she stuck the note into his breast pocket, patted it a bit, smiled at him, and walked over to Biddy's table to eat her collards and cornbread.

The hymn she had chosen was on page eighty-two and written by Fannie Cowper in 1882.

I'll Tell the World

"I'll tell the world.
I'll tell the world,
Tell all the sinners in the world.
I'll tell the world,
Tell all the world,
About the love of Jesus."

The message Beulah gave him burned a hole in Preacher Spotswood's pocket 'til he could get home, pull it out, and read it. He took in the hymn first, wondering what it meant but feeling a lack of air in his chest even before he read the notation. He rubbed his narrow mustache a few times as he read the message. "Meet me at Booker's Store Monday night at seven o'clock back beside the pickle barrel. Bring to me thirty of the dollars that our fine undertaker and church deacon puts into your hands once a month after he puts half that amount into the plate for the church. We don't mind him giving you money you can keep. Politicians do that all the time. We just want to be sure that ain't hush money. Right, Spotty?"

◆ ◆ ◆

Beulah had just placed two large dill pickles into a brown paper bag, then wrapped that in old newspapers to keep it from dripping when her minister came up to her quietly on Monday night at seven o'clock.

"How nice to see you in here, Preacher. I didn't know you shopped at Booker's Store. Booker, your clientele is improving every day," she said.

"Miz' Beulah Bazemore, what can I do for you?" asked Preacher Spotswood.

Boo didn't want to make him squirm. She just wanted to get this over with. So all she said was, "Brother Spotswood, a winsome young beauty, another one, yes, has found herself in a family way by a deacon in your church. And I'll bet your hat, ass, and overcoat that you know who it is. Why, yes, I see the light in your eyes. The biggest giver in your church who also thinks he's God's gift to women, especially young pretty ones. You have two choices. Tell him to give me the money to have this fixed, or you give me the money yourself."

He opened and closed his mouth like a fish just pulled onto the dock, but before he could say anything, she shushed him. "I know you're going to say he might not be the one," she said. "He'll of course deny it. But you and I both know he is. You know perfectly well what goes on in the choir room most every Wednesday night. I can tell you know. Another thing. You know that the local Ku Klux don't only burn crosses and carry on to scare colored folks. You do know that, don't you? That they also burn crosses in the yards of white men that are doing wrong by their wives and children to scare the hell out of them, too. Don't tell me how to talk. I'll curse you all I want till you come up with the money to fix up Felicia. And if you don't think I can't get the Ku Kluckers to burn a cross in front of your house as well as in front of our fine undertaker's, just give me a chance."

"Uh," he stammered, "Doc Haughton ain't no Ku Klucker. Neither is Big Dan Hardison. Who . . . "

"Do you think they're the only white mens I know? Who do you take me for?"

Somewhat watered down from his best preaching style, he tried to ask her quietly, without drawing attention from others in the store, "Why are you asking thirty dollars when that woman . . ."

"Mrs. Velma. She's a fine woman. A lady. And she helps out white girls, too. I 'spect your wife knows who she is even if you don't. Just don't be so high and mighty with me. You're starting to say she only charges fifteen dollars, and you're right. The other fifteen dollars is for Felicia for her agony and pain, to put aside for her high school graduation dress. All right? And if you don't have it with you tonight like I told you to, I'm charging you forty dollars, you hear?" All this was said in a firm, strong whisper. "If either of you give me a hard time, I can get other mothers of his babies to step forward and demand some money for those children, too, without even going to court. Do you doubt it, Preacher?"

He had no answer. Then he managed to say, "Miz' Bazemore, do you enjoy being self-righteous?"

"Bet your buttons, Preacher. Since I ain't never held myself out to be no saint in the first place, I don't have to pretend to be. The Lord knows I've got a long way to go, but before I catch that train you're always preachin' about—that train to Gloryland—it may have to leave without me. 'Cause I'm gonna get Felicia through high school first. Are we together on that, brother?"

He handed her, after looking around the store, a worn, clean handkerchief tied up by the corners. She could tell it had both bills and change in it. She didn't embarrass him by opening it and counting out the money. She straight away thrust it into her right dress pocket, then reached out and shook his rather lifeless hand.

"I've enjoyed doing business with you, Spotty," she said. Beulah pumped his hand and said this loud enough for the customers in that part of the store to hear. She marched out, smiling broadly and waving at everyone while carrying the thirty dollars planted deep in her pocket, along with all the keys to her house, Ben-Olive's house, Serena's and Doc's house, Mary Cavett's and Dan's house, and the Weeping Mary Baptist Church.

◆ ◆ ◆

"Qwitcher whisperin' in church, Mae-Mae. The preacher's gonna stare you down," said Sally Griffin, who was there to worship and pray.

"He ain't even in here yet, Sally. I'm just telling Miz' Crump 'bout Dan Hardison," whispered Mae-Mae. The visiting could get a little loud at Westside Methodist Church while the organist played hymns before the choir and preacher came in during the greeting hymn.

Even Miz' Sally Griffin was curious. "What about him?" she asked. So she leaned up behind the other girls with her arms crossed on the back of the old pine pew to hear Mae-Mae Lassiter and Mary Crump discuss the latest in politics. All three were "good" Democrats, as were their husbands—"yellow dog" Democrats. The kind that felt they had to swallow their candidates, guts, feathers, and all. They believed in the party first, last, and always.

The candidate, Lord love him, could do no wrong a'tall. "Except he's a son-of-a-bitch."

"Yeah, but he's *our* son-of-a-bitch."

That kind of Democrat.

"Well, Jack Haley just told my Lonnie in the yard outside the church that Dan Hardison is running for State Senate this fall, in November. Ain't that something? What'cha think?"

Sally Griffin had only just entered the conversation, but she grabbed a Biggs Funeral Parlor fan from the hymnal rack and started fanning distractedly, thinking.

"Well, you know, I ain't never thought of Dan as no politician. But he'd be real good at it 'cause he's—let me see. For one thing, he knows every farmer in this county." She glanced around to see if anyone had heard.

Just as she was arriving at her point, Mary Crump just had to say, "We gotta quit this yackin'! Brother John's fixin' to come in. But now that you mention it, 'most everybody does love Big Dan. All his hunting and fishin' and gamblin' buddies. He does favors for widows and colored people and whites that are down on their luck."

"What's that hymn? Page ninety-eight." She dropped the hymnal, wham! Grabbed it up again, looking about to see if anyone had noticed.

Everybody joined in gradually while rising up to "I am Thine, Oh, Lord. I am . . . "

◆ ◆ ◆

Persons from several counties questioned and discussed Mary Cavett's condition. At Mamie's Beauty Shop, the rumor of Mary Cavett's expecting was settled with alacrity. Fannie Mae Briggs leaned out from under her dryer to touch Maye Belle Hensley's knee. Maye Belle leaned out from under hers in response. Fannie May took a sip of her ammonia coke just brought in from Doc Haughton's drugstore. She slurped a swallow through the straw and then asked, "Does anybody not know about Mary Cavett's condition?"

Maye Belle responded excitedly, "Oh yes, I heard it at the oyster bar and again at church Sunday. That girl in front of me, that talks all the time behind her fan, tells more news than the *Enterprise*. If you want to know next week's news today, just keep one ear open around her. Not two, 'cause your ears will ring. She guessed, she said, it would be about January. Don't ask me how she knows. She just does."

◆ ◆ ◆

Mayor Charlie Mack sat in the back booth of the drugstore watching the door at ten o'clock in the morning to see if Mary Cavett and Cotton might drop by for their usual. He had heard the "news" about a baby and had confused feelings about it. When she came and sat at the first stool up front, he casually sauntered by, stopped, and asked, "Mary Cavett, what's this I heard this morning about Big Dan running for the legislature? Whenever did he get interested in politics? Fuh gosh sakes."

She laughed her pleasant laugh. "Can you believe that? No, me neither. But that Thomas Joyner, the agriculture boy, has convinced Dan he could go to Raleigh and get legislation through to help farmers, and also get more roads down here. 'To get the farmers out of the mud,' he calls it. And he could help improve some of the hunting and fishing laws. You name it. Dan's writing State College for brochures and information about all this. Do stay out of his way or he'll bore you to death."

Charlie Mack figured he would hear all about Dan's political venture on the houseboat the next Tuesday night, but somehow he just couldn't bring up the subject of Mary Cavett's expecting. It didn't seem gentlemanly.

◆ ◆ ◆

"Doc, can you hear me? I'm calling from the phone in the lobby," said Serena, telephoning in early August from the Arlington Hotel at Nags Head. She had moved down there for the summer. Doc usually drove down to join her on the weekends, making arrangements with a visiting medical student and a midwife to handle emergencies while he was away.

"Is that still the only phone at the hotel? I can hear you just fine. You don't need to holler. Are you all right?"

"Sure, baby, I'm all right. But do you remember Jack Bass from Tarboro?"

"Yes, he has the newspaper over there. Why?"

"Well, he's coming through Williamston tomorrow afternoon, and I thought I'd catch a ride with him and save you driving here. It's awfully hot. And I'll come back down with the first ride I can find. He's going home for a funeral. Mr. Robert Clark."

"Oh, my. I probably should go over to that funeral myself," said Doc.

"Oh, don't go, darlin'. We haven't seen those people in a long time. Besides, their daughter didn't write us a thank-you note when we sent a wedding present—those silver ice tongs."

"Maybe she didn't like 'em," said Doc.

"That's not the point."

"Don't be small, Serena. I can't let a pair of ice tongs keep me from going to a funeral if I feel it's my obligation to be there."

"Of course, honey. You do what you want. We'll be there about five-thirty. I'll bring fresh shrimp. Tell Beulah we'll just have a simple shrimp cocktail with sauce and lemon, crackers and butter, and a little potato salad. Okay? Is Beulah taking good care of you, honey? Now, if you'd rather eat at the hotel some, you just tell her, heah?"

"She does just fine! You know I'd rather suck my thumb than eat down there with all those people. I have trouble remembering all their names."

"Well, Daddy, I expect you two perfectionists are doing just fine." She still called him "Daddy" because that is what she called him in front of the babies, Mary Cavett and Chase, Jr., so they would learn to say it. Now here she was still calling Doc "Daddy" twenty-seven years later.

"Well, aren't you glad your doctor is a perfectionist? Don't you want your lawyer, doctor, and your brain surgeon to all be perfectionists?" Doc asked. "And your banker?"

"Oh, and Doc. Be sure Beulah gets the oil changed in that car soon, huh?"

"You just said she was a perfectionist. She's not going to let that car run out of oil."

"Well, it did on me, several times," Serena said.

"Honey, that's you. We're talking two different people. Tell the Midgettes and the Fearings I said hello, and I'll see you tomorrow night. Okay? And I love you."

Then he set about notifying the midwife and the medical student visiting this family down in Robersonville that he would be around for the weekend and they could relax unless he called. He also decided not to go to Tarboro for Bob Clark's funeral.

Friday, at five-thirty on the dot, Jack Bass and Serena drove up. She got out and hugged Doc good. The men chatted, and Doc took her bag and the shrimp. She gave five more pounds of the fresh shrimp, just caught that morning from the ocean in front of Kill Devil Hills, to Jack to take to Tarboro. She had an old metal box just for hauling seafood home over ice.

"Hey, this is awfully nice of you, Serena," Jack said. "Since Sally's still at the beach, I'll call my son and his family over and we'll have boiled shrimp for supper. Thank you, hear. A lot." He took off for Tarboro.

Serena and Doc walked into the house holding hands. Beulah greeted her and carried the shrimp back to the kitchen. Before Serena could unpack her valise, in fact, way before she unpacked, she got on the telephone to call three of her buddies to play bridge the next afternoon at one-thirty at her house.

On Saturday morning, Serena worked in her flowers that needed so much attention since she had been at the beach. She watered, plucked, topped, and weeded in her big straw hat while Beulah made her special spicy cheese straws from Serena's mama's recipe. Some of the cheese straws were for the afternoon bridge game, another batch was for Nags Head, and some were to keep around and give away, but most were for a tin to take to the Reverend Horton since she felt guilty for not having been to church in so long. She suspected the Hortons pictured her lolling on the Arlington's wooden porches, sipping gin and tonics at teatime—five o'clock in the afternoon—before going in to dinner after a long, hard day on the beach under an umbrella. Or maybe they suspected she was playing cards in the lobby, napping, reading, and visiting with those fascinating people down from Washington, D.C. and New York—writers, artists, journalists, and judges. The only problem was that the Hortons, if they did suspect these things of her, were exactly right.

As Serena was digging into her delicious dirt, Doc came home from the office, wandered out into the yard just before their lunch of shrimp salad and tomato aspic, and, strolling up to her, remarked, "You seemed so tickled to get to ride home with ol' Bass. I almost started to ask if you and he had something going on. Hey, what's he doing at the beach in the middle of the week, anyhow?"

She shrugged and asked, "How do I know?"

He went on. "Then I realized that he wasn't your type."

She sat back on her heels and removed her gloves. They were hot and sweaty in August. "What's my type?" she asked, curious.

"Me." He smiled his ol' blue-eyed crinkly smile, and she couldn't even remember why she ever went down to the beach in the summers, anyway.

However, she dragged herself up and flopped on the garden bench in the shade. "Sweetheart, he's down there with his wife because he's trained somebody to run that paper, and he can begin to retire. You've gotten so you won't discuss with me at all why you won't even try to get a young partner in with you. It's ridiculous, you practicing alone. It'll be years before Chase Jr., can come home and work with you. What if you get sick? Do you just like to be the only doc on the block?"

His smile had already faded. He hung onto the lower limb of a maple tree and reminded her, "How can I assure any partner a living wage? Could they feed a family or educate their children on the collards and chickens they might receive for their service? If I hadn't had those couple of halfway paying farms, I wouldn't be able to practice medicine at all, baby, not in Martin County."

They were distracted by Beulah singing, "Huh huh may zin hin hing grace, how sweet the sound . . ."

In the kitchen, Beulah Bazemore, Ben-Olive's sister, also raised by their grandmother Meemaw, came to Doc and Serena Haughton's house, two blocks from her own, six mornings a week. She prepared their breakfast and swept off the front walk, which seldom needed it. But she had the chance to visit with or speak to everybody coming or going anywhere and could report back in.

She "breshed up" the kitchen, "picked up" the house, "spread up" their twin beds, sent the laundry out on Mondays, and ordered groceries from Oscar Tice's corner grocery store every day.

Roosevelt Jones, who also worked at night out at Sunnyside Oyster Bar (where he knew everybody in the county and farther out), delivered the daily order by bicycle. The Sunnyside Oyster Bar was in a room attached to one side of the Sinclair Service Station on the edge of town on U.S. 17, which ran from New York to Miami.

Earlier that Saturday, Beulah had come in to scramble their eggs and fry their four pieces of bacon. Serena was in the living room playing solitaire, trying to get her head together so she could tackle her day. She had been up late reading the night before trying to catch up with the *Wall Street Journals* they received in the mail several days late, and *The New York Times* Sunday edition, which arrived about on Wednesday. She didn't care. She subscribed to it for the crossword puzzles, anyway, and to follow the January white sales that several New York department stores offered. She preferred sheets of four hundred threads per inch that rich people used, but Serena didn't want to pay full price for them.

Doc met his part-time bookkeeper, Hollis McGraw, at the office for three hours on Saturday morning whenever he wasn't at the beach. After that day's meeting, he stepped home for his fresh shrimp salad lunch, one of Beulah's specialties, along with her famous, really spicy tomato aspic.

She prepared enough for their Saturday lunch, an addition to Saturday's supper, Sunday lunch, and leftovers to take home. This classic, well-designed pattern worked well for everybody.

After the Haughton's lunch at twelve-thirty, the girls started arriving at one-thirty for a four-hour afternoon of bridge. Their mouths were 'bout waterin' to get started. They missed Serena when she was at Nags Head. They couldn't play at her house, smoke cigarettes, sip a little glass of sherry if they felt like it, or munch on Miz Boo's sharp, spicy cheese straws.

Why would anyone wish to leave this earth and go to some heaven when they might dwell in Williamston, the city of light in Martin County, and feed their five senses with all the basic pleasures? The faces of warm friends to smile upon, the sweet sounds of their laughter and their bridge bids, the taste of wine and cheese, the feel of well-used playing cards—satiny between the fingers—the odor of various summer colognes, and face powder. Serena's old, worn oriental rugs carried even more pungent odors after a July rain had made the house humid and damp. Gardenias brought in from the yard perfumed the room with summer sweetness (even though Serena didn't really love gardenias because they smelled like every summer funeral she had attended).

Doc relaxed in his leather chair and enjoyed being in the company of the girls, his wife, her cousin, Ruth Manning, Eleanor Parker, and Grace Rhodes. The reassuring hum of their pleasant conversations accompanied the cards. He was reading his Sunday School lesson for the men's class he had taught for twenty-five years at the Presbyterian church across the street. Ted Sessoms was always ready to fill in for Doc when he was out of town. That's why both prepared for it anyway. Doc was dressed in his regular weekday office, summer blue cotton cord suit and his wrinkled white shirt and tie. He tried to stay cool with a little electric fan running at his feet and turning back and forth directed right up on him.

Eleanor Parker asked, "Doc, why don't you just slip your coat and tie off and you'll be cooler?" He looked up at her from his lesson book with the most blank expression. She might as well have asked him to remove his pants. Then he went back to reading John 3:16, et cetera. He was one of those people who could concentrate on his subject, no matter where he happened to be.

The phone rang. After he picked it up and listened intently, he said, "I'll be right there." He hung it up, arose, and reached for his small black bag, mumbling, "Hetta Mae is about to deliver her baby. I'll be back after awhile."

"Wait a minute, wait a minute!" called Serena, vanishing into the kitchen. "I have something for you to take her."

Grace asked, "How many babies is that for her?"

"I don't know," he answered. "Five or six, maybe."

"Who's the daddy?" she went on. Doc didn't answer. He may have figured it was none of Grace's affair—or his, for that matter. But Grace was not to be outdone. "Somebody needs to talk to Hetta Mae about things, don't you think?"

"Well, right now, I'm . . . " he started. "Serena, I'm leaving, hear?"

"Here it is, here it is." Serena came bursting out of the kitchen with a clean cotton flour sack with tiny pink roses printed on it. "Here's cantaloupe, cucumbers, a cabbage, a quart of milk, cheese straws, and two new crib sheets from the January white sale in *The New York Times*."

"Lord, Serena, those vegetables are what Hetta Mae gave us from her garden two days ago."

"No, no, my darling," she twinkled up into his face. "Hetta couldn't have had a garden this year. She's been nigh onto a baby. Remember?"

"She's never missed having a garden since she was sixteen," he said. He shook his head. He lifted the flour bag of unrelated items and headed out the front door to his old, dark-green Chevrolet coupe. Serena told him to wait again as she ran upstairs. When she came down, she had a new box of Pond's bath powder in her hand. She kissed him lightly on the cheek as she threw the box into the flour sack.

"I gave you that for Christmas," Doc shouted as he left again.

"Oh," she said as she stepped quickly after him into the yard. "Tell her I'll be lending her Mary Cavett's bassinet, which was my grandmama's, and we'll get it over there the first of the week."

"Yes, ma'am, arright. Now let me go, hear?"

◆ ◆ ◆

About an hour and fifteen minutes later, Doc came in the back door and took off his baby delivery apron. He dropped it in the laundry basket on the screened porch for it to be washed on Monday. He washed his hands again at the kitchen sink, dried them on the nearest tea towel, came into the living room, and sat back in his chair, picking up his Sunday school lesson again.

"How'd things go?" asked Grace, who had been concerned about the size of Hetta Mae's family.

"Fine," he said. "A girl."

"Lord, what a crock of trouble little girls are, specially at about thirteen. Then you really have to start worrying."

"Why?" asked Ruth Manning.

"Shut up," said Grace.

Ruth said, "Did you play that last spade?" Then she looked at Grace Rhodes, her eyes twinkling, and said, "You remember the funny thing that happened over at Julia Love's house during a bridge party one night this summer? Tell Serena about it. It was while you were at the beach," she said to Serena.

Grace Rhodes couldn't wait to describe it. "You know how Julia won't let dogs in her house, not even Charlie Mack's dog, Brown Sugar. Well, she heard a "thump, thump" on the porch and jumped up to see what it was. She had been showing off her new pill box, with little sections marked Monday, Tuesday, Wednesday, and so forth, to everybody and left it on the table. You've seen 'em. The widow 'cross the street had seen Charlie walking the dog and asked him to come over and fix her broken light bulb. So he tied Brown Sugar's leash to the porch swing and stepped over there. The dog, of course, wanted to go, too, and kept jerking the leash to get loose. It made the swing keep banging the window, almost breaking it. Then Julia went out all upset, untied the rope, and ran over to see what Charlie was doing at the widow's house while she was playing cards. Now, the dog somehow got back into the front door, raced straight over to the card table, grabbed one of Julia Love's pills in her mouth, tasted it a moment, then spit it out on the floor. Julia ran in and got her out again and tied her to the lamppost this time.

While she was gone, your cousin here, school principal Ruth Manning, calmly wiped the pill off with her little lace hanky and put it back in the Tuesday slot. We continued to play cards. Then Miss Julia returned."

"You're terrible, Ruth," said Serena. "You ought to be ashamed."

"I am," said Ruth.

Then, and only then, Grace asked Serena, "Have you seen Mary Cavett since you got back?"

"I did, last night, why?" she answered while trying to figure out whether to open a weak club bid to get her foot in the door with this hand.

Grace tried to look innocent, but, failing, she said, "Well, I won't go into why I suspect so, but has it occurred to you, Serena, that Mary Cavett might be expecting?"

Serena stopped and stared. "You really think so? How do you know? Why didn't she tell me? Why didn't I notice?"

"Because," said Ruth, "you're not savvy about those things. You probably notice everything in the world except . . . "

Serena broke in laughing. "Except something important like the possible arrival of my first grandbaby? But what makes you suspect? She didn't look like she'd gained any weight to me. I don't want to mention it to her if she's not ready to tell us. Doc hasn't spoken of it either. Oh, I do hope so. We had sort of begun to wonder."

Grace threw in, "Why don't you ask Beulah Bazemore. She can tell by their eyes way before anyone else knows. That's how she gets all those jobs for her cousin, Easter, nursing new babies. Sleepin' in for a month to get the mama started nursing an' all."

"I believe I will. I'll ask Beulah when she comes back Monday. In fact, I'll call her today. Lord, I hope you're right. But tell me again what makes you think so?"

"I'm not sure," said Ruth. "She's been wearing sort of loose dresses, but then, everyone does. I think it may be the way she walks."

"Walks! What does that mean?"

"I said I don't know. It's just a feeling and I can't really explain it."

After about fifteen minutes of relative silence—except for the splaying sound of cards being shuffled, the "click, click, click" of the deal, and the soft, explicit voices of the bidding— Serena said, "Daddy, would you run me a little errand, please?"

"Sure, what do you want me to do, Serena?" he asked pleasantly.

"Just step down to the drugstore and get me a package of Camels, pretty please?" He headed out the door to drive the block and a half to his drugstore when she called after him, "Daddy, park in the back of the store in the shade, not in the front on the street. Then the car won't be so burning hot when you come to get back in." He left, and she turned back to the others.

"You can fry an egg on the dashboard this time of the year," she explained to girls. "And the leather seats will burn your hide."

They all nodded in agreement in chorus. "Sure could."

Six minutes later, the door opened and Doc entered empty-handed.

"Where are my cigarettes?" Serena asked, wide-eyed.

"Serena," he said quite seriously, "somebody had already taken that parking place. Now, where do I park?"

"Go to hell, Chase Haughton, you can just go straight to hell, you hear?" Then she returned to her cards without blinking.

The other three 'bout burst from not laughing, but they could hardly wait for the final hand. Then they could pile out of there and go to the drugstore to tell everybody these latest events concerning Doc Chase Haughton, his Serena, their Mary Cavett, and her Big Dan.

◆ ◆ ◆

On 5 January 1928, Doc Haughton and Serena rushed out to the tenant house with a doctor from Greenville who Doc had arranged to handle the very special delivery of their first grandchild, a boy, named Daniel Haughton

Hardison. A few weeks later, the new father, Big Dan Hardison, left for his first term in the state legislature in Raleigh. He sold himself as the champion of farmers everywhere and hunters and fishermen in eastern North Carolina.

8

Who'll carry the link
I said the Linnet
I'll fetch it in a minute
I'll carry the link.

IN early April of 1929, Mary Cavett dropped by her mother's house to ask if Miz' Boo could keep fifteen-month-old baby Danny that afternoon so she could go to a book club meeting. She saw Bymanishus Brown cutting Serena's and Doc's bright-green winter rye grass and mentioned something to him about sweeping up the grass off the sidewalk and the brick walk that led up to their house.

"Miz' Hardison, you' mama asked me not to sweep the walks 'round here long time ago, so I doesn't do it," Bymanishus told her.

"Why did she do that?" she asked, curious.

"Law', I don't know. It ain't mine to reason why. She just did."

When she found her mother in the house at her desk writing invitations to a bridal luncheon for the minister's daughter who would marry in June, she asked her why she wouldn't let Bymanishus sweep the walk. Serena, now curious in her turn, asked Mary Cavett why it should matter to her. This was not Serena's usual reaction. She was most often pleased and delighted to see her only daughter, anytime. However, she was addressing twenty-five invitations, all by hand in her best calligraphy, with the special pen she had ordered from Richmond. She was trying so hard not to make a mistake and have to order more envelopes.

Surprised, Mary Cavett said, "I just thought that since you have him here it would make a lot of sense to have him sweep the walks. Daddy doesn't have time to do it. and I can't quite picture you doing it, with your funny shoulder acting up. I'm not trying to meddle in your business, but I could save you a lot of trouble and time if you'd just listen to me occasionally."

Serena mumbled something, and Mary Cavett asked her, "What did you say?"

"Mer' Cavett," her mother answered, "I was just sitting here counting my blessings and . . . "

"Oh, Lord, when you start counting your blessings, that's when I know I should probably start leaving," said Mary Cavett.

"Oh, no, no," said her mother. "I was just thinking, wondering how in the world I managed, with only the Lord's help, to get from kindergarten all the way through four years of college, making more A's than not, found your Daddy, the finest man in the world—that I've ever met anyway. And to be fortunate enough to marry him and so thrilled to have his babies knowing they would come right straight here from heaven. And indeed you certainly did, because all I ever get from you some days is 'harp, harp, harp.' Some days, Mary Cavett, I feel you must be extremely unhappy or something, and you want me to suffer too. And you feel I'm the only person you can legally take your misery out on 'cause I have to take it. And your constant advice on how this incompetent here, your mother, should live and breathe."

Before Mary Cavett could catch her breath or speak, Serena went on, "The reason we don't have Bymanishus sweep the walks is because that is Beulah's absolute most favorite job around here. Every morning when Doc and I are eating breakfast, Miz' Boo says she wants to step out, take some air, and give us a little privacy. She insists on sweeping the walks whether they need it or not. She says that way she chats with everybody, both colored and white, on their way to work uptown or wherever and finds out everything going on all over Williamston. She checks out the children walking to school, finds out who's sick, who she needs to make chicken soup for . . . "

"All right, all right," said Mary Cavett. "I'd forgotten about that. You two live so crazy over here. I don't see how either of you gets a stick of work done. You're always making and carrying cakes, cheese straws, chicken soup, and who knows what all over town. I bet you take things to people you don't even know."

"Well, only," agreed her mother a little defensively if self-righteously, "if they are sick or new in town."

"Somebody called you the local volunteer Red Cross the other day," Mary Cavett started in again. She did want her mother to be, sometimes, more ladylike. A little more of a private person, self-contained, and not all over the place.

"Well, that's certainly an overstatement. I've never rolled a bandage in my life." Serena said, hoping that would end the discussion.

But no. Her most vocal critic continued, "It was Julia Love. She had heard that you and Beulah were out in the country at that sick Mrs. Hunley's who had all those children and an alcoholic husband. You were out there washing their clothes and sheets in her wash pot out in the yard, cooking them soup and even—Mama, I couldn't believe this—trying to comb the nits out of those children's hair."

Serena, caught again, could only say, "Well, Doc had done all he could do for her. She was too weak to get out of bed, and she has no people much around here."

At an impasse, Mary Cavett went over and hugged her mother. They both started laughing. "Well, why," Mary Cavett growled in her ear, "didn't you call me?"

Anxious to change the subject, Serena said, "I do need you to do something for me now. I have no cash handy to pay Bymanishus, and I need to write him a check. Do you mind stepping out there in the yard and findin' out just how he spells his name? I've never had to write it before."

In a bit, Mary Cavett came stumbling back in, holding her stomach from laughing so hard. "Oh, Mama, Mama."

"What is it, for heaven's sake?" asked Serena, astonished.

"Bymanishus said he had been waiting twenty years for you to ask him how to spell his name," answered Mary Cavett. "He said that his name is John Daniel Brown and that everyone calls him J. D. He said the first day he started doing your yard you asked him what people called him, and he said, 'by my 'nitials.' And you went on talking before he could say 'J. D.' and kept on calling him 'Bymanishus.' He always wondered how long it would take you to figure out . . . that day, you said something about, 'Oh, what a wonderful old Greek name, like Dionysius (the historian) or Diogenes, or Demosthenes. Why didn't somebody in my family think of that?' Or something to that effect. He was too startled to correct you and too shy to correct you later on."

"And he let me go on like that for twenty years? I am so embarrassed!" sputtered Serena.

"Oh, don't be, Mama," said Mary Cavett. "You wouldn't want to ruin your record."

"What record?" Serena inquired.

"Foot-in-mouth disease, the queen," her daughter crowed. Serena returned to her calligraphy.

Six months later, in October, the Crash came upon them all. Banks closed, stores closed, home building ceased, and Doc Haughton was paid even less often than before. Fortunately, Serena still had some of her inheritance from Monkey Top II, so they could afford to remain living in Monkey Top III.

◆ ◆ ◆

April 1931.

When Mary Cavett walked into her daddy's drugstore for the ten o'clock co' cola one Tuesday morning, the usual crowd on their work break were laughing. When they saw her, they stopped.

"Oh, don't let me interrupt the fun. Go right ahead," Mary Cavett said and smiled tentatively.

"Well," said Jerry, the soda jerk, "to be honest, we were laughing about you, Miz' Mary Cavett. Nothin' bad, you know."

"Oh, I couldn't have guessed that in this world. Can you tell me what it was, so I can laugh too?"

"Sure," started off Jerry, but Mayor Charlie Mack shushed him and tried to stop him. He wouldn't be stopped. He couldn't help it. It was a story about Cotton, her dog. One day he came trotting down Main Street hesitating at each store door, looking in as if he were trying to find Mary Cavett. He had something for her.

"What was it?" Mary Cavett asked, innocently.

"In his mouth," Jerry could hardly get it out for laughing, "he was carrying your pretty little pink brassiere."

Her face crimsoned so fast she could hardly swallow. "Oh, oh . . . that ol' story," she said. "It must have happened months ago. He got it off the clothesline, and he was just being the faithful friend. More than I can say for some people."

"Aw, Miz' Hardison, we didn't mean nothin'. At least we kept it out of the Williamston *Enterprise*. Somebody was tryin' to put it in there under the 'Williamston Merry-

Go-Round' column. But don't you appreciate it? The way we kept it out?"

She stared at Hizzoner, the mayor, Charlie Mack Griffin, but he smiled sheepishly and looked out over her head.

Reginald Ferraday, the retired schoolteacher, was sitting in the booth next to the Mayor and burst out, "I'd give my last dollar to have seen that dog coming down the street dragging that item of clothing. Where in the world was I?"

"What kind of talk is that? You're a teacher? I hope you didn't talk that way in the classroom all those years. No wonder our children are growing up with uncouth manners," said the mayor.

"Not from me," said Reginald. "I was a model major general in the classroom. Miss Ruth would've shot me if I wasn't. But my, it was tempting sometimes when the kids got smartmouth to try to take 'em and show them a thing or two. Actually, my students were rather remarkable, good kids. I must say."

"That's because their parents were, my friend," answered Doc Haughton, emerging from the back. "You, as a teacher, couldn't make them that way in fifty minutes a day in history class. It was their parents at home who made them read your book, prepare for your tests, treat you with respect."

Doc was just warming to the subject. He took his text. "Your students are only as proficient as their mamas and daddies are proficient at making them want to learn and respect school. Not to say teachers don't play a part, of course, in following up on their desire to learn. Did you ever think about it?" They all sat awaiting his sermon on education.

"There are some parents—like my longtime patients out in the country—who don't honestly want their children coming home smarter than they are. They don't want them speaking better grammar, quoting classical authors, reading poetry, or working quotients. It's embarrassing to them. Try to understand how they feel. I've treated many of these, and they resent some of their smarty educated offspring who might actually talk of going off to college.

"They'll say, 'I ain't never needed no collidge, and that scalawag, Homer, don't neither. If farming is good enough for me, it's good enough for him, I tells him. 'Sides, where'd I get the money to send him to collidge, or his sister, Ruthy, too? She wants to be a teacher. Damnation. Where'd they get all this fancy stuff from? Certainly not from me or their good mama. All we ever did was do for them, and now they want to run off to ECTC or somewhere and leave us out here by ourselves.' I hear this kind of talk sometimes," Doc said.

"Sounds like they want the children to hang around and look after them in their old age, and to take over the work," said Mary Cavett.

"Very likely. That's why they don't get them to school here regularly. They don't see much need for it," said Doc.

"How'd you come to all that, Doc?" asked Joe Sharpe, who owned the shoe shop.

"He didn't serve on the school board ten years for nothing," said Charlie Mack.

Doc went on back to his office.

"Not to change the subject," Charlie Mack said as he turned to Mary Cavett, "but, Mer' Cavett (he loved to say her name), I do think you ought to let us give the *Enterprise* that fine, picturesque story about your faithful dog, Cotton, trying to find his beloved mistress to give her a present."

"Charlie," she said, "it amazes me how all these years you have gone about trying to pass for normal. And, more often than not, you even accomplish it. May I congratulate you? Here's to our mayor," she said, and she lifted her co' cola.

Oh, they loved it. "Pass for normal." Oh, yes, they liked that. They couldn't wait to get back home or to their stores and offices to tell everybody what Mary Cavett Haughton Hardison said to Hizzoner, the mayor, Charlie Mack Griffin.

◆ ◆ ◆

Mary Cavett's wedding to Big Dan had taken place back in 1924 in early June, before everybody started going to Nags Head but after prep schools and colleges had let out. Mary Cavett was working with her mother out on the sun porch in April before the wedding when she asked, "Mother, do we absolutely have to invite Miz' Tiny Monroe? She just makes everybody miserable."

"Yes, sweet pie, we absolutely have to invite Miss Tiny and all the other beach people who have watched you grow up down there, held you for me when you had colic and I needed a break, and helped you learn to walk around the porches a year later. And picked you up out of the sand with skinned knees the summer after that. . . ." Serena was just warming up.

"But, Mama," interrupted Mary Cavett.

"Oh, I hear it coming when you start in calling me 'Mama.' What is your main objection? And keep it simple." Serena smiled sweetly as she looked up from the card table filled with the Williamston phone book for local addresses and her Christmas card booklet with out-of-town friends' addresses. Doc's medical society book for that set of people they encountered every year at the North Carolina Medical Society meetings at Myrtle Beach and Asheville was lying open there too.

She sat back with her arms crossed and her pencil behind her ear, ready and willing to follow this through to the inevitable conclusion. Her conclusion. After all, she was putting on this wedding, like it or not. Doc was paying for it, and they couldn't leave out their old crowd even if some of them were a bit prickly.

"Well, Mama, her presence will certainly be noticeable, as it is everywhere she goes," Mary Cavett said.

"Ladybug, her absence would be a whole lot more noticed than her presence, and besides, are you afraid she'll upstage you—outshine you on your big day?" asked Serena, teasing.

"Well, no," she answered primly. "It isn't that. Tho' she does interrupt every conversation she's involved in and even those in which she's not. And she has such flamboyant mannerisms. People that don't already know her are going to be overwhelmed and wonder where we found her." Mary Cavett's brow furrowed with those worry lines she seldom showed between her brows. She obviously wanted this event to be romantic, lovely, simple, and unruffled as far as it could be under the best of circumstances. But she was concerned about the flutter of hurt feelings in the wake of Tiny's tongue that seemed to follow Miz' Tiny everywhere she went.

"I can just hear her now criticizing whatever we do," continued a troubled Mary Cavett. "If I have a big, splashy wedding with twelve bridesmaids, six on each side, all carrying calla lilies, she'd go around saying, 'My, my. Just look at Doc and Serena showing off. He must have come into some money and wants everybody to know it. Now, if Mary Cavett was marrying a Vanderbilt instead of just a country boy, a football player, I might understand it. But really, all those hors d'oeuvres and that pâté, champagne, and caviar for her to hook up with a local yokel. I just don't get it.'"

"Ouch." Serena's stomach hurt, knowing it could be true.

"And," her daughter went on, "if I have a plain ceremony and reception, like I prefer to, with maybe two bridesmaids carrying bachelor buttons and daisies, and just a simple southern picnic supper for everybody—barbecue, fried chicken, potato salad, pimento cheese sandwiches—she'd come up with something like, 'Why that ol' skinflint, Doc Haughton, the tightwad. Why can't he open his wallet like everyone else and put on a decent wedding for his only daughter? He and Serena have us driving from all over eastern Carolina and southern Virginia for this?

You don't suppose Mary Cavett might be in a family way, do you? That's the only thing I can think of as an excuse for this pitiful affair. They just want to get it over with and forget about it.'"

Serena stared at her daughter. "I swear, honey, you've got her right down to a gnat's little eyelash. How do you do it?"

"Easy, Mama. Remember, she held me when I had colic and scraped me up off the steps at the beach. Later I was hostess at your beloved Arlington Hotel, and I had to seat her at her favorite table. She insisted on the best in the house, all those summers. Then I had to find a table for all the other people as far away from her as they could get and just place the Yankee tourists who didn't know her next to her. Or sometimes, in extreme cases, at the table with her. When that happened, she'd sit there with those innocent strangers and point out everybody in the room. She'd inform those fine Connecticut people, 'See that Jack Watson over there? He likes to remind everyone he was related to President Teddy Roosevelt. But he forgets to tell 'em he also has a brother in federal prison in Atlanta.' She kept them entertained, all right."

◆ ◆ ◆

Serena held several life patterns close to her heart and seldom broke them, even though the patterns of most of her days broke regularly. Certain yearly migrations she adhered to strenuously, in a way no different from the Canada geese that flew over Nags Head on the Outer Banks in the autumn heading south and back again in the spring to the north. Serena, fifty-three, trim, and stylish, always wore the latest new haircuts from Mamie's Beauty Shop on Main Street. This season the shop featured a short bob of her black hair with small, feminine flips in front of each ear, enhancing the twinkle of her bright-brown eyes. The hint of silver at her temples and the streak of silver over her left eye gave her a dramatic appearance that was not normal to most small tobacco towns in eastern North Carolina. She looked more like a Broadway actress. When accused of dying and streaking her hair, she merely laughed. "Keep them guessing," she told her husband Doc. (She did not.)

One of her migrations was to take a sleepover pullman to New York every year for the first week of December on a bridge and theatre train. She would buy Christmas presents and relax at high tea at the Waldorf every afternoon at four o'clock to check in with her friends. On rare occasions, Doc would join her for a short weekend, but he felt he couldn't stay away from his patients any longer, even when he found someone to cover for him. Finding someone to cover him was not easy to accomplish in Williamston. She was thrilled when he did join her and loved walking to little bars and dinner clinging on his arm up and down Fifth Avenue. So romantic.

They would select their Christmas gifts together and kiss—really kiss—one another right there on the sidewalk. It never occurred to them to do this on Main Street in Williamston. There, it was maybe a peck on the cheek like one would plant on an elderly aunt. Sometimes Serena would take Mary Cavett with her, or join old friends from

Norfolk or Richmond, Virginia, for the trip. She did not, however, buy clothes in New York. She selected those in Roanoke Rapids, North Carolina, a story in itself.

She encountered some of these Virginia friends regularly every summer on her other migration, when she spent three months at the old Arlington Hotel at Nags Head beach on the North Carolina Outer Banks. The hotel was near the spot where the Wright brothers flew the first airplane off a large sand dune near the ocean at Kitty Hawk. She was the somewhat unofficial hostess of the Arlington Hotel, partly because she and Doc had "gone on the note" of the fine Fearing family (who owned the hotel), and she had a vested interest in wanting it to succeed. The Fearings had the best dining room on the beach, and the cook was none other than Ben-Olive Bazemore of Williamston. He cooked there from 1 June through Labor Day, when he went back to Williamston, Biddy, and the children. There he cooked at the Tar Heel Hotel on Main Street again. He visited home every other Monday all summer, taking his money to Biddy.

Before marrying, young Mary Cavett was often the hostess in the dining room. She was good at her job because, coached by Serena, she knew the names of every guest who dined there if not the first time, certainly by the second. Of course, many of the guests were distant relations of hers and of one another, because most of them were from eastern Carolina towns—Elizabeth City, Edenton, Hertford, Roanoke Rapids, Weldon, Windsor, Roberson-ville, Murfreesboro, Greenville, "Little" Washington, Plymouth, and, of course, Williamston. Guests from Norfolk, Richmond, Charlottesville, Petersburg, Danville, and Lynchburg, Virginia, provided a good mix too. Still others from Baltimore and Washington had discovered this Outer Banks resort, calling it the best kept secret on the East Coast. The natives wanted to keep it that way. The charm of Nags Head was its simplicity.

The young people held barefoot dances before this fad hit anywhere else. Cookouts on the beach were popular, and "teatime" before dinner on the wide porches of the Arlington was everybody's favorite time of the day. People rocked in white, painted rocking chairs, feet propped up on the banisters overlooking the rushing, iced-tea cold waves. Northern currents that fed the water made it cold all summer. This was the epitome of these beach lovers' idea of a true vacation. One may wonder what was so exciting about such gatherings up and down the cool, breezy porches. Sit a spell, and the secret becomes self-evident. It was the conversation. Most of the people drawn there were wonderfully erudite, and many were well-read.

If they had been more materialistic, interested largely in social climbing, or in showing off clothes and jewelry, or given to throwing large fancy parties, they would have chosen Virginia Beach or Myrtle Beach. Or, if they could afford it, Palm Beach—and some of them could afford it.

One opinionated lady from Danville, Tish Van Zant, when invited to a porch party before dinner, was heard to say that she was in Miami Beach the past winter, and what the women did there was compare the sizes and prices of their diamonds and furs! Tish said that when one of the women looked at her hand to check out her diamonds, she quickly looked away because dam' if she was going to explain to her that she leaves all but her wedding ring in a lock box at the bank. Why should she wear jewelry around her friends who don't care what she owns. "I certainly don't wear jewelry to impress strangers," she'd say. "I don't care what strangers think. Or what they have." Something like that. Family heirloom jewelry might appear on special, rare occasions. Showy this crowd was not. For the most part, anyway.

Some of the guests were writers and journalists with newspapers in New York, Washington, and Richmond. One was a U.S. Supreme Court justice, and several were doctor/faculty members at the Medical School of Virginia. The president of the University of North Carolina was another. All of them mixed easily with those landowners from eastern Carolina who were fairly well-educated. Many were well-traveled, too, and all were individuals—one of a kind—each with his own wit and wisdom. These people drew Serena to Nags Head like a duck to a June bug. She hoped and even prayed that Doc would not be hurt when she stayed down there so long and tried to make his weekends there with her extremely pleasant. She introduced her handsome husband to all these people, most proudly, and she always marveled how he could keep up with the best of them. He assured Serena he wanted her to go down and enjoy her summers and her friends. The temperature and ocean breeze certainly made it cooler than home. Also, he understood this was a mentally stimulating crowd, and he saw no evidence of hanky-panky. When he retired someday, he looked forward to staying down there with her all summer.

The owner, Claude Fearing, knew the restaurant business. He stood just inside the kitchen door and thoroughly checked every single tray of food before the waiter carried it out into the dining room. He checked that the seafood was not overcooked or undercooked. He wanted sufficient parsley, dill, orange slices, colorful peppers, cherry tomatoes, or pimento slices to add to the platters' bright, fresh look.

"Presentation is everything," he always said. But he didn't believe it. A lot more than presentation kept diners up and down the beach coming to his hotel. One time Serena went into Claude's office for the express purpose of asking him why his baked potatoes were the absolute best in this world. What was his secret? He reached down to a large box beside his desk, lifted up a raw baking potato wrapped in pale green tissue (as all of them were in the packing container), and spoke with his authentic Outer Banks brogue. It was slightly salty with a tinge of a British's sailor's accent. Serena hoped she was developing an ear for it after so many summers at his hotel.

"Oi hev them shipped in twaice a week from Oidaho. We plaice two dozen of them in a 350-degree oven every fifteen minutes and baike them for forty-foive minutes. If they are nant served haht in the first fiftain minutes they are aout of the oven, then we daun't serve them et all. We give the customer a potato from the next batch aout of the oven, always served with real haomemade butter."

"Oh," she said. "Then you can use those leftover ones the next day for potato salad."

"Aoh, Serena, gaow on," he teased her. "Nao, dahrlin', we hev another special potato for mashed potatoes and still another for potato salad. Bai the way, hev you ever trahed our potato salad wi' fresh boiled shrimp in it? Thet's a winner, dearie, you can make thet at home. Ben-Olive can do it up for you at the Tar Heel Hotel when our season is done daown here."

Oh, Serena had the thickest little notebook smashed full of recipes she got from Claude Fearing, Ben-Olive, and other friends from all over North Carolina and Virginia. Everything from crab cakes to conch chowder. Still, somehow, no one ever caught her laboring over a hot stove in the process of translating them into a meal.

Not as long as Beulah Bazemore stood by her.

One hot summer when Serena was in the lobby arranging an armful of cattails she had cut from a ditch beside the highway on the way down to Nags Head, her son, Chase Jr., was on the beach sitting up on his lifeguard stand. Mary Cavett was folding napkins like fans in the linen room when a bell started ringing from the kitchen. Shouts came from the rear, and all general hell broke loose at the Arlington Hotel.

"Fire! Fahyuh! Fahyuh! Help, help! Everyone ran toward the kitchen, and some of the help came running out crazily with their clothes on fire. They rolled in the sand to put out the flames. There came Ben-Olive out the door with flames on his sleeves and back. When he saw Serena, he suddenly stopped short, bowed, and said, "How do, Miz' Serena. You all right?"

"Get in the sand, Ben-Olive!" she screamed. "Are you crazy?" They grabbed him and rolled him over in the sand 'til the flames were out. Someone summoned the so-called beach ambulance. Everyone was mighty lucky to have only first-degree and a few second-degree burns from a spilled hot grease accident the new employee caused. Ben-Olive took a lot of teasing over his good manners. No one from Williamston was surprised.

9

Who'll be chief mourner?
I said the Dove
I mourn for my love
I'll be chief mourner.

Autumn, 1932

LUVELIA Gannet's clothing covered the pink chenille bedspread as she unpacked on a late Tuesday afternoon after returning from her house over near Goldsboro. Miz' Alice had allowed her a short, Sunday-through-Tuesday vacation to visit home before returning reluctantly to her, Miz' Alice's, house for a big weekend. The tobacconists were back in town.

She had asked if she could go home on a Saturday so she could go to church with her mama and daddy at White Rock Baptist Church near their farm. But Alice had to laugh. "Are you demented, girl? Saturday night is our biggest night of the week. 'Specially during this Depression. The fellas need our place bad, these days," she said.

"I thought Thursday night was your biggest night, Miz' Alice, when the salesmen are in town," Luvelia said softly, still unsure of herself over there in Williamston.

"Nah, nah. Sometimes it is. If the politicians are coming through here or during tobacco season when the tobacco crowd's in town before they go home for the weekend. But Saturday night has always been a big one, honey. That's the night I hire Moses, from across the river. You don't think I'd hire a piano player for a slow night, do you?"

The dressing table featured a gathered skirt hand-sewn of pink dotted Swiss and tacked all around the top to cover what was underneath. The skirt was cut down the center and would pull out sideways, revealing three drawers on the left and a small stool, also covered with dotted Swiss. It was supposed to slide out from under the glass-topped dressing table, but it had been pushed under there to allow more space for the two girls who shared this bedroom.

The cracked mirror above the dressing table reflected several China dinner bowls decorated with pink dahlias and holding numerous partially used lipsticks, mascara, small dime store perfume bottles, rings, bracelets, earrings, safety pins, bobby pins, rhinestone pins, and necklaces.

So what was left to put in the three drawers? Handkerchiefs, undies, teddies, bras, petticoats, hose, socks, garters, bottles of lotion, unguents, oils, hairnets, hair rollers, old letters, empty envelopes, picture postcards from Carolina Beach, movie ticket halves, mementos from the fair, and discarded items from the dresser top.

Luvelia looked out the dirty glass where pink dotted Swiss curtains hung and noted the sun casting a golden glow over the tobacco fields. Sunsets always made her feel sad. Endings, she guessed.

Clarissa, Luvelia's roommate, wandered in, smoking a cigarette and still wearing a peach-colored chenille housecoat with coffee stains on it. Carrying her signature cup of coffee, she flopped down on the foot of the bed. Luvelia didn't want to offend her but could not resist asking her, "Have you been wearing that housecoat all day? Are you sick or something?"

Not a good decision. Clarissa got her back up. Just short of snarling, she said, "Since I've named you my official caretaker, you ought to make note of the fact that wearing this old number is an unofficial signal to Miz' Alice that I'm not feeling well so she won't send me outside to help clean her chicken house or work in her zinnia garden. She likes to put that stuff from the barnyard around the shrubs and on her famous zinnias.

"Sometimes I just ain't up to it. I believe in sharing the work and all." She softened and continued, "'Cause she's right good to us. But sometimes I just can't handle the work around this ol' place all day and trying to be so cheerful at night. By the way, how did you hear about Miz' Alice all the way over in Goldsboro, Luvelia?"

"The undertaker over there told me about her and he phoned Miz' Alice to call me. He thought I'd like it here. I worked around his place over there, and he knew I just couldn't stand dead people."

"My soul. What did you do for them?" Clarissa became really interested.

"Well, I washed them, if they needed it. Did their hair. Sometimes a beautician came in and we did it together, depending on how much the family paid us for the services. And I did their makeup and dressed them. Helped the family decide what they ought to be buried in. And you should a' heard some of the arguments the family had over what to bury them in and what jewelry they should wear and whether they should be buried in their wedding ring or not. 'Bout made me sick. One ol' rich man called his dentist and asked if he couldn't take the gold teeth out of his wife's mouth for him to have as a keepsake. Yeah, keepsake all right."

Clarissa laughed and asked, "What was the problem with the clothes?" She was all ears now.

"Sometimes the oldest son would object to his father being buried in his best Sunday suit," Luvelia said. "Even when the mom would say, 'Now, son, we bought that suit ten years ago to be your daddy's burial suit, and he'd be pretty disappointed if he didn't get to wear it. He picked it out up in Raleigh right after we had the good tobacco year in 1922. You ought to be ashamed. If you ain't, I'm ashamed for you.'

"'Well, I am ashamed,' he would answer. 'I have to go to church and funerals and weddings,' he'd say, 'wearing that ol' rag-tag, hand-me-down suit of Uncle Rufus' with a patch on one elbow. An' I don't dare take no nice girl out nowhere wearin' that ol' coat. An we ain't had a good tobacco season since 1922.'

"And the mama'd say, 'And furthermore, we've been having a depression lately, Big Boy, or haven't you heard? An' I don't know nobody, from a farm at least, that's been up to Raleigh shoppin' for nothing. Least of all a burial suit.' And so on. Just like I wasn't standing there listening. I might as well have been a bunch of turnips standing there waiting for them to decide."

Clarissa was enchanted. "You are a hoot, Luvelia. You ought to write a book. You could call it . . . "

"Yeah, what *would* I call it?" asked Luvelia with her mouth curled up on one side, right disgusted like.

"*Conversations Overheard in the Embalming Room*. No, that's too long," said Clarissa.

"Besides," corrected Luvelia, "those talks usually took place in the dressing room."

"Oh, par'n me. I've never been in either room. Not yet anyway," Clarissa defended herself.

Luvelia smiled and winked at Clarissa, cheering up a bit at the turn of this talk. "Don't worry, girlie, you will, you will, one of these great days. Unless you fall off a fishing boat at sea or something. An' don't you just wonder what your family'll be saying about you when that day comes?"

Clarissa pondered quietly for a moment. "They may not know when my day comes."

"Don't they know where you are?"

"Of course not. Daddy took off with a young gal and left Mama with six children. She couldn't manage it all, an' her mind went out an' she had to be put in the Virginia Institute for the Insane."

"What happened to the children?"

"My big sister took over, sort of, an' when I turned fifteen I left. I send her money every month when I can," said Clarissa, not bragging and not looking noble.

"Does she ask how you make it?" wondered Luvelia.

"Dear, no. Does your Mama ask you what you're doing over here?"

"She doesn't have to. She thinks I'm working for Biggs Funeral Home," said Luvelia matter-of-factly.

"Oh, well, we have a *few* things in common," said Clarissa. "We do have to put up with some deadbeats." Clarissa was thoughtful.

Luvelia changed the subject for some reason. "Hey, what's with this Big Dan Hardison guy? Why does he even come out here? All he ever does is play cards. Even solitaire, over there in the corner all by himself. He hardly ever talks to the girls. What's his problem?"

"Nobody really understands Dan Hardison. The men all like him and trust him. The girls do, too. One girl got herself messed up, and they say he helped her find that lady over in Bertie County that takes care of those things. And he even paid for it tho' he didn't have nothing to do with it.

"She couldn't afford to miss work that long or mess with no baby 'cause she's helping support her widowed father in a wheelchair and her idiot brother, who's doing for him around the house over in Robersonville. That is, when he's not lost out in the woods somewhere. She goes home every week on the bus, takes money, buys them groceries, and cooks up a mess of collards, soup, and oatmeal. Something to last them over."

"What's her name?" asked Luvelia.

"She probably don't want me talkin' about it. But it's Hattie Mae Roberson," said Clarissa.

"Was Robersonville named for her family?" Luvelia asked.

"I think for her cousins' family way back. They have lawyers and doctors in that branch of the family and an Episcopal priest!" Clarissa explained.

"Why don't some of them help out?" asked Luvelia innocently.

"Oh, they don't know how bad it is. Hattie Mae and her daddy don't never let on. They are very proud people," explained Clarissa.

"Very proud people. And her daddy takes her money?" asked Luvelia.

"He has no choice. And she insists. He thinks she works at a store downtown here, and most days she does. And on her days home, she cleans his house and takes him to prayer meeting on Wednesday nights—in his wheelchair. Pushes him down the road and back when it ain't raining. I've been home with her a few times, and I've seen what she does."

"What if she gets sick?" asked Luvelia.

"You mean gets vee dee? Well, she did get 'incapacitated' as Miz' Alice calls it. She was sick an' throwin' up 'round here all the time, 'til Mr. Dan helped her out."

"An' you're sure Big Dan ain't her . . . special?"

"Positive," said Clarissa.

"Why don't Miz' Alice help these girls out when they get messed up?"

"Oh, she does sometimes, when she knows. But she tries to teach them how to avoid it. Not to drink booze, for starters. Not much anyway. And when they keep havin' accidents, she just has to let them go. She can't afford but so many accidents, she says."

Impressed, Luvelia mumbled, "Damn, I'm 'bout ready to go back to the embalming room, myself."

"I wouldn't fault you, girl. I wouldn't fault you. Miz' Alice's Palace ain't for the faint of heart."

One day Luvelia asked Clarissa a question. "Clarissa, why do all these fellas seem to love to talk to us about politics and all? I get the feelin' some of 'em don't even discuss politics with their wives—do you?"

"Hey, good question," said Clarissa, putting on her mascara. Waving her tiny brush again, she said, "One, they must think we've been around and we know what's going on, and their wives don't know and don't care. And two, they may be right. And three, remember, we sort of get paid to listen. Don't you suppose? My guess is they think we're really interested in everything they say. You know how men are."

"Well," agreed Luvelia, "I will say that politics is more interesting than some of that stuff they talk about."

"Like what?" asked her roommate, smiling.

"Like how many possums they killt, how many herring they caught, or how many pounds of tobacco they get from an acre."

The girls laughed like conspirators. They might just as well work with the dead as feign interest in such brain dead living clients. But after the fun, Luvelia turned back to the dressing table and put herself together for an evening's work. Soon, she went down to the parlor, and Clarissa packed her suitcase. The next day she was gone. Didn't say where to.

◆ ◆ ◆

Back during Mary Cavett's high school and college summers after World War I, when she worked at the Arlington Hotel at Nags Head beach as hostess in the dining room, her brother, Chase Jr. worked on the hotel beach as the lifeguard. Their mother, Serena, held court in the lobby, in the rocking chairs on the porches, or under large, blue umbrellas on the beach. Serena embarrassed Chase Jr. by keeping an extra life jacket and Red Cross life preserver handy in case he got into trouble bringing a wayward swimmer in through the breakers. She had a long rope attached to the white life preserver, and she imagined herself throwing it out to him if he needed help. Fortunately, she never needed to test her throwing arm to help her son save a soul.

Then there was that lady who also stayed at the Arlington all summer, Miz' Tiny Monroe from Edenton. When Tiny appeared at the dining room door and paused a moment, the room grew silent for an imperceptible moment too as if holding its breath and wondering with whom Tiny might choose to sit. Whoever she chose had to welcome her. Usually, however, she would hail Mary

Cavett over with a, "Darlin,' have you saved me my favorite table, by the window?"

"Oh, yes, Mrs. Monroe, right overlooking the ocean," Mary Cavett would say. "There are so many gulls out on the beach today to watch. I kept three groups of people away from your table already, just for you."

"Oh, I'm so sorry," Tiny said. But she also smiled. She insisted on a table for four at the largest window, counting on two or three others to join her for her luncheon ritual—lots of iced tea and extra ice. And the general complaints about the food, the heat or rain or breeze, her room, the Yankees who had discovered the Arlington, and so on.

A bit about Miz' Tiny Monroe. Tiny was not tiny, of course. She was six-foot-one with long arms and long legs and nose to match. Some said her nose had a purpose—poking into other people's business. Her ears were wired, tuned to catch every negative vibration that hovered near. Her mouth, Tiny's tongue, famous for vinegary comments, expelled these sour notes at any moment, often dramatized with accompanying brass and percussion enhanced by a crash of tympani. The other summer guests would try to escape her—run if necessary—but she'd usually notice and hound bodies 'til they were forced to lunch or dine with her. The only real thread of companionship she shared with the other Arlington regulars was the tight thread of fear she wound around them, making them afraid to ignore her. She was about seventy but appeared to be eighty because of her lined, dry skin from smoking cigarettes—a habit she adopted well before it was accepted in polite society. Her hair was cloud-white with a light blue tint.

Serena once told Miz' Boo that Tiny would call her over after dinner to her sofa in the lobby, where she pretended to read books or magazines. But she was really watching everybody to see who was with whom and what was going on.

Serena would say, "I felt like she was getting ready to hatchet somebody and wanted my support. I'd tell myself, 'I'll sit there a while, but I'll just not listen.'"

"Good luck," said Beulah, who knew all about Miz' Tiny's tongue.

Tiny's husband had left her long ago. He lived over in "Easy City," Elizabeth City, with a waitress. Tiny wouldn't give him a divorce, of course. He never came to Nags Head, needless to say, even tho' he had grown up spending his summers there. He and his girlfriend went to Virginia Beach to more or less get lost, tho' that was impossible. Tiny received regular reports on their whereabouts there. How did she do it?

Her children had left her, too, best they could. Her oldest son was in California growing oranges. He tried to grow tobacco out there but couldn't make it work. Her youngest son was in London working in a bank and married to a milliner. Tiny's baby was a daughter named Mariana, now married to a Canadian she met at Nags Head one summer. He couldn't wait to get Mariana away from Tiny's nosiness, and he discouraged Tiny's visits to Montreal.

But Tiny still smiled warmly and proudly when she mentioned her baby—Mariana of Montreal, Canada, as if Mariana's husband owned part of it. Oddly enough, he did. When Mariana and Oswald came south to Florida every late winter, they would stop in to see her mother in Edenton. It was somewhat awkward to visit her father in Elizabeth City, and both were brief visits. Then they rushed off to visit their spring friends in Palm Beach. They repeated these short visits on the trek back in late April.

When her baby visited Nags Head, Tiny almost dissolved in pride and forced everyone within reach to sit with her and Mariana in the dining room so she could brag on her daughter's talents and contributions in Montreal. She was president of the Canadian equivalent of the Junior League, chairman of the Montreal Symphony, and leader of the Montreal Dog Show (which she sometimes won with her two Pekingese, Tiny—yes, Tiny—and Spinoza).

No one was unkind enough to ask Tiny when was she going to visit Mariana in Montreal.

As they all eventually had to accept her invitations to sit with her at a meal or at teatime, the one at five o'clock, they braced themselves for her comments. "Do you really think he/she is our sort?" Or, "I don't think she/he is to the manner born." If no one said anything, she'd try to soften it with, "But I do understand he has some land over in Pitt County somewhere." If still no assent was forthcoming, she might continue conversing with herself by adding, "Of course, it probably belongs to his wife." Or,

"He probably bought it cheap from some family that went bankrupt."

Tiny had cold, sharp brown eyes. When she looked straight at you, you felt you were being X-rayed.

When Serena tried to listen to Tiny at the table or on the beach, smiling pleasantly all the while, she couldn't help but think about what most people knew—that Tiny's grandmother was one-half Indian, one-fourth colored, and one-fourth English.

This might explain why Tiny was so outspoken about "our kind" and "quality" people—to refute the story that her grandmother was Mr. Jenkins' mistress for years before his wife died.

To the horror of the neighborhood, he married that mistress, who then bore one baby, Tiny's mother. This is how most of Mr. Jenkins' money came, eventually, to Tiny. His money supported her summers at the Arlington Hotel, where she held everyone hostage, required the table with the best view, and judged everyone who entered. She targeted their clothes, their hair, their family, their money and how they came by it, and the quality of bourbon they served at their teatime gatherings before supper.

"Really, such cheapskates," she might say. "Serena's cheese straws her maid Beulah makes for her, they're hardly ever crisp, and there's not enough good, strong cheese in them." Everyone listening who loved those dainties and wanted more of them wondered why Tiny ate Beulah's cheese straws and chocolate pecan brownies if she didn't like them.

"Doc," begged Serena, "why do I have to put up with Tiny every summer?"

"You're building character, sweetheart. Building character," her husband insisted.

"I wish you would be more original," she said sweetly.

"All right," he said. He came up behind her, put his arms around her from the back, and said, "Look at that wing-back chair there with the green velvet slip cover. Picture Tiny Monroe sitting there. Now, don't you feel sorry for her?"

"Chase, you must see something I don't see. I feel sorry for the people around her."

"Oh, no, baby. You're not being sensitive at all. Don't you see a person who has been deeply hurt, maybe irrevocably hurt? She has her back up, like a scared or angry cat or dog. Can't you try killing her with kindness? Just once?"

"Just once!" Serena shouted. "You know I've already tried that, many times. She still gets in her unkind cut. If not directly to me, then about some of my best friends. I have to avoid her when I can, don't I?"

"Oh, Serena, don't be a snob. You could melt Tiny better than anyone in the whole world. Just try one more time. You may be surprised." He was sure she could do it.

◆ ◆ ◆

In mid-September of 1933, after Labor Day when the weather gave the slightest suggestion of switching cooler, everybody in Martin County and several counties around had to make the first run of the season to Sunnyside

Oyster Bar for the first R-month oysters brought up from Nags Head.

Everybody was vying to get some before anyone else did. They'd brag about how many bushels they ate and how large, fresh, and delicious the oysters were. Somebody always had to tell the old thing about "the bravest man who ever lived was the first man who ate an oyster." Then somebody else had to say, "Or the hungriest."

Roosevelt Jones was their favorite person to open the oysters. Most ordered theirs raw. Some wanted them steamed just a little, and some, a lot. The sauce, of course, was the secret. And obviously the owner would never tell how he made it. Tomato sauce, horseradish, lemon juice, Texas Pete hot sauce, and Worchestershire were obvious. But nobody could figure out what the secret ingredient was. Some guessed crushed cucumbers and others spring onions. Still others guessed a touch of beer. However, one could purchase a quart jar full and take it home for shrimp or whatever. One woman, a bank president's wife from Raleigh, would phone down and have the owner send her two quarts by a highway patrolman coming toward Raleigh before she had her large parties or church affairs.

Senator Big Dan Hardison often carried his out-of-town political buddies there whenever they came through Williamston. They could laugh over legislative adventures in Raleigh and joked about how their voices sounded so drunk, southern, and uneducated whenever they did radio interviews.

◆ ◆ ◆

As Serena and a friend were rocking on the porch of the Arlington enjoying the August 1934 sweet breeze, Anna Blue Henderson walked by. Someone later heard Serena say to Sally Seton, "I wonder why Anna Blue just let herself go like that. That's rather a shame. She was such a grand-looking girl at St. Mary's. All the boys calling on her."

"You know what having babies does to us," said Sally. "Of course you just snapped back to your original size like a rubber band, but most of us keep some of the weight with each baby. We all hate you for it, of course. It isn't fair."

"Oh, do you think it was easy for me to give up Beulah's hominy grits, biscuits, corn pudding, and pancakes? My mercy, I thought I'd starve."

"Why did you do it, then? Did you just want to look like the cute little sweetheart Doc married? Isn't that sort of childish, Serena? He was certainly in love with more than just your slim waist, narrow hips, and thin arms, wasn't he? If not, that doesn't say much for Doc's character now, does it?"

"Well, I'd sure like to think," mused Serena, "that Chase would still care for me if I let myself go, or lost my mind or came down with TB or something. But somewhere I read that men are often attracted to women who *look like their mothers looked when they first recognized them*—their young mothers, that is. These men have a mental picture of this beautiful, smiling creature who swept them up out of their cribs, held them close to their breasts all warm and cherished, cuddled them, or even fed them milk from those wonderful breasts. She smiled down on them, kissed the tops of their heads, and tickled their little feetsies. This is the woman they spend the rest of their life searching for, and sometimes they even find one like her. At least they think they have 'til after they marry and find out she's really different from the beautiful young mother they remember. According to that article, men are much more romantic than we think they are. The point was, I suppose, that what can it hurt to try to stay the girlfriend they think they married as long as we can, considering that age and the laws of gravity are going to take their toll anyway? Maybe I'm silly."

"Well, granted, you are a little crazy, Serena," Sally said.

"Thank you, Sally. You've always said I was, but coming from you, I accept that as a compliment considering what you say about other people. You're so honest and practical. You don't cover up anything. If someone lies, cheats, or steals, you just say so while the rest of us try to say they're just a little "funny." We could count on you, even at St. Mary's, to tell it just right. What's the difference in you and me? Hmm? Am I a liar?"

"Oh, Serena, the difference between us is so obvious. You're a romantic, an incurable romantic, and I never was and never will be. Maybe I just see black and white. I'll bet you even dream in color, don't you?"

"Of course I do. Doesn't everyone? Don't you?" asked Serena.

"I'm not sure I even dream at all. My head hits the pillow and I'm out like a light. If I dream, I don't remember them," said Sally softly.

"Oh, why that's terrible," said Serena. "Dreams are wonderful fun. I hate to be waked up in the middle of one. I want to see what's going to happen next. Sleep doctors say that dreams are the way the mind lets off steam and stresses at night. Dreaming helps us keep sane and manage our real daily lives. Hey, Sally, maybe you're the crazy one and not me, you having to see everything just the way it really is. How do you stand it?"

Sally looked at Serena as if in deep thought, figuring. Serena then asked, "Sally, is your cute husband, Beanie, a romantic?" Beanie, of course, was short for Stringbean.

"I don't know," Sally mused. "I have to admit I've never really thought about it. Ha! Beanie, a romantic. What a funny idea."

Serena continued to sit, rocking and staring out at the waves but thinking sadly that, yes, Beanie was a romantic. So romantic, in fact, that he had a sweetie down at Little Washington that he went to visit about every two weeks. Everybody pretty much knew this, of course, but nobody ever mentioned it to Sally.

Serena was older than Sally by a couple of years, but she wondered for a moment if the pragmatic, forthright Sally would have told her if her Chase—the beloved Doc Haughton—had a "girlfriend." Just a passing thought. However, she stopped rocking for a moment.

"What's the matter?" asked Sally.

"Uh, oh, do I see porpoise jumping, rolling out there beyond the breakers?"

Sally said she didn't see any porpoises.

Later, Sally broke the silence and said, "I don't mean to gossip, but did you hear what Tiny said to that pitiful Mrs. White who has to roll around here in a wheelchair? She had the unmitigated gall to ask her to her face, 'What in the world sin did you commit to cause God to punish you this way?' Serena, what are we going to do about her? About Tiny?"

Serena just shook her head, remembering what Doc had said.

◆ ◆ ◆

One school morning in September of 1935 at eight o'clock, Danny was still at his place at the breakfast table with his daddy, Big Dan, sharing fried liver pudding, cheesy eggs and grits when Miz' Beulah Bazemore came through the back door bringing fresh chicken broth she had made earlier at Serena and Doc's.

"Mist' Dan, what are you still doing here lolling over breakfast? Why ain't you out at the farm gettin' those people outta bed to do they stuff?"

"I've already been out there and back, Beulah. I like to have breakfast with Danny and drop him off at school."

"He oughtta be walkin' to school. Do him more good," said Beulah.

"He usually does. This is a treat," defended Dan.

"Oh, well. Here's some chicken broth for Mary Cavett to make her corn chowder. To use as her starter. All right?"

Looking at Danny's breakfast, Beulah said, "Danny, you got to eat more bananas and oatmeal so's you can be sure to get your 'tassius every day. Oranges give you 'tassius, too, so you tell your mama to give you oranges or bananas every day, you hear?"

Mary Cavett came back into the kitchen saying, "Yes, Dr. Bazemore. We hear you and we appreciate your house calls any time you can make it, especially when you bring your homemade chicken broth. Thank you." But Beulah was already out the door, Dr. Bazemore was making her morning rounds.

Suddenly, Beulah bustled back in the door, telling Danny, "Yes, and I saw your granddaddy, Doc, giving you another Snickers candy bar down at the drugstore th' other day." To Mary Cavett and Dan she said, "I swear, I tells him he cain't give that boy all that sugar and chocolate every day like that and him a doctor. Besides giving him bad teeth, it will also give him the green-apple quick-steps in the middle of the night." Before they could comment, she really was gone.

◆ ◆ ◆

As sure as the seasons changed and wild ducks flew south, Serena and other birds of her feather drove two counties northwest in the fall and back again in the spring to Roanoke Rapids to Golda's. They would select and purchase a special outfit for college football games in the fall and Easter in the spring. Some of these eastern North Carolina women also went in early summer and winter, four times a year, to buy the newest fashions for summer at the beach and for the winter parties. The really rich women with generous husbands or some money of their own (or who wished to appear rich) would buy extra dresses for the Christmas parties and wedding affairs in June.

Many more would carry their debutante daughters to Golda's to buy clothes for the girl, her sisters, the mother, and even the grandmother to wear for the magical four days in Raleigh every September when a hundred girls from across the state were presented to "society." This was a yearly ritual presented by the Terpsichorean Club, a men's dance club. The members of the Terp club, not to be confused with Twerp club, considered themselves to be the most eligible bachelors in the state. They invited older, former debs to assist them in selecting the most elite nineteen-year-old ladies from the mountains to the sea for the fellas to look over every year the first weekend after Labor Day, a mating ritual if you will. When a daughter was invited to be presented, even if the family secretly thought the process was barbaric, a father was hard put not to let her accept for several reasons. One, the mother was probably thrilled to pieces to play Queen Mother for awhile. The girl loved to play the princess and select her chief marshal and five more young men to be present to dance with her and her friends.

The sad side was that sometimes her best friend might not be invited, and the girl felt disloyal in going to Raleigh if her friend could not. Also, of course, sometimes the smartest girls were not invited, or the most beautiful or the most stylish. The criteria were extremely vague. Just to say it was all "society" or "politics" didn't quite explain it. A secret committee in each town, or one dowager, perhaps, was chosen from Raleigh to make the choice. No one was supposed to know who that person or group was. It was assumed that former debutantes would perform this local duty. Naturally, relatives or friends of these women would be considered first, and the services the parents had performed to the community, county, or state might be taken into account. If the girl's daddy had been the richest bastard in the county, mean, selfish and self-centered as all get out, it might not keep the daughters from being invited. The mean bastard or his wife might have been a cousin or brother to one of the committee members. Some years the selection committee in a smaller community might not send anyone at all, which, supposedly, made it a greater honor to be invited "your" year upon turning nineteen.

If a person from Mars had landed in Williamston and asked for an explanation about the Debutante Ball, Mary Cavett would have been hard-pressed to give a believable, logical explanation. No man would have even tried. If anyone gave it a moment's thought, he or she would have assumed that Serena Haughton was, no doubt, on the committee or even was the committee. However, no one ever dared to ask her. She couldn't help but notice that the mothers of girls and the girls themselves during their freshman year at college became even more friendly than usual. They gave lots of compliments like, "Miz' Serena, you're just looking younger every year. What in the world is your secret? You're even prettier than you were ten years ago, and you were the best-looking woman in town then." She might have been rather mystified by all the attention if she was not on the committee.

Serving on a debutante selection committee seemed a little out of character for a woman who was accused of being the local Red Cross, carried soup to sick families, and scratched nits from the heads of children with sick mamas. She certainly seemed to see every girl the same, as if she adored them all, her own Mary Cavett included. Serena never appeared to be sizing them up as debutante material to represent Martin County at the big ball in Raleigh, where they would be presented to the governor and his wife and to society across the state of North Carolina.

The fathers probably did not like to send their hard-earned money to the Raleigh Junior League to be used for their charities. Oh, yes, it could be referred to as a charity ball, but the charities were in Raleigh, not in Bear Grass. Then the mother reminded the daddy that, who knows, maybe Drucilla would meet Mr. Wonderful over the long weekend, go to college one more year, and marry him or another deb's brother. That would be the perfect scenario, of course, but nobody ever did a study on how often it actually happened. However, it happened often enough to keep the mothers, the girls, and the girls' reluctant fathers coming back, for the same reason a man keeps going fishing or returns to the gambling table.

Deb time was easily Golda's most lucrative season, and she was very proud of her girls and their mamas for being among the best-dressed women at the ball. Although it was only a small shop on the main street of a mill town, Golda's was really a *couturier* clinic. Golda was the doyenne of fashion for a wide area. Ladies came from all over Eastern Carolina and Raleigh, as well as from Norfolk, Charlottesville, and Richmond, Virginia.

Before Mary Cavett made her debut in Raleigh back in the twenties, she and her mother had ridden up to Roanoke Rapids to Golda's shop in July to select their clothes for the big September weekend. Ben-Olive drove. Serena was nibbling on a fresh cucumber right out of Beulah's garden, and on it she had sprinkled salt and pepper.

She said, "Ben-Olive, please tell Biddy to come and take a lot of these wonderful cucumbers Beulah brought us. We can't put up but so many jars of pickles, especially after we did all those jars of watermelon rind pickles. I have to give Biddy and you some of those, too."

"All right, Mrs. Haughton, but Beulah gives us buckets of cucumbers, too," he said.

"Oh, well, maybe Doc can take them down to the office and give them to somebody." She want on, very seriously, "Mary Cavett, you know, I've always thought you looked really sweet in soft green. Wouldn't you like a dress in this cucumber green chiffon? It would look lovely with the deb pearls your daddy gave you. And you could have your satin shoes dyed the darker green of the outside of a cucumber and carry a dark green velvet little evening purse for the Saturday night dance. Everyone else will be wearing pink or blue, and you'd stand out, don't you think?"

"Mama, I swear you are really going off the bridge. Can't you just see the item in *The Atlanta Journal* social pages: 'Atlanta boy, student at University of North Carolina, Grainger Thompson, III, son of Atlanta attorney, serves as chief marshal for Carolina debutante at Raleigh statewide ball, Miss Mary Cavett Haughton. She was wearing a gown of cucumber green.' Next thing, you'll want to buy me something the color of eggplant or squash."

"Actually, Mary Cavett, I was thinking of a suit of eggplant purple for me to wear to the tea at the governor's mansion, the day you wear that tobacco-brown dress we bought last week. It looks so handsome and unusual on you. No one else, I guarantee you, will be wearing tobacco brown—that golden, rich color with the hat and gloves to match. It is so perfect for fall. That Golda is a genius. I wonder who we'll run into today up here?"

"Mama, I don't even want to do this deb business." She folder her arms, hoping to be taken more seriously. "Remember?" said Mary Cavett. "If Grainger could not have been my chief marshal, I don't believe I could stand to do it at all. But if I hear much more about clothes and hats and gloves and shoes dyed to match, I might just . . ."

"Don't say it," her mother pleaded. "I'll change the subject. I promise."

When they arrived at Golda's, they parked out back in the alley and came in through the rear service entrance (which was the custom of her regular customers). Golda and her assistant, Hannah, both hugged them with sincere affection. Golda said, "Oh, this is going to be a day you'll never forget, Mary Cavett. I have one of your friends from Rocky Mount here—Betty Ann Garner—and her mom, a bride from Edenton, and her mother and grandmother. Also, the governor's wife from Virginia will be in about twelve o'clock on her way to Wrightsville Beach. She can't stay long—just long enough to buy some beachy things for her two weeks' stay down there. They go to the Surf

Club there, you know. But she says she wanted to get here in time to have some of our wonderful hot dogs with the rest of you girls.

"Does that man across the street still steam the rolls to keep them hot and soft?" asked Serena, smiling.

"Absolutely," said Golda. "And he always piles them with juicy chili sauce he makes. But the first time he drips sauce on one of my gowns when he delivers our lunch, I'm going to call the sheriff. Well, girls, let's get to work. Go back there with Hannah, get your robes on and your shoes off, and we'll start you modeling the things I've selected for you. Serena, you have the dressing room on the right with all the jewelry in it. The hats are down the hall."

Unlike any other store in the world, Golda's clothes were all in the back, hidden until a customer was decked out head to toe in the correct shoes, gloves, hat, and jewelry, especially the perfect pin, necklace and belt. The client never saw herself in a mirror until she was presented from the back with Hannah towing her in and over to the three-way mirror with special lighting about it to glamorize and dramatize the subject. She would receive ooohs, ahhhhs, and even applause if Golda's concoction was truly fetching (no matter how unattractive the model.)

All of her customers made their appointments weeks and even months ahead, telling Golda what special occasion was coming up. She'd often buy in New York with these special customers in mind and was always sure no two people would ever, ever be caught wearing the same dresses or even jewelry. Her pins were spectacular. For instance, she wouldn't put a large or dramatic pin on a small, shy or reticent lady. Her color sense was magical. She could dramatize the most mousy matron of any age.

If asked where she vacationed, she loved to tell of the world's most famous hotels, from New York to Paris, from London to Rome, where she would sit in the lobbies and watch fashionable women come and go. She'd make mental notes and the written kind also in order to be prepared when she went to New York to buy for a season always months ahead. She had to buy in January for September, much to her chagrin. She feared a new shade of a color, or hang of a skirt, or turnback of a satin cuff with rhinestone buttons would come in a moment too late for her Christmas customers. She wanted to have the very latest, from scarves to evening bags.

However, she always clung to the classics, never the chic. This was why her clothes were considered a good investment, the women assured their husbands, because they could wear them at least five years. Often longer.

"Mary Cavett, who's going to be your chief marshal?" asked an interested Elizabeth "Betty" Ann Garner from Rocky Mount. "That Thompson boy from Atlanta? Your roommate's brother?"

"That's right," broke in Serena before Mary Cavett could answer. Mary Cavett did not object. She thought these conversations inane.

Then Betty Ann volunteered that hers, her chief marshal, was Peter Rascoe from Windsor, and her five assistant marshals were . . . she proceeded to list all five, their hometowns, their fraternities at which colleges and, as Mary

Cavett feared, who their mamas were and what their daddies did for a living: doctor, lawyer or plantation owner.

Another old joke about eastern Carolina was: "How do you know if you've just met a person from eastern North Carolina? She doesn't say, 'It's so nice to meet you.' She'll take your hand and ask, 'Honey, who's your mama?'"

Then Betty Ann's mama, named Elizabeth Ann and also called Elizabeth Ann, not "Betty," spoke up to further inform the group all sitting there in Golda's faded housecoats (some had safety pins holding them together in place of a long, lost button) about her older daughter, Sarah Jane. "Betty's sister, Sadie Jane, chose as her chief marshal that Valentine boy from Richmond. She met him when she was at St. Catherine's, and two years after her debut they got married and are living in Charlottesville, where he is in med school."

Mrs. Garner could say a lot in one sentence. The obvious response to such a comment would normally have been, "My, she hit the jackpot, didn't she?" But the responses she received were more like, "How nice. Do they have children yet?" or "You must enjoy visiting Sadie in Charlottesville. That is a beautiful old university town, the gardens and all."

Golda, in the meantime, was sitting there, listening pleasantly and sponging up all the information she could absorb about these people so she could recognize the pecking order and dress them accordingly. Incidentally, she and all the ladies who waited on the clients, yes, clients (not mere customers), always wore black. They wore plain, long-sleeved, high-collared black frocks in order to enhance any outfit sent out on a client to the front to the romantically lit three-way mirrors in view of their friends and family for all to admire. Golda was a psychiatrist of the first order and had a flare for theater and "presentation".

She would ask a few leading questions during the private fashion show. She once asked Serena, "I heard you were at one time engaged to that handsome attorney Vance Millikin, from Rocky Mount. How did you happen to marry your hometown fella from Martin County?"

Serena's answer to this question was her usual, "Just lucky, I guess." It didn't quite satisfy some of the others.

Gertrude Hastings from Elizabeth City commented, "She was more than lucky. She was smart. Vance drinks too much and has already walked out on two wives, but he goes to Virginia Beach now instead of Nags Head, so Serena doesn't have to run into him anymore."

Golda pushed it a little further. "Really now, Serena. How were you wise enough to know?"

A little cruelly, unlike Serena's usual demeanor, she said, "Golda, I knew I wanted children, but I didn't want to marry one."

Golda nodded and said, "Why, of course." The others laughed appreciatively.

The Virginia governor's wife was enchanted. She finally spoke up. "You North Carolina people amaze me. How did you get so smart about people, about reading character? I can't wait to ask Boyd if we can't move to eastern Carolina when his term is up. You people aren't stuffy at all. I've never heard conversations like this in Charlottesville or Richmond either. That's why we love to go to Wrightsville Beach. The Wilmington people are like you, too. Down to earth. Say what they want. Put people at ease. I love it."

"Humph," snorted Elizabeth Ann Garner. "Wilmington people are the snobbiest in North Carolina. All eastern seacoast towns are like that. You have to be born there at least seven generations back. Savannah, Charleston, Beaufort, South Carolina. Why, Elbert Peel from Williamston came back from visiting an Episcopal priest friend of his, the rector in Beaufort, South Carolina. He said the priest walked him out to the church's graveyard from the 1700s to show him a gravestone. On the stone was engraved a kind and generous statement: 'Though a stranger amongst us, we loved him yet.' The deceased had lived in Beaufort sixty years."

Before the Virginia governor's wife, Saravette Harrison, drove away with her friend and her driver to join her husband, Boyd Harrison, in Wilmington, someone asked her how it felt to be inaugurated as first lady of Virginia. Her sincere smile and twinkling eyes accompanied her answer, which people carried home to at least three counties. "If I may be completely honest, I felt like a little girl playing grown-up," she said. She was in.

This was also the day that Serena advised Mary Cavett, concerning her debutante events, "Never forget. If you are invited to a party, it is not for you to *be* entertained, it is for you to *entertain*. Your grandmother told me that my deb year, and I'm obligated to pass it on to you. Also, be especially nice to the mamas and do not flirt with the other girls' boyfriends or with their daddies, no matter how rich and handsome they are."

"My stars, Mama. How did you know? That is exactly what I was practicing to do—flirt with the fathers! Good Lord."

◆ ◆ ◆

In early March of 1937, Danny came home from baseball practice with the fifth grade intramural team. He ran up the steps, almost knocking over a rocking chair on the porch, and skidded into the dining room just as Mary Cavett and Dan were sitting down to pork chops, mashed potatoes, green beans, and some of Beulah Bazemore's tomato aspic that Serena had sent over. Dan, Mary Cavett, and Danny had moved into the "big" house when Danny was about two years old, as had been planned years before.

Doc and Serena had moved down Church Street to a bungalow house a block away. "All on one floor," they were happy to say, and so was Beulah. Happy about the lack of steps. They had built it right after the big war because Williamston needed a "teacherage." They had the parts shipped in from Sears and Roebuck on the back of a train, and local carpenters threw it up in a jiffy. It was solid as a rock with good, hardwood floors. It housed six single teachers, two in each of the three bedrooms. The price was reasonable, and everybody was pleased for awhile.

By 1928, it was not large enough, so the county bought the old Pope family house, renovated it, and rented rooms out to ten single teachers. This was perfect for Doc because he wanted to give up the big house, yard, goldfish pond, smokehouse, and storage building to the young couple and let them worry about it. He did insist upon taking all his dahlia plants. Serena left her roses. She said, "They don't move well, anyway." So Mary Cavett, Big Dan, and Danny had been living in Monkey Top III on Main Street for seven years since 1930.

Mary Cavett only had occasional part-time help. She thought that with just one child, she could manage. However, the house, the yard, and Danny's activities kept her from ever going to Raleigh during the legislature to the big receptions, the women's Sir Walter Cabinet meetings, and the parties, so she really had no idea what Big Dan's life was like up there. She had heard that the women dressed up for everything, wore hats and gloves, and had their hair and nails done for all the political events. She would not relish that lifestyle anyway.

"Wash your hands, son, before you sit down, hey?" reminded Big Dan.

His mother said, looking at him, "Wash your face as well." While he ran back to the bathroom behind the kitchen, Dan told Mary Cavett, "I guess I ought to prepare you. We're having Governor Hoey down here in early April for a Democratic political barbecue at Smitty's Warehouse. I'd like to have him and ten or twelve other people over here first for drinks before we go down there, okay? Can you get some help? We'll keep it simple."

"Uh-huh, I've heard that before. Why is he coming here? He's just barely been elected last November and sworn-in in January," she said, eating more tomato aspic with homemade mayonnaise than potatoes or pork chops.

"You may not realize it, Mary Cavett, but Clyde gives me—well, yes, dammit—he gives me credit for carrying at least six counties for him down here. This is sort of a thank-you trip. He thanks me and the fellas, and I figure out what we're going to ask him for. Another road, getting the logs cleaned out of the river to allow more river boats, a coupla' state jobs for some of my people . . ."

"Oh, that's not right, Dan. Let him hire people for those jobs who are qualified or have experience. Don't send some halfway loser that can't keep a job down here up there to be paid to be the third deputy assistant to the second lieutenant to the assistant director of the highway department, at taxpayers' expense!"

"Well, Mrs. smalltown know-it-all. No, I don't mean that. But I didn't even know you cared. And besides, we may very likely know people down here who are qualified. For instance, nobody thought that Thomas Joyner, the fellow the agriculture development department sent down here, could do a dam' thing. And looka' here. He's turned the whole county around. Farmers are making a good living, sending their children to college. A few years ago a farmer here was just scratching in the dirt and losing his hat, ass, and overcoat."

"Shhh. Don't talk that way in front of the boy," she warned.

"He didn't hear it. For instance, what if the state needed a new state medical director? Couldn't your Daddy do it as well as anybody, Mary Cavett?"

She looked at him as if he had lost his mind.

"Probably, but he's too old to start off in something new. And besides, a job like that shouldn't go to somebody's relative just because he's a good country doctor. It should go to a qualified person who has studied public health and disease prevention. And Daddy's been so busy sewing people up, delivering babies, taking out tonsils. He'd have no idea what they're doing in Asheville or Charlotte, or what should be done. You men amaze me when it comes to political appointments. Nothing but payoffs to somebody's son or brother-in-law, to somebody who's given a bunch of money to some candidate. Don't even tell me about that sort of thing. I don't want to hear it."

In the meantime, Little Danny had taken his seat, dug into a barbecued pork chop, buttered his mashed potatoes, taken a few green beans, and turned his freckled nose up at the tomato aspic. He wanted to interrupt their hassling, so he finally waved a paper up between them.

"What's that, son? Did you make an A?" asked his father.

"Nope, not yet. I haven't turned it in yet, but I wanted to read it to you first. Remember? I had to make a two-page report on the Roanoke River. I wrote big so as to make it three pages."

"Just like your daddy," mumbled Mary Cavett.

"Thank you," mumbled Dan back. "Somebody's got to think big around here."

"Well, I have my report on the Yangtze River. You saw that A that I made, so I thought I'd turn this one in early and maybe . . ."

"Son, if you do too much of that, the other chirrun will think you're bucking for good grades and call you teacher's pet," his daddy warned.

"Dan," said Mary Cavett. "I can't believe you said that. What's wrong with trying to get something in early? He's a Boy Scout, and they swear they'll always try . . . "

Danny broke in, "'To do my best for God and my country.'"

"Lord, God," Big Dan swore. "It's worse than church around here. I'm surrounded by Boy Scouts and mother superiors. I surrender!" He threw his hands up high in surrender, then picked up a pork chop bone to suck it.

Little Danny wiped his mouth and said, "I'll read you my report right after dessert, Mama. What's for dessert?"

"Tapioca pudding," she answered mildly.

"Tapioca! Mama, that's just pap. Baby pap. Tasteless."

"I thought you liked tapioca."

"Maybe when I was a baby. Why can't we have chocolate something?"

"Again, sweetheart? I made that chocolate cake last Saturday, and you ate on it for three days. Besides chocolate gets you all riled up. You can't sleep."

"Well, then, where is the rest of it?" said Danny.

"I sent it over to Granddaddy's."

Danny reminded her, "Granddaddy says chocolate and sugar are bad for me."

"Yes, but he forces himself to eat it upon occasion—and eats every crumb."

Big Dan couldn't resist. "I tell you what. I'll settle this whole discussion. I'll eat my share of the tapioca and Danny Boy's too. Then we won't have any more problem."

"Oh, no," Danny jumped up. "You get yours and I'll have mine, thank you. No fair, you having yours and mine too." Mary Cavett and Big Dan pretended not to hear. She reached over for the silver tureen on Grandmother's side-board and started spooning tapioca into compotes.

"Mama, not fair! You made chocolate tapioca." Mary Cavett gave her most saintly smile and said not a mumbling word.

"Mary Cavett," said Dan, "about the rally at the warehouse. If you would get some help here that Thursday night around five o'clock. We'll have about twenty over here first. We'll just offer bourbon and soda, Scotch for the fancy Scotch drinkers, boiled peanuts, souse meat soaked in vinegar with soda crackers, and small cornbread squares with a spoonful of ham-flavored collards on top and a nice bite of old cured ham on top of that. All right?"

"My soul," she said. "Are you trying to kill him, kill the governor? Souse, collards, and old ham?"

"No, I'm trying to give him a night he'll remember, Mary Cavett. Oh, and add to that the best liver pudding we can find. It's made out in Bear Grass at the Rogers farm, I think. We'll serve that on crackers, too. But a lot of fellas like to pick up a spoon and just eat it straight. Specially if it's fried a little so's it's crispy on the outside. Oh, and you don't have to go down to the warehouse unless you want to. It still smells so strong of tobacco, and you're allergic to tobacco. You know how you are. The governor won't eat anything there. Or drink. He doesn't like to shake hands or talk to people with his mouth full. So we're taking him on down to the houseboat afterwards for some of Ben-Olive's rock muddle. Clyde is excited about that. He's been hearing about the houseboat for years, he says, and actually asked if he could go aboard. An' I said sure. And to make it even better, I'd like Little Danny to meet the governor. I want you and Danny and your mother and your daddy to meet us down at the river. Unless your daddy would like to come here first and go to the warehouse with us. Okay?"

"My mercy! I never heard you say so much in one breath in my life, Dan. When did you figure all this out? Are you quarterbacking again?"

He shrugged. "It really isn't so much different from working out a fourth-down play with a run for goal. You just try to keep everybody covered every moment. I'd ask Ben-Olive to drive you down, but he'll already be there cooking. I'll arrange a ride for you. Maybe with Charlie Mack or one of his boys out at the car place."

"No, no," she said. "Danny and I'll just come to the warehouse. He'd enjoy the band playing and so would I. And maybe he'll like hearing those political speeches. They're not my cup of tea, but I can take it for one night."

"Daddy, do you make those warehouse kind of speeches in the legislature?" said Danny.

"I sure do, Danny, in spite of your mother. She's never even heard me speak about roads or agriculture in the legislature. But I can't touch Governor Hoey. Listen to this,

Mary Cavett. Clyde made this speech just the other day in Charlotte. I've a copy."

"Really, now, Dan, " she said.

"I won't read it all. It's plain and clear. At a supper for six hundred young farmers from sixteen counties, he titled it, simply, 'Farming Is a Business, Agriculture Is a Science.' It begins, 'The future successful farmer must understand the chemistry of the soil, must be acquainted with its needs, and must be capable of diagnosing its capacities. He must also know the character of the soil best-suited for growing various crops and be schooled in the knowledge of the value of rotating these crops so as to feed the soil, increase its fertility and productiveness, and at the same time, save it from erosion. This is a new country, but we have wrought such havoc on our land in the last century that soil conservation becomes a vital necessity in this day unless we wish to develop a dust bowl here similar to those in the central western states!'" He looked up and said, "And it gets better."

Mary Cavett watched him curiously. "Well, you're certainly a convert. I 'spose it would be nice for Danny to hear those kind of talks. But we can't stay out on that crazy boat very late. After all, it's a school night. No, actually the next day is a holiday."

Danny was finishing his second serving of chocolate tapioca pudding with some added graham crackers he had discovered and said, "I want to go, Daddy. I want to meet Governor Hoey. Is he the one that wears a fancy tail suit all the time and has a carnation in his buttonhole?"

"That's your governor, son. And he'll enjoy meeting you too. Now read us that paper about the Roanoke."

Danny cleared his throat, stood up, looked back and forth at each of his parents, licked his lips, and wiped the back of his hand over his mouth. Then he wiped his hand on the back of his pants, shifted back and forth from one foot to another a time or two, and cleared his throat.

"Get on with it, boy. You're worse'n a baseball pitcher making a spitball," said Big Dan.

"Okay, Daddy, here goes. Now I didn't make it all up. Some came right out of the book at the liberry."

"*Library*," said Mary Cavett.

"*L-i-berry* ," said Danny.

"Mary Cavett, why in the world don't you teach English at Harvard?" said Big Dan. "What are you doing hanging around Williamston when you could be teaching at Harvard? Huh?"

"Good question," she said. "Go on, honey." He cleared his throat again, and this was Danny's report.

The Riddle

Runs all day and never walks
Often murmurs, never talks
Has a mouth and never eats
Has a bed and never sleeps
What is it?

"It is also deep and narrow. It springs from the eastern divide of the Blue Ridge mountains of Virginia between the high towns of Roanoke and Lynchburg. Its course is formed by the marriage of two mountain streams, Big Otter and Goose Creek. The two join in the hills near Alta Vista. A third oversized creek, shown on the map as the Little Pigg, joins forces. Then the three together flow toward the North Carolina border as one. The Banister River, and the more famous Dan River, join the young Roanoke northwest of Clarksville.

"The river cuts through Warren and Halifax counties, brushing the small historic towns of Warrenton, Macon, Littleton, and Thelma before rumbling over the rocks at Roanoke Rapids and then rushing on her way to and through the Albemarle Sound to reach the sea. As she flows around and bounds the eastern border of Martin County, she picks up speed, heading past the high ground planted with corn and tobacco on her right. On the left bank sleep miles and miles of mushy conine swamp. There are no roads on the swampy side by which fishermen can reach the river.

"During the spring 'run,' this river is the site of every known fishing device—trot lines, poles, seines, dip nets, and drift nets. Moving up and down this river are barges, oil tankers, and fishing boats. But few are pleasure types, for the Indians named the mighty Roanoke "River of Wild Song" for a reason. Some say *Roanoke* early on meant "River of Death." She is deep and narrow, heading southward from the mountains, which makes her swift and vicious. She specializes in snags, fast-floating logs, and evil sucking whirlpools that cause her to be unsafe for Sunday afternoon family outings. Whenever you approach the mighty Roanoke, treat her with great respect. Thank you, Daniel Haughton Hardison."

Big Dan and Mary Cavett looked at one another over his head. She felt sure as rain he was going to grow up to be a doctor like her daddy. Dan was sure as shootin' little Dan was going to grow up and to be the governor like his good friend Clyde R. Hoey and give fine speeches. All starting in the Friday assembly gatherings at Church Street School in Williamston, North Carolina, in Martin County, as the Roanoke River ran around it on its path to the sea.

10

Who'll carry the coffin?
I said the Kite
If it's not through the night
I'll carry the coffin.

THE barbecue at the tobacco warehouse, planned by Senator Dan Hardison and Mayor Griffin and long touted as the swellest Democratic rally in this part of North Carolina went well, as expected. The high school band played, American flags flew, politicians ranted, the governor orated, and people repeated jokes. Several people quoted Will Rogers, who had once commented, before he was killed in the plane crash, "I don't belong to any organized party. I'm a Democrat."

Somebody informed the governor that there was a small—very small—town over in Bertie County named Republican.

"My gracious," he said in his old southern colonel accent. "Does that mean there's a cache of Republicans hiding out over there?"

"Oh, no, there's only one. But he's such a rare phenomenon that they decided to name the town Republican because it is such an oddity. Actually, they are not sure that fella even knows what Republican means. He just wanted to do something different from his daddy. Kinda' like rebelling against authority."

The governor's eyes twinkled. "That's not all bad, either, friend. Everybody, every young person, should be encouraged to have a mind of his own. He shouldn't be required to join the same church or political party as his father. He should have a chance to figure out things of importance for himself."

"I'm surprised to hear you say that, Governor Hoey," said the retired schoolteacher Reginald Farraday. "You don't think the faith of our fathers or the party of our fathers is sufficient for these young squirts? Uh, thinkers?"

"You're right. That's what I'm expected to say. But as a former newspaper editor and journalist, I admit to preferring that we teach everybody to read, encourage them to study both sides of an issue, and make up their own minds," said the governor, smiling kindly.

Doc Chase Haughton was standing there listening and said, "I'd give my best hat to see your campaign manager, my son-in-law, Dan Hardison . . . to see his face if he heard you say that, Clyde. As hard as he's been telling everybody in six counties that the faith of their fathers *is* the Democratic Party and they'd better accept it—guts, feathers and all—and vote for you in a snowstorm."

"Grand, grand," exuded the governor. "Good for Dan. He's our man. I wouldn't change him for the world or refute anything he tells the voters. He's telling them the truth."

"But you just said . . . " started Reginald Farraday, the retired schoolteacher. However, the governor had already slid on over to another group and was flashing his election smile, shaking hands all round, and making everyone feel very comfortable and happy they came.

Within the next group that came toward him was a hog farmer named Booger Bear Brown. No one remembered where the nickname "Booger Bear" had come from, and he wasn't telling. His wife was with him, and someone introduced them to Governor Hoey. The governor commented on her silver bracelet.

"That's a mighty fine bracelet you have there, Miz' Brown."

She began to take it off.

"Don't show the governor that thing, Lucy. He don't want to see that ol' thing."

"Yes, he does," said Lucy Brown, showing the governor the inside. "He had a good year last year and bought this for me in Raleigh with this inscription inside that he made up himself."

The governor took it and read the inscription out loud. "From Boogaloo to my waterloo." Booger's face turned quite red.

Amid hoots and hollers, Hoey added, "That is delightful, Miz' Brown. Truly the most original inscription I have ever read or heard. It really is. I wish I could have come up with something that original for my wife, Isabel. But the only thing I can think of that rhymes with Hoey is 'fooey.'"

Getting over his embarrassment, Booger Bear decided to tell Governor Hoey that he remembered meeting him over in Greenville when Big Dan took him and a carload over to a rally when Clyde was first running for governor.

As they were driving back to Williamston that night, Booger had asked Dan if Clyde R. Hoey was to be the next governor. Booger went on to inform Governor Hoey that Big Dan had said no.

"Why not?" Dan was asked.

He had announced, "Because Clyde can't spit on the floor."

The governor exploded, "Well darn his time. I never knew he had ever once said such a thing as that, or thought it!"

Dan, of course, was coming up behind them and heard most of it. He added, "Miracles do happen, you know. Miracles do happen. You did actually get elected, even tho' you never did learn how to spit on the floor. I'd take you 'round to all these country stores hoping you could learn to be one of the fellas. I was about to give up hope until I learned one thing about you, and that saved your hide down here."

"What was that?" the governor and all the others wanted to know.

"You can evermore tell a dam' good story. Also, you'd rather hear a good story than go to a fire."

"Well, Dan, my friend, I'll have to tell you what I've learned about you down here, visiting in Martin County today," said the governor. "It's another miracle."

"Whatever is that?" asked Big Dan.

"The people," answered Governor Clyde, "are both pleased, amused, and even delighted and proud that a good ol' farm boy who loved to play baseball and football should end up being one of the most powerful men in the North Carolina State Senate. And chairman of a major committee, highways. And respected by both Democrats and Republicans in the legislature."

"Hell, you never heard all that," said a disbelieving Dan Hardison.

"Oh, that and more," said the jovial governor. "Furthermore, do you know what I told them?"

"Don't make me guess," said a curious Dan. But he was not prepared for the answer.

"I quoted to them one of my favorite short passages from the Bible, Psalm 118, verse 22: 'The same stone which the builders rejected has become the chief cornerstone.' What do you think of that?" asked the governor.

"I say," said an amused Dan Hardison, "whatever makes your ears flap, go for it."

"Hey, governor, here's somebody you've gotta meet," said Big Dan as he directed the guest of honor over to a fella drinking iced tea with his barbecue. "This here's Warren Goff, the preacher's kid who always got us in a pack of trouble. He cussed so bad our mamas tried to get us not to play with him. Warren, meet Governor Hoey and get ready, 'cause I'm gonna tell him about you."

"He looks perfectly innocent to me," said Governor Hoey, shaking his hand.

"Oh, he's calmed down by now. He's a model husband and father. Sings in the choir. And I ain't heard him cuss in years."

Dan went on, with Warren blushing under the dubious praise.

"I'm no psychologist," said the governor, "but I've always heard that preacher's kids often feel a need to act up in order to convince their peers that they are regular fellas and not 'different' somehow. "

"And sometimes they overdo it," finished Charlie Mack, who had just wandered up and caught the gist.

"Hey, Charlie, tell the governor 'bout Warren and us killin' snakes." Big Dan pulled the mayor forward.

"Yes, I've heard that expression down here. Somebody was doing a thing vigorously, like killin' snakes. What does it mean?" asked the governor as three, four others gathered around.

Charlie warmed to his subject as he told about how he, Big Dan, and Warren, back in high school, borrowed guns and a motor boat to make an annual spring trip down the Roanoke River when the snakes were first waking up and venturing out to lounge about on low-lying limbs hanging out over the river. The boys would motor up under the trees along the edge of the swamp. When they spotted a snake on a limb, they thought it great sport to try to shoot at it and watch it zing off that limb and splash into the water. They never knew if the bullet hit it or if the gun just frightened it. Great sport.

One spring, known as a "snake spring," when they seemed to be everywhere (perhaps after a warm winter), the boys puttered up under a large limb and saw a great big ball of snakes wrapped up on it.

"Great dam' balls a' fire," shouted Warren. Before we knew it, he was firing off his daddy's gun into that big ball of snakes.

"And of course, you know what happened," Charlie continued. "The whole pile landed, whop! Right in the boat at our feet. Such scrambling you never saw." Charlie went on, "I don't know who was the scaredest, them or us. We were so busy diving out of that boat that we never even counted how many there were. Before he jumped out, however, Warren here, bless him, shot—yes, shot—at the snakes in the boat at his feet."

"That's understandable," offered the governor, fascinated.

"But, governor," countered Charlie Mack, "he shot the dam' boat and it started sinking!"

"Oh, my mercy!" said the governor, and everybody howled for the umpteenth time. They had heard the story about the preacher's kid, the football player, and the future mayor over and over and reveled in it like the litany over at the 'pistopal church. This was a Martin County litany, in truth.

"What in the world happened then?" the visitor wanted to know.

"Oh, you don't want to hear it," added Warren. "We were miles down the river from home, three scared boys clinging to the sides of a sinking boat filled with snakes in the fastest-running, deepest river on the eastern seaboard.

Just accept it that the Lord looks after drunks and fools. None of us drink much, and we're all still standing here."

"It doesn't sound like you fellas had the time to drink much, or needed to. You were just as wild stone sober as anybody else would be high as a kite. You boys must have come by it naturally," said the governor, his faced ringed with smile wrinkles. "And now I know where 'killin' snakes' came from. Martin County folklore."

"Oh, wait'll you hear another Warren story," Charlie went on. "We were all out with some coon dogs in the swamp one night, five or six of us, trying to see if these expensive dogs really would 'tree' a coon for us. "

"What in the devil would you do with a coon if you caught one?" interrupted the governor. "People don't eat them, do they?"

"Not that I know of," said Warren. "Sometimes we'd shoot them for 'sport,' they call it, but a lotta' times we'd take them home in a bag to the children to keep as pets in a pen in the back yard. Raccoons are cute little fellas. They look like bandits with a thing over their eyes to disguise them. And have you ever watched their paws? Like when they are trying to scoop up a fish in a pond? They look more like real hands than they do animal paws. And they look at you so intelligent like."

"Oh, Warren's taking too long," broke in the mayor. "One night, over in Conine Swamp, the dogs spotted a raccoon and we thought we saw his eyes shining out at us way up in this big ol' cypress tree. Warren said, 'Wait a minute. Let me take this bag up there, climb up, and grab him to take home to my little brother.' The poor creature seemed petrified, the story went, frozen in fear on that limb and frightened by the dogs' barking. So we held our fire and up he climbed, bag in hand, while we tried to watch in the near-total black darkness," explained Charlie. "One fella had a small kerosene lamp he carried with him. It's a wonder we didn't start a fire, too."

"So what in the world happened?" asked the governor.

Warren looked down at his socks and seemed to blush again as the mayor pushed on to the worst moment in Warren's life. "Governor, the next thing we knew, here came Warren scrambling backwards, almost forward, down that tree, dropping his tow sack, his face white as a ghost. And he almost fainted when he got down to us and tried to say, 'Run!'"

"We all started to run, men and dogs, except the dogs wanted to stay there and bark some more. "'What are we running for?' I asked Warren, puffing and blowing.

"'I got up there,' he said, 'eyeball to eyeball with that ol' coon. But you know what?'

"'What?' I said, all out of breath.

"'It won't no raccoon. It was a Conine Swamp wild-cat.'"

"Good Lord, a'mighty," said the governor. "Well, son, like you said, the Lord looks after drunks and fools. Especially in Martin County. You people, obviously, live charmed lives down here. Why would anybody ever want to leave?"

"Haven't you noticed, gov'nor? Not many do," said Big Dan. "That's what's wrong with us. There's too much inbreeding. Makes us 'bout half crazy. When I was in

Raleigh at State, I couldn't wait to get back home to my mama's cooking, to her good sausage biscuits. I felt like Brer Rabbit in the briar patch and never wanted to leave here again, especially just before exam time."

"And here you are up there in the State Senate chambers every other spring acting like you own the place. You must have learned something down here, son," said the governor. Looking around at those assembled, he remarked, "The folks up there sure like your man."

◆ ◆ ◆

After the big rally on that evening of 9 April 1937, the sun had just set over the fields of young tobacco when Big Dan's newest car, a Chevrolet this year, pulled out of the sandy parking lot beside old Hardee's tobacco warehouse. Dan, the governor, Charlie Mack, Mary Cavett, and Little Dan had slipped out the side door after most of the shouting was over to go down to the *Swamp Monkey* for the "highlight of the events," according to Governor Clyde. "I've always heard that the most congenial place to be caught in a rainstorm was aboard this old houseboat with your particular group of Martin County Democrats, enjoying some of the local Bear Grass brew, cards, and some of what's-his-name's cooking," he said.

"Ben-Olive," said Little Dan from his spot in the back seat between the governor and Charlie Mack. His daddy and mother sat up front.

"We're tickled you'd come down here, Your Honor," said Charlie Mack, who was really a lot more than just tickled to have the governor visit his little town of five thousand souls even if his buddy Dan was responsible for getting him down there. He'd take a governor any way he could get him.

"Well, I'll 'Your Honor' you, too, Mr. Mayor, Your Honor," the governor said. You did a fine piece of work on that rally—with the barbecue, the music, the flags, the speaker's stand up on a fine stage with all your dignitaries seated up there. And the nice red, white, and blue flower bouquet there in front of the podium. Don't think all those things go unnoticed. I'm very aware of how much planning and work you boys do to pull these events together, get out a crowd, and have all your friends cooperate with you to make it a success. I want to compliment you for all your time and trouble. You're an asset to the party, your country, and your state. And I wish to thank you."

"Lord a'mercy, Clyde. You can get off your stump now," Dan responded quickly. "You're beginning to sound all the time like you're giving a speech. It's just us now and you can relax. Okay, buddy?"

Mary Cavett, appalled, turned around and looked over her shoulder at the smiling, elegant governor. She rolled her eyes as if to say, "Look here, just don't pay him any mind."

But Governor Hoey said back to her, with a wink, "You dear southern lady. You just might not understand. Your husband and I have our own system of checks and balances. He tries to keep me from getting out of line and I can't really afford to check him too often. He knows it, of course, because your boy there very largely got me elected. Especially down east here, where he is, in case you're unaware of it, possibly the backbone of the Democratic Party in this part of the state. This is important for many reasons. The least of which, there are so few Democratic counties in the mountains, and every county down here counts. So your boy there can tell me anything he so chooses. If you think you dear people are answering to the governor, you need to know, but don't tell just everybody, that the governor is answerable to *you*, the good people who got him into this tail suit here in the first place."

"Lord, God, in heaven! There he goes again. If you give him one half a'minute and a little breath, he'll turn it into a political speech in the first two seconds. What are we going to do with you, Clyde?"

Charlie Mack intervened. "If you ask me, a mere onlooker, I'd say Mr. Hoey doesn't need you to do anything. He does very well in Charlotte without you. And they have how many thousands of votes more than Martin County has? I'm not convinced the governor here needs so much advice from a Martin County farmer. All due respect, you understand, Dan."

Mary Cavett was shaking her head looking down at her hands at this conversation, and Danny was looking from one to the other. The governor put them all at ease. "Big Dan here can tell me, advise me, suggest to me anything he so desires. He is one of the straight-arrow true men in the whole great state that I totally trust to level with me. He will tell me the honest lay of the land and the thoughts of the people. And if he wants to tell me to quit speechifying, he can do that, too."

Before Mary Cavett, Charlie, and especially Danny could take these last words in, Dan said, "If you had just left out the word 'great' before the word 'state' in that last sermon, it would have almost seemed like a true statement of fact instead of a state pronouncement. Remember, oratory is the bulldog of the intellect." The governor stared at Dan in utter amazement and forgot to close his mouth.

To change the subject, Mary Cavett asked the men how they felt about the smaller gathering (she wouldn't call it a cocktail party) at their house.

"Oh, delightful, Miz' Mary Cavett," said the governor. "I really appreciated the chance to speak closely with the leading lights—political, that is—from at least seven counties about here, in a smaller setting, more personal. You understand. They could tell me what was happening in their counties, who was for us and who wasn't. Matters we really cannot attend to at the big rally with all the hoopla, food, and music going on. Dan was a genius to plan that for us at your lovely home. Not many county rallies afford me this much of an opportunity to reach out. Your gathering was very valuable for all of us. It didn't hurt your husband, either. He's up for a number of good committees and could be chairman of any one he chose to be. He's a political magician, if you don't mind my saying so."

"Well, please do me a favor, Clyde, and don't ever say that out loud again—what you just said," Big Dan laughed. "That would ruin me. I don't want to be no magician, if you don't mind. And any fool knows I ain't no genius. So let's leave all that alone, if you want to do me a favor."

Governor Hoey was thoroughly enjoying his ride through the country on the way down to the houseboat. "Hey, let's give this politics business a rest for a while, heah? I do love seeing this part of old eastern North Carolina. I feel at home. I believe in another life I must have been born and bred right down here. I feel so relaxed, as if I've just come back from a long trip and I've finally reached my true home place."

"I swear, man." guffawed Dan. "You've polished up that ol' saw so shiny from saying it to the voters in the mountains, and up in Charlotte and Durham, and here you are trying to pass it off on us dirt dawbers down here. It won't fly, Clyde. It won't fly."

Unmoved, Governor Hoey insisted, "No, honest, Dan. See that sign right there? I feel like I've not only seen it, in that very spot, but I feel like I was the little boy who painted it and nailed it up there."

Dan, Mary Cavett, Little Dan, and Mayor Charlie Mack all looked to the right, and there was this big, hand-painted, crude sign that announced, "Puppies for sale."

"Oh, that's Willy Johnson's house!" Little Dan exclaimed. Shouting and pointing, he asked instantly if he couldn't have one of Willy's puppies. "Let's go back and pick one out, Daddy, hey?"

"Nope. We have enough dogs, son. Sorry."

The governor apologized for bringing it up. The Hardisons assured him not to worry. Little Danny pouted with his arms crossed and gently kicked the back of the front seat of the car behind his daddy.

"Oh, my," said the governor. "There's another one. Free kittens. Dan, don't you think I ought to take Miz' Isabel a nice little Martin County kitten? To show her I remember her on all these trips? How 'bout going back?"

"Well," mused Dan, "not from the Fergusons' farm back there. They probably don't have any kittens. That old sign is just a ploy to get people to turn into their farm so they can sell you some of their canned tomatoes, beans, corn, and fig preserves."

"Wonderful. Do let's go back there," said the governor, turning his head back to look. "Isabel had rather have all that than a kitten, anyway."

Big Dan continued, "Then what they really want to sell you is their pickled pig's feet, souse, liver mush, and canned chitterlings. They won't let you leave without it."

Clyde's face turned pale while his stomach just turned, and he murmured, "You people certainly are enterprising folks down here, Dan."

"You got it. You should recognize it, Clyde. Remember, this is where you grew up in another life, right?" Dan smiled. Clyde smiled. "Do you still want me to go back and let you shop? You can pick up a coupla' votes while you're at it," Big Dan teased him.

"Maybe another time. We'll think about it. You probably already have their votes lined up anyway, don't you, Dan?" the governor said.

"You can count on it. And Charlie Mack? You heard him say, 'We'll think about it?' That should be his rallying call. Almost every matter that comes to his attention in

Raleigh, he smiles, shakes your hand, puts his left hand consolingly on your right shoulder, looks into your eyes. and says, 'I'm listening.' Or, 'We'll look into it!' 'We'll take that into consideration.' Or, 'We'll think about it.' Now ain't that some way to run a state? Always sittin' on the fence?"

"Isn't, not ain't, Dan," said Mary Cavett.

Loving this, the governor said, "Hear, now, Dan, what's a poor politician to do? Make half the voters mad every time he opens his mouth? I'm just doing what you taught me."

"What the hell did I teach you?" asked Dan, amused.

"You distinctly informed me," returned the governor, "'Keep your mouth shut, Clyde. Let people suspect you're a fool, rather than open it and confirm it.' And besides, you said if my mouth was shut, I couldn't put my foot in it."

"Lord knows I wouldn't say a fool thing like that to my governor. Charlie Mack, you know I wouldn't, now would I?"

"I know you would," the mayor retorted calmly, only half smiling.

Little Danny was taking most of this in, the parts he could understand. Mary Cavett was gazing out the window with her hands folded in her lap and holding a clean, handmade lace, perfumed handkerchief her grandmother had given her. Heaven only knows what she was thinking.

Governor Clyde turned his head quickly again, taking note of another road sign painted by hand that said "Bioled Peanuts" in large letters. He couldn't wait to remonstrate with Senator Hardison. "Hey, senator, don't you teach your voters down here how to spell? 'Bioled?' What kind of education system do you folks use in Martin County?" he joked.

Big Dan did not remove his eyes from the dirt road in front of him. Mayor Charlie Mack, Little Danny, and Mary Cavett all watched him, wondering what he would tell the governor.

Dan said, "Spelling ain't no prerequisite to selling nuts, governor."

The governor, already knowing this would be a night unlike most of his political visits to Asheville, Winston-Salem, or Charlotte, told him, "Look here, you pseudo-farm boy, any fella that can use the word 'prerequi'—what? sit?—certainly knows the difference between a double negative and a . . ."

Mary Cavett interrupted, cutting her eyes out the window, "Governor, I've long since given up on him. He insists Martin County is the double negative capital of the world, and he doesn't want to do anything that might besmirch our reputation. If a former English teacher cannot convince her own husband, how can you expect anything else?"

The governor couldn't resist. "Dear, if sharing bed and board with your student won't change him, I suppose nothing will. Mary Cavett, if you ever entertained the thought you could change this particularly hard-headed man of any bad habits at all, I am sure you have disabused yourself of that notion."

She agreed. "Look here, every one of you," Dan broke in in his own defense. "Why should I go roun' all time talking down to my constituents? Tell me that?"

Mary Cavett said, "Using correct grammar isn't talking down to them. It's just the proper, educated thing to do. Our senator should set a standard."

"Well, not this senator. I speak their language. They know I'm one of them. They trust me. I trust them. These here farmers know we're all in the same boat, 'bout to go down. And we're hanging in here together, few good roads, no industry, no nothin'. But I've already mentioned that, haven't I?"

Mayor Charlie Mack had been sitting in the back seat trying not to stare at Mary Cavett. At least he was trying not to let Big Dan catch him if he glanced in the rearview mirror and saw him staring at his wife. Charlie decided he had to get into this conversation whether he wanted to or not, rather than to just sit and enjoy their rattling on and gazing, when he could, at Mary Cavett's dimple. "Mentioned it," he said. "So many times we could dance to it, Dan. Why don't you leave the poor governor alone and let him relax and enjoy his visit? He'll never come back the way you're nagging him all the time."

"Hey, here we are," said Dan. "There are some folks down here at the dock waitin' for you."

They were at the top of the high bank that bounds the river and started driving slowly down. Dan worked the brakes.

"Who all is it?" asked Mary Cavett. "I didn't think anyone was supposed to know where we were taking him."

"Half the folks in the county know where he was going, but most of them know better than to just show up down here," Dan said. "There are some places you don't go uninvited, and most people know that."

"You are sounding like a snob to me, Dan," said the governor. "And you know I can't afford to get around with any certified snobs." Governor Hoey smiled and winked at Mary Cavett.

"Well, that's just the crowd that's supposed to be here. The sheriff, Timothy McKinnon, you met him at the rally, the Ford dealer, Bill-John Bellamy, Charlie Mack's competition in Williamston. "

Charlie Mack threw in a fascinating fact. "Dan trades cars every two years, before they start wearing out," he said. "One year he trades with my competition for a Ford, and then two years later he trades with me for a Chevrolet. Two years each. Ever faithful."

Charlie, if you don't mind," Big Dan interrupted, "I don't think the governor could be the least bit interested in what brand of car I drive."

"Oh, but the governor is," Governor Hoey declared. "That's an outstanding characteristic. It shows great commitment to his friends and to dealing and buying right at home. Great quality in a politician."

"Politician! Now, don't call me no politician. I'm just a plain ol' dirt farmer. Sometimes I'm even honest. But I ain't no politician."

"Whew," whistled both men. "No politician. And if that's the truth, then I'm the Pope," said Charlie Mack. "And I'm Winston Churchill," said the governor.

The nonpolitician's wife, Mary Cavett, asked, "And when was the last time you made a scratch in the dirt, hmm?"

As Dan pulled to a stop, the governor asked, "Quick, who are those other people? Catch me up. Have I already met them?"

"Yeah, some of them," answered Dan. "The sheriff's lady friend there is Charlie Mack's sister, Dr. Dorothy Griffin. You haven't met her. There's Lawyer Martin and Lawyer Peel. You met them at the rally. Peel is smoking the cigar—chewing it, rather. And the tall man with his arms crossed is Mary Cavett's father, Doc Chase Haughton. And the guy with him is . . . someone I don't recognize," Dan lied.

"Is Dr. Dorothy a medical doctor, too?" the governor asked Charlie.

"Aw, naw," said Charlie. "She teaches English at ECTC. One of the first lady pea aich dees they ever hired there. She's my sister."

"You should be proud," said the governor.

"Oh, I are," said Charlie Mack, winking.

Mary Cavett rolled her eyes and swung her head back and forth again. She couldn't wait to get out of the car and did not wait for any one of these "gentlemen" to open her door.

11

Who'll bear the pall?
We said the Wren
Both the Cock and the Hen
We'll bear the pall.

THIRTY minutes later, all were safely aboard the *Swamp Monkey*, having crowded into four motorboats. Ben-Olive was finishing up his rock muddle, collards and ham bone, cornbread, sliced tomatoes soaked in vinegar and sugar with cucumbers, and lemon pie with meringue two inches high.

Doc Haughton had introduced his guest, Dwight Carter from Norfolk, to everyone. While the beer from the barbecue place plus the "attitude adjustment" offered there (B & B) was performing its social duties, those gathered joked and teased while they "sought once more for amiable insults" and "fought for friendly retaliation."

Dwight, the visitor from Norfolk, chatted awhile with Sheriff Timothy and his girlfriend, Dr. Dorothy Griffin, the mayor's sister. He almost asked about their children, then noticed just in time that neither of them was wearing a wedding ring. So he thought better of it. He approached Doc later and asked from a mild curiosity if they had not married.

"No," explained a mystified Doc. "They have courted many years, every other weekend, either over in Greenville where she taught or here when she visited her parents one weekend a month. All I ever heard, she never invited him into her house for some reason, just onto the porch. They ate out and attended the movie. Then, one night, he wandered on in the house for some reason. To his utter dismay, he found the little six-room house, a bungalow like the one Serena and I live in now, packed, filled up to the waist with stacks of stuff, with a small path to walk through from room to room."

"What kind of stuff?" asked Dwight.

"Well, books, magazines, papers, playbills, church bulletins, home-canned goods friends had brought her, sheet music on the piano and everywhere else, recordings on the Victrola, houseplants (mostly dead or dying), boxes of papers, trash. Apparently she can't throw anything away—can't decide what to throw away or when. The sheriff tried to tell me about it, but I'd never seen anything quite like he described. I've read about it in psychology books. One nickname for it is 'packrat.' The real name is 'hoarding.'"

"I've heard about that," said Dwight. "Is it an obsession to save things?"

"Right. And if they married, him being the sheriff over here, she'd have to possibly give up her good job teaching, organize and pack up all her rooms full of collections and what all, and move over here. And she hasn't figured how to go about it."

"After ten years?"

"Um hmm. We keep thinking they'll figure out how to manage it. They seem to get along real well. They both like books, lectures, concerts in Greenville, Chatauquas. And every year they say next year they'll get it straight. Who knows?"

Dwight asked, "Do her belongings give her a sense of security?"

"Again, who knows?" said Doc, shrugging his shoulders. "I'm no psychiatrist."

They moved toward the group standing around Governor Hoey. Dwight decided to go inside to the big room, sit down, and collect his thoughts, having not been aboard this craft for ten years.

Mary Cavett, with Little Danny in tow, had previously gone inside to get away from the mosquitoes and allow the men to tell some of the off-color jokes they had been known to recall when the ladies were not present. Danny had brought two decks of cards in his pocket for his mother or somebody to play Go Fishing and Old Maid with him if matters got slow, so they sat at a table and he started dealing the cards. "Okay, Mama, you start. And why do the mosquitoes just bite you and me and not Daddy and Granddaddy and all those others?"

"I don't know, honey. Maybe because most of them are smoking. If you were a mosquito, would you go through all that cigar, pipe, and cigarette smoke just for a bite? Actually, I think I read somewhere that mosquitoes are more attracted to blondes than brunettes. Something about their chemistry—the way blondes have a different odor than brunettes."

A voice from the window seat said, "Is that why they go for me? Because I'm blonde?" A tall man walked from the shadows at the window seat over to the card table and stood with his hands in his pockets looking down at Mary Cavett. He also added, "It could also be that blondes have one less layer of skin than brunettes and are easier to bite, do you suppose?" As it happened, he had spent at least two years in medical school before flunking out.

Ben-Olive said something like, "I hope those skeeters don't bite me none. I've got to get out there and rinse off these pots and pans in the river. " He went toward the screen door on the swamp side of the boat with his arms full of pots and pans and bumped the door open with his thin, bony hip. Danny called to him, "Hey, don't fall overboard, hear? The river's high this week."

"Don't worry 'bout John Norman," Ben called back as he shoved out the door and let it slam behind him.

"John Norman?" The slender blonde man asked Danny. Danny shrugged and played his card. His mother said, "It's just a local expression." She glanced up at him a moment and then lowered her eyes back to her cards, staring at them. He, meantime, kept looking straight at her, then put out his hand as if to shake hands and introduce himself. She placed her cards in her left hand and took his with her right, gazing up at him.

"I'm Dwight Carter."

She smiled slightly and said, "I'm Mary Cavett Hardison, and this is my son, Danny Hardison. Danny, shake hands with . . . Mr. Carter." Danny reached up to shake hands with the man, but his mother said, "Danny, practice what your Daddy said, now."

Danny then put his cards down, stood up and shook Dwight's right hand neatly, looked him in the eye, and said, "I'm pleased to meet you, Mr. Carter."

Dwight, clearly impressed, said, "I'm very pleased to meet you, Danny."

There was an awkward pause. Then Danny looked at his mother and said, "Can we play cards now, Mama?"

The adults both said, "Sure."

Dwight asked the boy, "How old are you, Danny?"

Glancing up, the boy said, "I'm nine, be ten next January."

Dwight nodded slowly, put his hands back in his pockets, rocked back slightly on his heels, then rocked forward again several times like a college professor mentally computing the answer to a math problem, all the while watching the little boy engrossed in his game. Finally, he looked at Mary Cavett, touched her on the shoulder slightly, and asked, "Mrs. Hardison, how old are your other children?"

Not looking up from the cards, while mumbling "my turn" or "go fishing," she shook her head in the negative and said, quietly, "There are no others." Dwight watched her and the boy a few moments, maybe a full minute. Then he walked slowly over to the window and leaned against it, looking out at the men on the river side deck of the boat.

He scrambled in his pants pockets feeling for a package of cigarettes, pulled it out with a box of matches, and fumbled to lift out a cigarette. Then he reached into the small box for a match and began trying to light the cigarette. This was not simple, as his hands were shaking. There. He glanced sidewise at the boy at the table then turned back to gaze out the window at the other men.

Big Dan announced, "The governor here can sure tell a good story, and he loves to hear 'em too. Elbert, tell him the one about the traveling salesman in the trunk." Haw, haw, haw, haw, they all laughed even before he told it while mentally deciding which of their best they should try to tell tonight.

Ben-Olive came banging back in from the swamp side of the deck with his river-washed pots and declared, "Almost ready, folks. You can be washing your hands."

Danny said, as he gathered up his cards, "In the river, like those pots?"

"Sure thing. Okay by me," said Ben-Olive, laughing. "Let's chase those talkin' bigshots out there in here or they'll be out there all night. Go get 'em, boy!" As Danny ran out the door with this important duty to perform, Ben-Olive and Mary Cavett started arranging chairs to the table. As the men were still slow to break up their goings on, Ben stepped out the door with a dinner bell and a soup ladle and banged the men in to their supper.

Thirty minutes later, well into the riverboat meal, Danny was ensconced at the head of the T-shaped table between Governor Hoey and his father, Big Dan. Hizzoner, the mayor, Charlie Mack Griffin, was on the other side of the governor and so on down to the bottom of the table, where the last two persons sitting across from one another were Mary Cavett and Dwight Carter. Dwight spoke neighborly across the table, "How is it your son is sitting between his honor, the governor, and your husband, and not you? The pretty hostess of the evening?"

Mary Cavett actually smiled. "I'm not the hostess of the evening. Actually, these affairs are not my choice. I'm here only because Dan asked me to please come. I suggested he have Danny sit up there instead of me and not force me to make small talk with his honor all evening. I just let the fellas have at it. I don't follow politics."

"From what I understand," Dwight chatted on, "the governor would greatly admire sitting next to the well-known Mary Cavett Haughton of St. Mary's College fame. I heard you were May Queen there? And well thought of all over eastern North Carolina. He would enjoy your company immensely."

"Oh, I'd be a great disappointment. After I asked after his family, Mrs. Isabel and their daughter, I'd have nowhere else to go. I don't read all his speeches like Dan does. I don't follow politics on the radio. What would a country girl like me have to discuss with a governor?"

"May I suggest you're not exactly a country girl just because you live in a small town? And besides, don't you ever go to Raleigh with your husband? During the legislative session?"

"No, hardly ever. The Sir Walter Cabinet, the wives, are a group of ladies that meet, have speakers, play cards, and such. But I have to stay here with Danny."

"Is that not putting a child's concerns before the concerns of a husband, Mrs. Hardison? Is that a good idea?" He watched her closely.

Mary Cavett put her spoon down. "What is this? The third degree? Are you a detective? A psychiatrist?" He smiled at her, and she couldn't help but smile back at him. And smile, and smile.

Suddenly, she snatched up her spoon and tried to start back eating the rock muddle stew. Actually, she wasn't able to eat very much. She seemed to have lost her appetite somewhere. Then she accidentally knocked her fork to the floor. Dwight leaned down quickly to retrieve it, and upon picking it up down there at the end of the table, he caught sight of her graceful, beautiful crossed ankles. They were still tan from the Nags Head summer sun, and he had to look at them a long moment. He almost reached over to touch one ankle but realized he might fork it. So he came to, sat up, looked at the fork, stood up, and strolled over to Ben-Olive to get Mary Cavett a clean fork.

Mary Cavett watched him with curiosity. Then she turned her head to see how Danny was getting on with the governor.

The governor seemed entranced as Danny told him about a boating accident the past week on the Roanoke River. Danny had read all about it in the Williamston *Enterprise*.

"You actually read the newspapers?" said the governor, astounded. He had started out in the newspaper business himself in Shelby, North Carolina, at a very young age.

"Why, yessir. I'm nine years old. My grandfather's brother is the editor," he said proudly.

"Well, that's just grand," said the governor. "I'll bet he gives your daddy some fine political write-ups, describes the bills he introduces and all he accomplishes in the Senate, doesn't he?" Danny looked a little confused.

"Well, I guess," he mumbled. "I've never read anything about my daddy in the paper, tho'."

"Actually," intervened Big Dan, "Mary Cavett's uncle is not exactly a fan of mine. He's careful not to ever mention my name in his paper and does not. Only that Mary Cavett, Danny, and I have motored over to Greenville for a Sunday afternoon to visit Aunt Sally. The society editor writes that junk. The paper has never mentioned that I introduced a bill for better roads in eastern Carolina to get us out of the mud. The very roads they are riding on ever' time they leave town."

"Why, that's astounding." The word "astounding" was one of the governor's favorite exclamations. "You enjoy the total unmitigated support of the people of Martin County, and a wide area all about including many other counties, all without the support of the local paper owned by your uncle?"

"Well, he's not my uncle. He's Mary Cavett's father's brother. And that may be the problem. To him, I'm just an upstart farm boy from down in the swamps near Dymond City who played ball at N.C. State while the editor got a degree in journalism at the University of North Carolina at Chapel Hill. All of which is exactly the fact," he announced with an ironic smile, nonplused. "A spade is a spade."

The governor still looked a bit mystified. "Oh, he says nothing against me. He just says nothing. If I want anything in the paper—to explain my vote or ask for a letter to the voters—I have to buy it," said Dan.

Though looking puzzled, the governor offered as if in explanation, "Perhaps, following old newspaper ethics, he just doesn't want to appear to give too much of the paper's political space to his own nephew, don't you suppose?"

"Probably so," said Big Dan, smiling agreeably.

The governor looked down at Danny. "You know, your Daddy doesn't even need the support of the local paper. He's got all the people here and in the surrounding counties pulling for him just because they like him and trust him."

"Why do they trust him?" asked Danny.

"Because," said the governor, "they know he will never let them down. And because his friends know he will never embarrass them."

"Lord, God!" piped in Hizzoner. Big Dan put his finger over his lips and glanced at Little Danny. "'Scuse me, Danny," said Charlie Mack and went on. Danny had not even heard it.

"Big Dan embarrasses me all the time. Every chance he gets. What're you talkin' about? You just don't know him a'tall, do you, governor?" said Charlie Mack.

"Why, yes, I think I do know him, very well. I also know what he's capable of, maybe better than you, Mr. Mayor. Maybe better than he even knows himself. He may be called a farmer down here, but I've seen him put a campaign together in Raleigh to get a bill through, line up his people one at a time—one by one recognize his opponents, and render them nil or overwhelm them, all the while smiling and asking about how their Mamas are doing. It's a beautiful thing to watch. Like watching a . . . a . . ."

"A football game, right?" said Charlie Mack. "And Dan's the quarterback."

"That is the biggest bunch a' malarkey I ever heard," broke in Dan. "Now let's allow the governor to say a few words for everybody, hey?" Big Dan raised his voice. "Time to let the governor give us some words of advice while he's amongst us, hey? I don't think I have to introduce him. Sorta' like the way we're supposed to introduce the president. We don't go on about who his mama was and all his accomplishments. We just say, 'Ladies and gentlemen, Mr. President.' So tonight I'll just say, 'Miz' Serena, Mary Cavett, Dr. Griffin, gentlemen, the governor.'"

"Where'd he learn all that mess?" someone whispered.

"Yeah, yeah." Clapping and whistling followed.

Ben-Olive clapped his hands, too, and sat down on a cucumber pickle barrel after having got quiet with the dishes.

The governor rose, wiped his mouth with his monogrammed, white linen handkerchief, and clapped Big Dan and the mayor on the shoulder. He looked about the room—yes, the whole strange room—with deep affection and smiled at all the people in it with warmth. A glow of kindness showed in his eyes, as well as, possibly, a glow also from the famous Bear Grass rotgut. However, he lifted his shoulders, his head, and his right arm and said, "Friends . . . friends from Martin County, Pitt County, Bertie, Nash, Washington, and Halifax counties. You have no idea how tickled I am to be down here on this old houseboat. Having had that fine fish dinner prepared by the famous hands of Ben-Olive Bazemore, from the skillet of a culinary genius."

Ben-Olive lowered his head and swung it back and forth in total wonder at the governor's words, rather like Mary Cavett had done that afternoon riding down.

"I'm sure you're not expecting or wanting another speech tonight," the governor continued. Certainly not one of the more serious speeches as I tried to bring you and your friends at the warehouse earlier this evening. "

"That won't no serious speech, governor," said Big Dan. "Par'n me for appearing rude, but you almost disappointed me. We bring you down here, braggin' on your speeches and concern with local matters, and you go on about stuff up in Raleigh. An' here we are down here chokin' in the dust on all these dirt roads. Takes us longer to get to Nags Head than to Raleigh. And Nags Head, by the way, is a . . . a gem . . . a jewel! And one of these days you people up there in Raleigh will catch on fast that our beaches and mountains are still waiting to be discovered. They'll bring blue millions of dollars every year from tourists, free and fancy. And those nice tourists will leave all their money in our beautiful state and go home. And for that money you won't have to provide them with schools, hospitals, jails, mental asylums, nothing. Just roads. Give them highways to get down here to spend their money and to get back home on. Not to mention getting our farmers out of the mud so they can get their crops to the market."

"Shut up, Dan. Let the governor talk," somebody said.

"No, no. Dan here is right," the governor said. "I do usually try to discuss local matters, and Dan's right. I've never been down here before and I should talk with you about your problems and what's being done—if anything—about them, and what you think we can do to help you. Governor Morrison certainly improved your roads a great deal, but there's still much to be done so your school buses can run more efficiently. And, yes, to get business and industry to move in down here and bring more jobs, to have more happening for you than pigs, cotton, tobacco, corn, and mules. Don't you need more tractors?"

He was interrupted. "Yeah, yeah, you're right, governor." Little Danny's eyes were so big in the midst of all this. And in a moment, the governor's eyes grew big as Danny's when a loud, mesmerizing "hoooooooonk, hoooooooonk" came roaring across the water.

Suddenly the boat began to rock and flop mightily. Ker-flap! Ker-flap! Large waves hit the boat, causing her to lose her smooth, floating demeanor and go crazy with the swashing up and down. The men caught hold of the table or a chair trying to stand and steady their legs squarely to ride it out. Some laughed and some cussed as they tried to hold onto their drinks without spilling them.

"Grabba hold, everybody," shouted Ben-Olive, holding on to the cooler part of the wood-burning stove. Finally, the whopping and flopping subsided enough for the governor to collect himself and ask, "My soul, what in heaven's name was that?"

"Hey, don't be ashamed, Your Honor. It's just an old lumber barge heading down to the sound, riding high and fast on this spring rise in the river. They usually honk at us sooner than that so we won't be caught off guard. I guess the captain was so busy takin' that curve up there he didn't notice us 'til a little late. Sorry it gave you such a turn. We're kinda used to it," said ol' Mr. Perry from Bertie County.

"Well, I do say," said the governor, quickly recovering his dignity. "It wasn't anything short of an earthquake, I suppose, never having been in one—an earthquake, that is. I imagine an earthquake experience must be very mild to that shake-about you sustained right there." Talking seemed to soothe him.

Mary Cavett and Dwight at the foot of the table had taken in every word, watched it all, then looked at one another and smiled. Suddenly from nowhere, he asked her, "Where, if anywhere, Mary Cavett, would you rather be than here?"

"Why do you ask that?"

"Just wondering, sort of wondering."

"I hardly know. Maybe home with a book. But that suggests that I'm bored, and I'm not."

"You chose this life, didn't you?"

She shrugged.

"Don't you think," he began as he leaned closer to her, "what those fellas up there are talking about is what your life down here is all about? Don't you even care to know what's going on with your tax dollars? With the farmers? The economy? With your daddy's patients?"

Mary Cavett smiled, rather accusingly, and asked, "Are you preaching at me again?"

He said, "Maybe at me. Actually, probably at me."

Suddenly curious, she asked, "Don't you have a daughter, Mr. Carter? How is she doing?" Mary Cavett tried to change the subject.

"She, uh, her name was Heidi."

"Yes," Mary Cavett nodded. "How old is she now?"

"Heidi died when she was about Danny's age, of polio."

She blushed. "Oh, I'm sorry. Really, sorry." Then she asked softly, "You have other children?"

"No, I was divorced after that."

"Oh, I didn't mean to be prying. I can't say anything right."

"Don't apologize. No need," he said gently.

"By the way," she asked as it occurred to her, "what brought you down here again after so many years?"

Dwight answered her cautiously, "I'm just filling in for a fella who's been sick. We're afraid he has cancer. I'm usually covering northern and central Virginia. I certainly didn't expect to see all these people. Your daddy said, 'Come go somewhere with me,' at the drug store while putting on his coat after we finished our order sheet. He didn't say where. Just made me come with him. You know how he is."

"Oh, yes. Very persuasive, yes. And as to your question, I never expected to come back here to live. Visit, of course, but it never occurred to me I'd come back here to spend out the rest of my life and die here."

"I recall," said Dwight, "that at one point you thought you'd be living out your days in Piedmont Park in Atlanta, having Sunday dinner after church at the Piedmont Driving Club."

"How did you know about that?"

"Norfolk girls go to St. Mary's too," he said with a quirky, know-it-all smile. Then, suddenly, Dwight stared at Mary Cavett.

He leaned over to her and begged, "Mary Cavett, tell me some things about Danny–what he does and says. I can't sit outside the schoolyard watching him. Does he get along with other children? Is he a loner, hiding behind a tree, swinging alone on the swings, doing homework during play period? What is he like?"

Mary Cavett warmed up. "Oh, he's so funny. The other day I was after him to change his socks more often—every day, in fact—to avoid athlete's foot and to scrub his feet really good with Octagon soap. He detests doing that, and do you know what he said?"

"Can't imagine."

"He said, 'Mama, don't you know dirty, smelly ol' socks are healthy for me?'"

"'In what way?' I asked him. I fell for it."

"'They keep mean ol' bitin' dogs away from me, and cars and school buses won't run over me neither,' Danny said."

Dwight laughed. He loved it.

"How can you argue with logic like that?" asked Mary Cavett. "He made it up on the spot, I'm sure. It was too corny for him to have heard it anywhere else, don't you think?"

"Absolutely. Dam' he's smart." He turned away again.

"And he's all boy. Dirty ol' socks. Dam', dam', dam', " Dwight mumbled to himself.

Shortly, Doc Haughton said he and Miz' Serena would have to leave a bit early for him to check on Mrs. Hatem (who was suffering from hives), and to see old Preacher McGuire (who was down with arthritis) for a few minutes. They slept better if he popped by and patted their hands or cheeks, massaged their shoulders, and gave them a little something—sometimes a sugar pill, sometimes a real painkiller. He tried hard to keep his patients from getting too accustomed to painkillers and sleeping pills. He might sit by their beds and rub the affected areas 'til it seemed to calm them down. After he went home, he could sleep better as well.

He insisted that his guest, Dwight Carter, should not leave early with him but remain aboard the houseboat for the whole evening and ride back with Hizzoner, the mayor. Charlie had arranged for someone to send out a car from his Chevrolet place, as he had ridden down with Dan and the governor.

After Doc and Serena had left, being rowed back across the river in one of the boats that used both a motor and rowing apparatus to slice across the swift Roanoke, the governor stepped over to Ben-Olive with something on his mind. The men from Bertie County had also left a little early.

"Ben-Olive, you and I are both grown men," the governor began. "We can talk honestly with one another, man to man. Now, don't you worry about those problems over in Bertie County. Martin County doesn't give you problems like that on election day. You just go out and vote your conscience. Vote for Big Dan or whomever else you want to. It is nobody's business what you do behind that little curtain on voting day. When those folks at the door try to grab you and say, 'Vote this, vote that, vote for my brother,' or what all, you just smile, walk on in behind the curtain, and do what your heart tells you to do."

"He's saying, 'Vote for Governor Hoey, you hear?'" said Sheriff McKinnon as he walked by with his lady friend Dr. Griffin on the way to get an extra slice of lemon pie.

"No, no," said the governor. "I can't run again. Remember, North Carolina only allows one term. One four-year term. The legislature is afraid that during an eight-year term—one four-year term right after another—a governor might build up a powerful statewide political machine by using payoff jobs, giving appointments, and handing out titles. And he would get too many voters obligated to him, too many supporters on the state payroll have too much power. Tar Heels don't want their governor or anyone else to have too much power. We are a true democracy, and I'm proud to be a part of that great heritage. Power to the people, not to the politicians. And your vote allows that to happen. But you must vote, you hear?"

"Lord knows, I thank you, Mr. Governor, I do, I do. An' I'll never miss another chance to go vote on votin' day," Ben-Olive said. "Just wait 'til I tell Biddy," he thought proudly. "She won't believe me, of course." He could hear her saying right now, "What wuz you doing holding up the governor, huh? He was down there to visit with Mr. Hardison, Doc Haughton, an all a' them folks, not you," she would surely remind him.

"Naw, naw. He come over to me not once but twice," Ben-Olive would reply. The other time, he say, 'Now Ben-Olive, I also want you to read the newspapers, too. Read the papers and learn about who is running and what they say. I understand the local paper may not cover much statewide news. So also read *The News and Observer*, okay?'"

"He say all that to you?" Biddy will ask, impressed.

Back to the party: "Well, actually," he told Governor Hoey, "I don't take no paper. It's not exactly in my budget, you know?"

Then challenged the governor, "Go by the library and read it free, hear?"

"Not to quibble, Your Honor, but some of those nice old ladies that works down at the library ain't so happy to see us black folks come in the door. It's like they's afraid of us or something."

The governor looked perplexed. "It's a darn public, tax-supported county library, Ben-Olive. It's for everybody," he said.

"We have a little library for the colored folk over in my part of town, but I ain't sure they get no *News and Observer* from Rolly in there every day. But if you say so, I'll ask about that."

The governor turned around to Big Dan, who had been listening to the latter part of this discussion. Dan said, "We'll do a little checking on this, Clyde. We'll look in on the library. You can count on it, hear?"

"I'm certain I can," the governor had replied.

The governor walked over to speak to the lovely Mrs. Hardison and said, "I'm really impressed with a nine-year old young gentleman who already reads the newspapers!" Turning to Danny, "I predict when you grow up you'll go a long way. Just grow up like your daddy and accomplish a great deal for your people down here. We hope to heaven you'll have your daddy's roads by then and can start bringing in industry in your area, son. Good jobs for everybody, you hear? Keep that in mind, boy, all right?"

"Yes, sir," Danny replied.

"Oh, now, Governor," said Mary Cavett lightly. "You can just leave Danny alone. He might want to grow up to be a doctor, like his grandfather, or a sheep farmer in Australia. Who knows, maybe a poet, or artist, or . . . "

Little Danny was staring up at his mother in pure astonishment with his lower lip dropped. "A poet! Mama, are you crazy? Australia?"

"Mamas really are wonderful, surprising creatures, aren't they, Danny?" said the governor. "They never cease to amaze you. You should hear some of the things my wife, Isabel, comes up with sometimes. I've no idea where it comes from. Sometimes I think women read too much for their own good. Maybe we allow them too much leisure time that they spend it reading poetry and travelogues."

Mary Cavett and Dr. Griffin, who had just come up on this, were both pointing their forefingers at him like guns and sending daggers with their eyes, though smiling with their lips. "Maybe we should put them back to work out in the fields like the pioneer women," Dr. Griffin said.

He rolled blithely on, but not for long. At Danny's confused look, he said, "No son, I'm only teasing. The best thing that ever happened to men was educating women. Remember, the hand that rocks the cradle rules the world. Countries that hold back women don't go very far."

Big Dan watched Danny's expression, trying to take all this in. Even if it was a school night, how many nights—or days, for that matter—would Danny have a similar opportunity? Maybe he could write a paper about this evening with the governor for extra credit if none of the other children knew about it, Dan thought. Just him and his teacher. He didn't want his boy to appear overprivileged.

Ben-Olive stepped over from the sink to hear better.

Hizzoner, Charlie Mack, asked, "Governor, do you really believe all that business about women ruling the world?" Charlie knew this would grab Mary Cavett's attention.

"Well," the governor said, smiling, "maybe the really smart ones don't actually let on, but sometimes they can help men get it done correctly. Except, of course, when the males are all hell-bent for death and destruction. This glandular thing for war, winner take all, bang their chests like Tarzan of the Apes—in fact, acting like the gorillas who raised Tarzan in the jungle, yowling through the trees—not even a woman can stop them when they think they've found an excuse to run off to war. Except now, in 1937, instead of sticks and stones, clubs, and bows and arrows, they're flying airplanes instead. They're designing more tanks, more explosives. Yes, you've heard about that man in Germany, Adolf Hitler, starting a Nazi Party, strutting up and down the square and playing nationalistic band music."

"What kind of music?" asked Charlie Mack.

"You know, soldier music!" said the governor. "'Kill 'em dead' kind of music. 'Fight, fight, kill, kill' kind of music. The kind that drummed our little Southern boys off to the Civil War to defend slavery, for God's sake! When hardly one in a hundred of those poor boys ever owned a slave. Wasn't that a fine joke? A joke on those boys? The rich fellas convinced them, 'If you'll go out there and give your blood and life for the "Southern way of life," I'll see to it that you won't ever have to work on my plantations for low wages because I can buy me some slaves who'll work on them for free and do exactly like I say, which you probably would not do.' The 'Southern way of life' way down South in the land a' cotton, where one man can buy and sell another an' put a whip to his back if he takes a notion." Clyde Hoey was warming to his subject. "Thousands of men died for a system that kept the white man down as well as the black man. Kept us all in the ditch—except the few that owned the slaves."

Bill-John Bellamy, the Ford dealer, asked, "How's that, Governor? How did slavery keep the white man down?" He glanced at Ben-Olive. "Just wondering," he said.

"Let's see, now. You can count, I'm sure. What percentage of the population owned those three or four thousand acre plantations, mostly down here in the east? They were certainly not in the mountains, and not many were in the Piedmont."

"Oh, I guess, less than one percent," said Bill-John.

"On the nose! Yes, less than one percent," said the governor. How many white men struggled along on ten or twenty acres—hardly enough land to support a cow and grow vegetables, much less support a money crop? They were called to fight and die too. Po' white trash. North Carolina had only a few really large plantations, and about 330,000 slaves. And, son, many of those fine small farmers left their families to run off and fight for the big landowners, marching to the pipes and drumrolls and sporting uniforms that looked pretty neat at first, for awhile. But they got dirty or muddy in a fight, and smelly. Who do you think washed and ironed confederate uniforms? Let me tell you. My granddaddy told me. Nobody. All to save the slavery system."

Bill-John thought he'd ask, "Governor, you wouldn't happen to be a communist, would you?"

"Heavens, no, Mr. Ford dealer. I'm as big a capitalist as you'll ever want. I just think it is a healthier idea to have each tub on its own bottom. You'll see a great big ship on the river that can and will swamp the little boats trying to fish for a living. Rather like that barge that came by earlier tonight. He 'most took up all the river. I don't often get carried away by a subject like I just did. But the Civil War was such a tragic waste. More men died than . . . Makes my chest pain just to think about all that wasted, spilled blood. All those lives. The South hasn't caught up yet. It may never."

"Well, sir," said Charlie Mack, "if you don't mind, those families had bought that land, or inherited it. Some had it for generations. However, they worked like the dickens turning it from swamp and woods into farms, growing cotton and food for everybody. They sent lumber back to England, where they needed it. The English had little land to grow trees on and were thrilled to get the lumber. All they could send back to us were bricks for ballast to weigh their ships down in the water because they had so little else to send us. There was some furniture, silk, and books for our few rich people, but they really needed our lumber, tobacco, tar, wheat, and corn. How could the owner of a two-thousand-acre plantation do it all by himself, even if his ancestors had cut down the original trees and broken the ground themselves? Thousands of small farms could hardly accomplish the overseas sales, the business that plantations could produce. I'm sure there's an answer."

"They could have tried *paying* their farm workers. Not buying 'em," said the governor quietly. "Of course, that's a good question, and I don't have the best answer. It's a good thing I wasn't governor in 1860. Defeated, I'll get down off my stump now, but my heart still hurts when I think of all those dead Tar Heel boys who stuck at the front like tar and wouldn't run away for anything. We lost more men than any other Southern state. We owned the fewest slaves of any state in the South. We were fighting for pride, and you know where pride goes. You're right—before the fall. Should we still be proud, or just sad? I only wish they had been fighting for something different. A cause to *give* somebody freedom, not take it away. To protect people from an evil enemy. All that blood . . . "

Ben-Olive had ended up across the room at the back of the small group. He leaned against the wall with his arms crossed on his chest and stared down at his shoes. He looked up when Big Dan smiled and spoke to the governor.

"Clyde, we're kinda glad you didn't launch into that lecture," Dan said. "And it was a good one, at the tobacco warehouse. Ben-Olive and I know what you're talking about and most of the others here. But there are some of 'em lost their granddaddies in that 'cause.' Whether po' white trash or not, they responded to the call to save 'Southern pride.' Whatever that is, or was. They didn't know much about glands or band music, but they loved that ol' Confederate flag, states' rights, and, all right, the right to buy slaves. And they gave their all, lost cause or not. Some are still pretty touchy about it, ain't they, Ben-Olive?"

"You better believe they are. Yessir, they's some subjects we just don't bring up around here, nowhere, no time," said Ben-Olive, almost under his breath.

"You're right, of course, Ben-Olive," said the governor. My granddaddy died at Antietam. Maybe that's why I get so wrought up. But my response to the whole thing is to get mad at . . . at the waste. Ah, me, I launch into a dam' symphony of rhetoric about the darndest things."

Changing the subject suddenly, the governor leaned over and asked Dan, "What's that nice sheriff's name, the one who's been courting the lady Ph.D. at ECTC for ten years? The fella who graduated from Davidson and is a sometime poet? Who can run all night to catch a bootlegger and then walk him in without handcuffs? Who is president of the North Carolina Sheriff's Association?"

"And furthermore," said Big Dan, "he can't even spit on the floor. We don't know how in the heck he keeps getting elected."

"Well, if that's a criteria, I couldn't get elected either, right?" said the governor.

"Right!" said Dan. "But about Timothy, Tim McKinnon there, Clyde, if you can remember all those other things about him, why'n hell can't you remember his name?"

"I don't know," said the governor humbly. "That's just where my gift lies. My strengths and my weaknesses. I can remember a body's face, the details, where he went to school, and his wife's physical outline, but I can't recall his name for the life of me. That's why I need friends like you to protect me, hide me, and save me from embarrassment. You'll not let me down, will you?"

"Well, maybe not this time—if you'll just get us some dam' roads down here, you hear? If you don't get something started, I'll expose your tail all over eastern Carolina," promised Dan.

"And I'll get the roads, if you'll quit talking crude like an ol' worn-out football player," promised the governor.

They both laughed heartily, punched each other in the chest, and bopped one another up by the ear, just like a coupla' bear cubs playing in the woods. Or rednecks down at the country store, or po' white trash, mountaineers, baseball players, state senators, and governors on the politickin' trail.

"Hey, boys," said the governor. "I've gotta get to the hotel and that right soon, for as you know . . ."

They all listened, knowing it was a parting shot before he climbed down into the motorboat.

So he said with full effect, "He who hoots with owls at night will never soar with the eagles in the morning." After a salute, he stepped down. The boat promptly vanished into the night.

12

All the birds of the air
Fell a-sighing and a-sobbing
When they heard the bell toll
For poor Cock Robin.

THE elderly, windup clock over the stove in the *Swamp Monkey* was covered with dust caught in greasy smoke from frying fish, pork chops, squirrel, or chicken. Looking at it closely after the big supper for the governor, one might make out the time as 11:45. Only three men were left aboard for the final haul across the swollen Roanoke River: Ben-Olive (who was still the captain in charge of his ship), Charlie Mack Griffin, and the traveling pharmaceutical salesman from Norfolk who looked like a tanned, blond tennis pro—but a rather tired tennis pro.

Ben-Olive was scrubbing up, washing up, sweeping up, and finishing up the place, smiling to himself and trying to remember all he wanted to tell Biddy when he got home.

Charlie Mack had wiped off the tables and spread them back out again from the long, T-shaped plan they had employed so everyone could sit at the same table as the governor.

He placed the chairs back at the separate card tables, thinking all the while that this was one of the times he had to admit he rather enjoyed the title of mayor. Everyone—the political heavies from the surrounding counties and the governor—seemed to have no trouble remembering his name. When Charlie came to the table where the blond fella from Norfolk was sitting, seeming to look at something in the bottom of his glass of bourbon and water which he was twirling, he sat down across from him. It occurred to him that the man, whose last name was Carter, had enjoyed right many of those glasses of bourbon this evening. But of course Charlie hadn't counted. He had only poured a few of them.

"What did you think of our governor?" Charlie asked.

The Carter fella didn't answer him or even look up. Charlie Mack glanced over at Ben-Olive, but he was still busy, so he tried again. "Hey, Carter, what did you think of North Carolina's governor?"

Without lifting his eyes from the sand in the bottom of his glass, Carter said slowly, "He certainly had some, uh, unusual views about the South's part in the Shivel . . . I mean Civil . . . War. I know what he meant. We have the last letters my great uncle wrote to my Aunt Virginia before he was killed at . . . at . . . somewhere."

"What were his letters about?" asked Charlie, being polite. "Maybe about how the officers counted the men to see how many had run off during the night?"

"My great uncle was an officer. He was concerned about a couple a' buttons missing from his jacket. There weren't many needles or seamstresses in the army. As if he was dressing up to go to a dam' party, a killin' party. All nice FFV manners, you know. Had to dress correctly before going to the party. Ishn't that something? A fine, grown man with a wife and children at home, an educated man from the University of Virginia—my school— reduced to worrying about proper buttons on his chest as he went off to kill somebody. Or to be killed. That was only, what, sixty some years ago?" He had not looked directly at either of the two men in the room. He was just talking to himself. Then his head turned to Charlie Mack, his eyes a little red and watery. "Are we any shmarter than we were then?"

"Well, let us certainly hope so, fella. Here, can I get you something to eat before we go home? Some cornbread and butter maybe?" Ben-Olive's cornbread with butter was guaranteed to brighten up a body's mood.

The fella would have none of it. He struggled up from his chair, saying, "No, no thanks," and walked wearily to the long window seat with the single bed mattress on it. He laid down on his back, looking up at the flypaper dotted with fly carcasses hanging from the ceiling.

"This has been the second worst night I've ever had. No, the third," said the Virginian, looking at the flypaper.

"Might as well wander along with this," thought Charlie Mack.

"The worshe, uh, worse—a very bad night—was the night my little girl Heidi died of polio. The very worst."

Charlie Mack thought the man might start crying.

"The second worst night was the night Big Dan came home and caught us, by dam'. I'd been here on thish dam' boat that night, too. Is this thing cursed? This ol' boat?"

Charlie Mack and Ben-Olive looked at one another. Ben-Olive had stopped mopping. What was this guy talking about?

"And then tonight, I find out that all these years, nine years, for God's shake, I've had a little boy."

He had not looked at them yet during the whole time he'd been lying on the window seat. They felt like they were eavesdropping, but it did not occur to them to stop him. Not now.

"A son, a little boy. And I never knew it. She never tol' me. He has to be mine. Looks 'zactly like my baby pictures mother kept on the piano. Same hair, eyes." He closed his eyes. One hand was across his forehead, and the other hung down off the window seat. He had left his last drink on the card table. His chin trembled for a moment.

Ben-Olive asked Charlie Mack what the fella was talking about. That's when Ben noticed Hizzoner's face. It looked frozen and red at the same time. He did not blink as he stared at the man on the mattress.

"An' then that bastard of an ol' football player comes home early that night. And I had to shlam outta there, first the back door, no the front door. He always comes in the back. I had to run out the door like some kind of sneak thief. In such a hurry, I left my coat with my dam' wallet in it and all the cash the druggists had been paying me. Hadn't been to the bank yet. And you know what?"

Charlie and Ben both mouthed, "What?" But they didn't need to.

"That big bashturd never did send my money or my coat to me." He blinked a second, then pulled himself up slowly to a sitting position on the side of the window seat, put his elbows on his knees, wiped his eyes, and stared at the brown and green linoleum. "But under the circumstances, I don't guess he'd be expected to. Still . . . hell."

Somehow, Charlie Mack actually wanted him to continue. He heard himself ask the man, "Why didn't you come back and demand your coat and money?"

"You think I'm crazy? I, un, changed my territory to Northern Virginia. Later, my little girl died, my wife divorced me, and my daddy died. Mother went to a nursing home. I shtumble back down here, jus' doin' my boss a favor. Doc Haughton says, 'I want you to go somewhere with me.' And he takes me to a tobacco warehouse, to a barbecue, a political rally. Is that what it was?"

"Yes, a Democratic rally," said Charlie.

"Well, we're all Republicans where I come from," Carter said.

"You must have felt bored and out of place," said Charlie.

"I didn't feel anything. Haven't for a long time. An' I didn't count on seeing Mary Cavett. So he brings me down to this dam' boat, and there she sits playing cards with a little boy that looks like I spit him out."

Charlie Mack had pulled himself out of his chair by now and was standing over leaning against the wall, against his newest Griffin Chevrolet Company 1937 calendar. His arm was covering the blond cutie in white shorts who was leaning against the hood of the red convertible as if she owned it.

"If you had known, what would you have done about it? If you had known you had a little boy down here?" asked Charlie.

Dwight blinked a moment, not quite comprehending.

Charlie repeated, "Would you have come down here and claimed him, and her? His mother?"

"I don't know. What the hell could I have done? That man seems to . . . to think the boy is his. But they've had no other children. Obviously, it isn't her, uh, problem. Surely he knows." He shook his head. "But he didn't let on tonight. He acted like the boy is his, didn't he?"

"You'd better believe," said Charlie. "Big Dan is smarter than the average bear. He raised Danny like his own son. He is a good father. The best. Absolutely."

Ben nodded, too. "That's right," he agreed.

Dwight wearily let these words slip out as if he was thinking out loud, not directed to anyone. He seemed to be counting his losses on his fingers. "Yes, I guess he took me for all I had. My sweet lady, my son, my coat, my wallet, my money, my self-respect—if I still had any."

Charlie Mack quietly started to protest—a futile gesture—but nevertheless, he said, "Well, it won't exactly like that. I mean, what would you have done if you had been in his shoes? Hmm?"

The very drunk Virginia gentleman from Norfolk began to pull himself up unsteadily and looked about vaguely, asking, "Hey, where's the bathroom on this thing?"

Ben-Olive started toward him and said, "We don't 'zactly have no bathroom in here, but out there we got the whole river." He pointed toward the door.

Dwight, now seriously inebriated, started stumbling toward the door on the river side, and both men started toward him to catch him and to help him out the door.

"No, dammit. Leave me alone. I guess I can take a leak if I want to without two dam' rednecks holding my hand, thank you. Who do you think I am?"

Ben-Olive had never been called a "redneck" before. He thought he'd have to tell Biddy about that, too.

Dwight pulled himself through the door. Shortly after it slammed, all hell broke loose and the greatest racket started up. "Hoooooooonk, honk! Honk. Hoooooooonk. Honk. Honk," came from a deep-throated barge horn that commanded drawbridges to open or warned smaller craft of the giant wake on its way over to the side of the river. Fuh-lap! Fuh-lap! The big waves started pounding the houseboat, making it rock like it would in a storm at sea, back and forth, side to side. Kuh-whump! Kuh-whump! Kuh-whump! The two men looked at each other, and both raced toward the screen door, getting through it as fast as two grown men could at the same time.

13

Good Friday, 1937

THE Martin County schools were "let out" back then for the students to honor Good Friday, and this is the way they did it. When school let out on Thursday afternoon, Maundy Thursday, they went home all over North Carolina and started boiling fresh eggs. As there were not many Catholics in Martin County, not many people made much of Maundy Thursday, except possibly, some at the 'pistopal church. A few would show up over there on Church Street, and they would drape the cross with black cloths as a symbol of Christ's death.

The children didn't attend, as they were home dying eggs and wondering what the Easter Bunny would bring them on Sunday morning.

"Mama, tell him not to bring boxes of raisins and chewing gum this year. Tell him I really do want a chocolate rabbit," said at least one wishful bunny rabbit pulling out her bunny costume to wear to an Easter egg hunt the next morning. Churches or Sunday school classes offered most of the hunts, plus there was a big one every year—a giant production by the Lion's Club.

Mary Lane Davis' mother was thrilled when her six-year-old Mary Lane came home from the Lion's Club hunt, and in her basket was a giant, foil-wrapped, chocolate Easter rabbit. "Oh, honey, how beautiful!" she said. "You've never found one before, not ever."

Little Mary Lane didn't seem so tickled about it somehow.

"Where did you ever find it?" her mother pressed. She knew that all the bigger children knew the hiding places and pretty much got everything. Mary Lane looked up at her mother and said mildly, "The man who said "Go!" gave it to me."

"Oh," said her mother. "Well, we'll chop it up and sprinkle it over our ice cream for Sunday dinner."

Mary Lane looked up, horrified. "Not my rabbit, you won't. I'll keep it in my room and eat two bites of it every day until it's all gone," she said.

Her brother, David Jr., walked by and could not resist saying, "Unless the little ants get in it and eat it all up because you're not sharing."

Mary Lane was rather wise for her age and called after him. "You mean a big ant named David. Mama, don't let David Jr., get my rabbit. It's my first one. Can't I keep it?" Her mother was trying to figure out where Jesus was in all this. Then Mary Lane went on, "And this year they had some little glass eggs that broke open in half, and there was money in them—pennies and nickels!"

"Did you little children find any of those?"

"Nope," said Mary Lane, unwrapping a pink candy egg. "The big children got all those too." She didn't seem too upset. Apparently she knew her time would come.

"And what did the Lion's Club ladies serve you when it was over?" she asked, just to keep her talking.

"Oh, hmm, they had pink lemonade with a cherry in the bottom of each cup and white cupcakes, vanilla ones, you know with little jelly beans on top." Even at six, Mary Lane was good with details.

"Did Danny Hardison find a lot of eggs?" she asked. He was their cross-the-street neighbor.

"He didn't go."

Then Mary Lane's mother remembered seeing Mary Cavett heading off walking to town that morning, as if taking him with her to the drugstore where she had her daily co' cola every morning at ten o'clock except Sunday. Cotton stepped along with them, all shiny and white, running aside occasionally to chase squirrels up trees.

Danny suggested to his mother that since he missed the Good Friday morning Easter egg hunt, couldn't he have his one candy bar a week on Friday instead of waiting 'til Saturday at the afternoon cowboy movie show? She relented, saying he could have his choice, and he chose between a Snickers, Mr. Goodbar, Baby Ruth, Mars bar, or

Three Musketeers. He didn't care for all the coconut in the Mounds bar.

"Danny," she asked him, "how did you have so much trouble with your multiplication tables last year when you have total recall of every candy bar ever made or that you ever ate?"

"Aw, Mom. They're different. Who wants to remember nine times twelve, anyway?" he said.

What his mother, Mary Cavett, did not know, of course, was that her father, Doc Haughton, or the pharmacist, Doc Bennett, would slip him one or maybe even two other candy bars each week. They'd also slip them to his friends if they were tagging along with him with just that fond hope in their heads. Granddaddy Doc Haughton was beyond his daughter's control—and his wife's too, if you heard Serena tell it.

"Mary Cavett," Serena would say, "I am on your side. I beg that man not to give the boy candy. 'Doc, dear, please don't give Danny candy. It upsets Mary Cavett so. And for good reason. All the sugar rushing through his blood makes him nervous, and when the rush goes down, he feels draggy. I can even notice his reaction to sugar.' And remember, your daddy died of diabetes."

"You told him all that?" asked Mary Cavett.

"Oh, that and more. But as you can see, it does no good. And he's a doctor, too."

"But he's a granddaddy first," said Mary Cavett wryly.

That day, Mary Cavett told Danny he would have so much candy over Easter that he should just get a comic book that morning.

"Flash Gordon," he snapped.

"You already have too many Flash Gordons," she informed him matter-of-factly. "We'll talk about it later. Also we can buy the dye for the Easter eggs this morning and a dozen extra white eggs."

"Mama, why do you have on that dress?"

"What dress?" she asked, looking down.

"That dress." He pulled slightly at her sleeve. "I've never seen it before. With yellow daffodils on it."

"I guess I haven't worn it for a long time, Danny. I'd almost forgotten that I had it. Does it look like Easter?"

When they arrived at the store, Danny ran to the comic book shelf, sat down on the floor, and dived into the comics as Cotton curled around and plopped himself down beside him. Supposedly, he was selecting which one he wanted to buy out of his allowance (his mother also urged her father not to give him free comic books, as she wanted him to learn to pay his own way). Problem was, he was such a fast reader, he could read most of them all the way through before she could turn around and touch the ground.

"Aren't you going to go back and speak to Granddaddy, honey?" Mary Cavett said.

"Mama, his door's closed. That means he and Mrs. Skinner are both out or gone home."

"Why, that's strange. Daddy's usually right here all morning 'til lunch, and sometimes he doesn't make it home then."

She looked over behind the soda fountain for an answer.

Woodrow, the soda jerk, was drying glasses. He shook his head and shrugged his shoulders saying, "I don't know where they went, Mrs. Hardison. A fella came in here while ago and ran back there. The three of 'em came steppin' outta there like keystone cops, dashed through the front door without a word to me and tore off down the street."

"Was he carrying his bag with him?" asked Mary Cavett.

"You know, I don't remember. I was too startled to notice, I guess. What would you like to drink, Danny?" Woodrow said.

"Mama, may I have a Dr. Pepper this time?" Danny asked.

"If you have one now, you can't have another one, or a co' cola today, you hear? Besides the caffeine, there's the . . . "

"Oh, I know. It rots my teeth. Ech. Mama, you love to take the fun outta things."

"It's not just the sugar, honey. Cola drinks get you all riled up too, like chocolate. Just too strong for children. But Woodrow, I will take," she said meekly, "a small Coke with ammonia, please."

"Ammonia! Mama, are you crazy? That's what Beulah cleans the kitchen pipes out with, an' you're gonna swallow it down your stomach?"

Mary Cavett smiled sweetly at her son, amused at his consternation, and even wondered at herself and the contradictions she exposed so regularly. It was always much easier to recognize weaknesses in others than in herself. She sat at the round, marble-topped table where Doc and Serena had sat during their courting days sipping ice cream sodas. She remembered how Serena had teased and taunted her for boiling every bottle and nipple she had put into little Danny's mouth as a baby.

Serena would accost her, "You never gave that baby milk, water, or juice except in a boiled bottle with a boiled nipple. But then you'll turn around and snatch a pacifier he dropped up off the dirty floor and slip it right back in his mouth quick as a flash." Mary Cavett smiled just thinking about it and then remembered Serena saying, "You young mothers just kill me. You spend days warming bottles, milk, water, and juice so nothing cold could possibly get near his dear little tummy. And then you'll turn right around and feed him ice-cold frozen ice cream! Am I crazy, honey, or are you?"

"Me, Mama, it's me." Mary Cavett would laugh and say, "I'm the crazy one. You're right. I was convinced that cold milk from the ice box would make his stomach hurt and that room-temperature milk might make him sick. And, frankly, I never even thought about frozen ice cream giving him a stomachache. I'm just full of contradictions, I guess."

Serena had hugged her and said, "Honey, don't let my teasing upset you. I was just as bad as you in my way."

Mary Cavett noticed Scott's Emulsion, which her mother always kept, on the shelf, as well as 666 for cough and cold and quinine for malaria. Then she became aware that young John Hackney had run into the store yelling to Woodrow.

"Hey, come on! Down to the river! They're bringing up that guy," he said.

"What are you talking about?" Woodrow asked.

"Where you been, boy?" said John, incredulous. "Didn't you hear? Some joker fell off the houseboat last night. A traveling salesman from Virginia. They didn't expect to find him, river's so high. Then they spotted him in a log jam at the roots of that big cypress just below the boat."

Danny jumped up, all excited. "Hey, was he still alive?"

"Lord, no. Nobody can swim that river, high as it is. The sheriff's bringing him up, the coroner's there. Oh, that's your daddy, ain't it, Mrs. Hardison? Come on Woodrow! Miz' Hardison, you'll stay here so's he can come, won't you? Nobody'll be coming in here anyway. Everybody's down at the dock."

"Miz' Hardison," asked Woodrow, "do you think Doc would mind? I don't want to put you out none."

Mary Cavett seemed to mumble something like, "Okay."

"Mama, Mama, I gotta go, too. I'm going too, hear?"

"Oh, no. No. Danny, you can't go," she said softly.

"What? I can't hear you," he said.

"I said no. No, Danny. You cannot go down to the river."

"Oh, Mama, you never let me do nothing."

"Anything!" she said dumbly.

"Anything!" said Danny, turning away, crossing his arms, and pouting. "That's what I said, nothing!" Danny insisted. "You never let me have no fun. Double negative this and double negative that. No co' colas, no candy, no Flash Gordon. I ain't never seen a dead person before. Everybody has but me."

He noticed Mary Cavett had not corrected his 'ain't never,' and he turned around and looked sideways at his mother.

She tried to stand up. Then she sat back down and stared out the window at the sunshine reflecting on the cracks in the sidewalk, best he could tell. She seemed not to know he was there. So he turned and ran out the door.

Through a strange blankness, again she noticed Scott's Emulsion on the shelf beside the 666 for coughs and colds. Where had she seen that before? Oh, yes, up in Sarah's room. She seemed to smell Sarah's room. She smelled argyrol, Ben-Gay, and unguentine for scrapes and burns.

Then Ben-Olive stepped slowly through the door and stood looking at her. She did not see him.

"My goodness, Mrs. Hardison. What're you doin' here by yourself? How 'bout I give you a ride home. You haven't seen my new pickup truck yet."

Dazed, she asked, "You have a new truck?"

"Well, it ain't exactly new. Maybe eight years old. But it's new for me, and Mr. Charlie Mack says he'll keep it running like a sewing machine. Oh, Beulah boiled a great big hen today over at your mama's house, and she's taking the hot chicken broth over to your house. She might be there now."

"Whatever is she doin' that for?" asked Mary Cavett, confused.

"You know how she is," he said quietly.

"Then, I guess we'd better go home and let her in." She spoke and moved like a movie running in slow motion.

"I lent her a key to go in," Ben said. "But she'll be looking for us."

Mary Cavett started to walk toward the door ahead of him like a good little girl going to Sunday school with her head down.

As they approached the door, it burst open, and they heard, "Yoo-hoo! There you are. They told me at your house that you would be here at the drugstore, and here you are. Hello, Ben-Olive. Fancy meeting you here."

It was Tiny Monroe. Herself.

"I was just on my way to Raleigh to one of my board meetings, you know, and I always like to stop and take a break in Williamston and see my old good friends, Serena

Haughton and Mary Cavett and you, too, Ben-Olive," Tiny said. "I thought you cooked down at the Tar Heel Hotel." She went on before he answered. "I don't expect any lunch or anything, but I did think I might get a co' cola or something here at Doc's drugstore. Where is the soda jerk?"

"Oh, he's stepped out a while, Miz'Tiny, but he ought to be back soon," said Ben-Olive.

"Well, is Doc Chase here? I'd love to speak to him if he isn't too busy. He is absolutely—your father, Mary Cavett—the handsomest man of his age I've ever laid eyes on. Your mama's a lucky lady. If I'd been younger I'd have given her a run for her . . . well, is he back there in his office?"

"He's stepped off, too, Miz'Tiny," said Ben-Olive, "and also his nurse. They had an errand."

"Well, this is a funny way to run a business or a doctor's practice. What's wrong around here? Are you all right, Mary Cavett? You look a little pale."

"I was gonna give her a ride home in my truck," Ben-Olive told her.

"It's only two blocks. Why can't she walk it?" Tiny said.

"She, ah, turned her ankle. I don't mind taking her."

"Well, look here. I have my driver right out there just waiting. I insist on driving her home. Come here. Let me have her."

Suddenly, Mary Cavett spoke her first words since the intrusion. "No, Tiny. I'm riding home with Ben-Olive. He came to tell me that his sister, Miz' Boo, had just brought us some chicken soup."

Then Mary Cavett looked up at the shelf. "Oh, look Ben-Olive. There's an old blue-and-white croup kettle like Sarah always kept in her room, just for me, to help me breathe when I had asthma. May I take that home?"

"I'm sure your daddy would be glad for you to have it," he said as he reached up on the shelf to lift it down. Then he gently led her by the elbow out the door to his truck. That is the way Mary Cavett rode the two blocks home—carrying two items in her lap, a croup kettle and a Flash Gordon comic book. Cotton had scrambled through the truck door with her and was lying across her feet.

The End

turn the page for Ben-Olive's favorite recipes

Fifteen Favorites
of
North Carolina
Sound Country Cooking

BAKED ROCK OR FLOUNDER

2 to 3 pounds fish, dressed whole
4 or more strips of bacon
4 medium potatoes, sliced and peeled
2 large onions, sliced
1 lemon cut in wedges
1 small can of tomato sauce
parsley

Salt fish inside and out, cut slits on top side of fish. Put in greased Pyrex dish and top with bacon. Bake in hot oven until fish browns slightly. Steam potatoes and onions until tender. Reserve liquid from potatoes and onions. Take fish out of oven and put potatoes and onions on top of fish. Pour tomato sauce and enough liquid from potatoes and onions to keep the fish moist. Bake in hot oven for 20 minutes or until done, basting once. Before serving, place lemon wedges and parsley as desired.

◆ ◆ ◆ ◆ ◆

SCALLOPED OYSTERS

1 quart oysters
1/4 pound salted crackers
1 cup milk
3/4 to 1 stick of butter
salt and pepper to taste

Place a layer of oysters in a 9 x 13 inch baking dish. Sprinkle with salt and pepper, then add a layer of cracker crumbs. Repeat layers until all oysters and cracker crumbs are used, ending with cracker crumbs on top. Dot generously with butter. Just before baking, pour milk over casserole. Bake at 350 degrees until lightly golden in color. Serves 6.

BEN-OLIVE'S CRAB AND CHEESE CASSEROLE

1/3 cup butter
1/4 cup chopped onion
1/4 cup diced green pepper
1 1/2 cups milk
1/2 cup flour
1 teaspoon salt
1 teaspoon pepper
1 teaspoon dry mustard
1 tablespoon lemon juice
1 teaspoon Worcestershire sauce
2 (6-ounce) cans crabmeat, flaked
1 cup shredded cheddar cheese
1/2 cup buttered bread crumbs
Dash of cayenne (optional)

Melt butter in saucepan over low heat. Add onions and green pepper and cook slowly until tender. Remove onions and pepper. Blend flour, salt, pepper, cayenne, and mustard together; stir into butter. Add milk, stirring constantly. Cook until sauce is smooth and thickened. Fold in lemon juice, Worcestershire, crabmeat, 1/2 cup of cheese, and the sauteed vegetables. Spoon mixture into 6 individual casserole dishes or shells, or a 2-quart casserole. Blend remaining cheese with bread crumbs; spread around edges of dishes. Heat at 325 degrees for 15 to 20 minutes.

◆ ◆ ◆ ◆ ◆

SOUND COUNTRY SHRIMP SALAD

3/4 cup hot mustard (Dijon or Creole)
3/4 cup salad oil
1/4 cup catsup
1/2 cup vinegar
1 bell pepper, diced
3 green onions, chopped
2 to 3 pounds cooked, cleaned shrimp
hot pepper sauce to taste

Combine all ingredients and chill. May be served with toothpicks as an hors d'oevre, on lettuce as a salad, or as an entree. Yields 8 to 12 servings.

SEAFARE BACKFIN JUMBO IMPERIAL CRAB

1 pound backfin lump crab meat
1 1/2 tablespoon mayonnaise
1 1/2 tablespoon Durkee's Famous Sauce Dressing
1 tablespoon Lea & Perrins Sauce
1 cup cracker crumbs, coarsely rolled
1 tablespoon paprika
1/8 pound butter, melted
Green pepper, diced (optional)
Chives (optional)
Pimentos, chopped (optional)

Combine crab meat, mayonnaise, dressing and sauce. If desired, add peppers, chives and pimentos at this time also. Blend lightly. Mound into 4 crab shells. Combine paprika with cracker crumbs. Pat onto the filled crab shells. Pour water to 1/4" depth in a shallow baking pan. Place crabs in pan and bake in 350 degree oven for 12-15 minutes, or until top is golden brown.

◆ ◆ ◆ ◆ ◆

CLAM AND OYSTER STEW

6 medium potatoes
2 large onions
2 cups water
1 quart milk
1 pint clams
1 pint oysters
1/4 pound sliced salt pork

Simmer potatoes and onions in water. Fry out the pork after it has been cut into small cubes and add to above mixture. Add milk and clams and season to taste. Cook 2 minutes. Add oysters and remove from fire.

STRIPED BASS ROCK ISLAND

1 Rockfish (6-8 pounds)
2 ounces salt pork
2 cups of your favorite bottled dressing
1/2 to 1 cup half and half
butter for pan
salt and pepper

Dress the striper with the backbone remaining in the fish. Score both sides, making cuts about 2 inches apart. Put the dressing inside the fish near the nape and fasten over the scored cuts with wooden toothpicks.

Place fish in a buttered roasting pan. Bake in a 450 degree oven for 1 hour. Pour in enough of the cream to cover the bottom of the pan and cook for 15 minutes longer, basting occasionally, until fish is light brown.

◆ ◆ ◆ ◆ ◆

BAKED FLOUNDER

1 whole flounder (medium to large)
3 to 4 slices bacon
2 tablespoons flour
1 large onion
2 to 3 potatoes
salt and pepper to taste

Score, salt and pepper flounder and place in 9 x 13 inch baking pan. Fry bacon slices in a skillet. Extra oil may be needed. Add flour to drippings and brown. Add water to make a medium gravy. Add salt and pepper to taste. Pare and slice onions and potatoes. Place over fish. Pour gravy over fish, onions and potatoes. Bake at 400 to 425 degrees for one hour. Baste occasionally.

SAUTEED SHAD ROE

1/4 cup butter
2 shad roe (about 1 pound)
lemon wedges
1/2 teaspoon salt
dash of pepper

In a covered 10-inch skillet over medium heat, in hot butter, cook roe (turning once) 8 minutes or until roe loses its pink color and is tender when tested with a fork. Sprinkle roe with salt and pepper, serve with lemon wedges. Yields 4 servings.

◆ ◆ ◆ ◆ ◆

CRAB AND SHRIMP CASSEROLE

1/2 pound mushrooms, chopped
1/2 cup butter
1 cup cooked chunk crab meat
2 cups cooked shrimp
1/4 cup butter
1/2 cup flour
1/2 teaspoon salt
1/4 teaspoon pepper
2 cups milk
2 tablespoons sherry
1 cup grated cheddar cheese

Saute mushrooms in 1/2 cup butter. Add seafood. In a separate pot, prepare a medium white sauce; melt 1/4 cup butter, add flour and cook until bubbly. Add salt and pepper. Remove from heat. Add milk, return to heat, bring to boil, stirring constantly. Add white sauce and sherry to seafood mixture. Mix well. Pour into a greased 9 x 13 inch baking dish. Top with cheese. Bake 20-30 minutes in a 350 degree oven.

BATTER FRIED FISH

1 egg
1 ounce vegetable oil
1 pound fresh fish fillets
1 packet instant mashed potato flakes
salt and pepper to taste

Combine egg, oil, salt and pepper and beat until smooth. Dip fish in batter and roll in potato flakes. Fry in hot oil until golden brown. Yields 4 servings.

◆ ◆ ◆ ◆ ◆

SOUND COUNTRY CLAM CHOWDER

1 quart clams, canned or fresh
1/4 pound salt pork
1 quart diced potatoes
1 onion, diced or chopped
1 quart rich milk, scalded
salt and pepper to taste
butter, if desired

Remove black parts from clams, saving the liquor. Cut pork in small pieces and fry until crisp and golden brown, then remove small pieces of pork from the fat. Discard fat. Add potatoes and onion to a pot, with just enough hot water to be seen through the potatoes. Cook over low heat, just simmering, until done.

When potatoes are done, add clams and pork. Cook for 2 minutes after coming to a boil. (Longer cooking will make the clams tough.) Remove chowder from heat and let stand for a few minutes, then add hot milk, the clam liquor, and seasoning to taste. (If seasonings are added before the hot milk, chowder may curdle.) May add butter to each bowl, if desired. Note that chowder is usually better if left until the next day. Yields 6 servings.

SAUTEED SHRIMP

2 green onions, chopped
1/2 cup butter
garlic salt
4 tablespoons sherry wine
2 pounds peeled, raw shrimp
1 pound fresh mushrooms, sliced
grated Parmesan cheese
juice of 1 lemon

In skillet saute onions in butter. Season with garlic salt. Add sherry, lemon juice, shrimp and mushrooms. Sprinkle with Parmesan cheese. Simmer until shrimp are done. Serve with the juices or over pilaf rice. Freezes well after cooking. Yields 4 servings.

◆ ◆ ◆ ◆ ◆

CAROLINA SOUND COUNTRY OYSTER PIE

2 pints oysters
3 cups thick white sauce
hot pepper sauce
Worcestershire sauce
salt and pepper
2 packages saltines, crushed
1/2 pound cheddar cheese, grated
2 (2-ounce) jars pimento peppers
buttered cracker crumbs

Heat oysters in a pan. Drain off liquid and reserve. Keep oysters warm over very low heat. Make 3 cups thick white sauce using the following recipe. Season with hot sauce, Worceshershire sauce, salt and pepper. In a greased casserole, layer cracker crumbs, grated cheese, pimentos, oysters, and white sauce. Repeat layers and top with buttered cracker crumbs. Put in 400 degree oven until it is thoroughly heated and the cheese is melted. Yields 8 servings.

Thick White Sauce

To make a thick white sauce, melt 3 tablespoons of butter in a saucepan. Add 3 tablespoons flour and stir until blended. Add oyster liquid and milk (equivalent to 3 cups) to butter mixture and stir until thickened.

◆ ◆ ◆ ◆ ◆

BEN OLIVE'S BREAD PUDDING WITH SCUPPERNONG WINE SAUCE

1 3/4 cups soft bread crumbs
3 1/2 cups milk, scalded
3 eggs
1/3 cup sugar
1/4 cup melted butter or oleo
salt and vanilla to taste

Add bread crumbs to milk. Beat eggs slightly and add to bread crumb mixture. Then add salt and vanilla and melted butter. Pour into buttered pan and bake 45 to 50 minutes at 350 degrees.

Wine Sauce

1/4 cup butter
3/4 cup flour, creamed together
1/2 cup sugar

Pour 4 cups boiling water over this mixture, beating to keep lumps out. Let boil, add pinch of salt, take from fire and add wine to taste (about 1/4 cup). Other sweet wines will serve as well such as blackberry, sherry, etc.

Rockfish

Rockfish is also called squid hound, rock bass, striper, striped bass, green head, and sea bass. It is olive-green with a white underside. A series of spots on its sides give the appearance of stripes running from head to tail. Rockfish range in size from six inches to three feet.

The rockfish, known for its size and fighting ability, is a challenge to catch but a delight to eat. A six to eight pounder makes a tasty entree. Larger ones can be broiled or flaked for salads. The mild flavor of this fish lends itself to a variety of sauces and recipes, from the simplest to the most elegant, from rockfish stew, or rock muddle, to sweet and sour rockfish, to rockfish florentine.